FLIGHTLINES

FLIGHTLINES

JOHN F DEANE

POOLBEG

Published in 1995
by Poolbeg Press Ltd
123 Baldoyle Industrial Estate
Dublin 13, Ireland

© John F Deane 1995

The moral right of the authors has been asserted.

The Publishers gratefully acknowledge the support of The Arts Council.

A catalogue record for this book is available from the British Library.

ISBN 1 85371 555 7

Cover illustration by Camille Souter
Cover design by Poolbeg Group Services Ltd
Set by Poolbeg Group Services Ltd in Janson Text
Printed by The Guernsey Press Ltd,
Vale, Guernsey, Channel Islands.

One

She was still an elegant woman. She was silent during dinner, silent but smiling quietly to herself. She took a little melon and port; it went down the throat like honey-water, the melon-flesh soothing the heat of her insides, the port warming up again the chilled ends of her veins and nerves. And then a little, oh ever-so-little, yes, turkey breast, a dab of cranberry sauce, just a spoonful of sweetcorn. No potatoes, no thank you, nor stuffing, no. It must all land light as a feather on the delicate ground of her stomach. To rest there, benevolent, a grace. Afterwards, the merest touch of Christmas pudding, it was so heavy, you see, but she simply must have just a mouthful, after all, after all . . . And cream, yes, a little cream moistened again with a nice dash of Irish whiskey; in that refreshing pool she could float the bit of pudding, ease it down smoothly, relish it the more. Then she sat back quietly in her chair, satisfied, touching her lips with the red serviette, prepared to undergo the entertainment Abbey View House had laid on for them.

She grew quiet, then, her eyes open, both hands resting on the edge of the table. Around her the other old ladies and gentlemen grinned and dribbled and muttered, applauding sometimes, but most often staying wide-mouthed and wondering, like kindergarten babies, at the goings-on of the distant, irrelevant world. Come to intrude a while on their reveries. But the elegant woman remained perfectly still, as if all her attention were devoted to the young volunteers and their little acts. And when they came to take her back to her room for a short nap, they knew at once she was no longer there. Someone had come from the awful, wonderful Elsewhere and tapped her silently, but firmly, on the shoulder of her living. She had suffered a stroke. A second, but a massive, stroke. On Christmas Day.

"And she was so animated during the dinner," Mrs Weston told the family. "She pulled a cracker. With Mr Fox, I believe, and laughed heartily at the bang. She won, too, and read out the little joke to the rest of them. And wore the green paper hat that popped out. So serene. Happy, even. Blessed." And Mrs Weston sighed professionally into the phone, touched her cuffs and hung up.

The nurse got her into her nightdress and laid her down peacefully in her bed. She was breathing gently. Her eyes were closed now, her pulse normal. But there was no movement. No reaction to touch or sound or light. No presence. She was – *gone*; it was the only word. Gone. Not there. Elsewhere. Gone into the twilight world that is neither life nor death.

The doctor came and gave her a thorough examination. Delicately. She was more fragile now than an old delft jug. He discussed the situation with her family; he advised against intravenous drips. There was no point. She was gone. Really. A drip might make her suffer needlessly. She would be dead in a number of hours. By night-time surely. But really, wasn't she blessed . . . ? To go like that . . . ?

The family stayed a little while. They stood silent, perplexed. They moved restlessly. A child played with a tassel on the end of the curtain. For what do they know, the children, what do they know of such absences, such differences, and wouldn't it be better when this useless old woman at the remotest edges of their lives, this old woman who had intruded on their Sunday afternoons and now on Christmas Day (Christmas Day!) would at last have disappeared?

They all went home for a while; there were guests . . . they would be back in the evening . . . or if there was any news.

At four o'clock precisely, and as usual, an elderly man entered the foyer of the home. He, too, was fragile. But standing proud. The attendant at the desk smiled at him familiarly, then remembered her instructions and pursed her lips. He asked once again to be allowed to visit her. He asked if he might be allowed to see her. Just for a moment. Please.

For the only time in many weeks the woman at the desk hesitated. She knew. She knew some of the before, most of the now, and she knew, she thought, all of the future. So she allowed pity to touch her face for a moment and that pity grew in her eyes as she saw him, come back for the thousandth time, pleading.

He sensed her softening and the heaviness in his heart became suddenly light. He allowed himself one moment's hope. He fell at once on his knees, there in the high brown foyer, so that the woman, middle-aged and hurt herself this Christmas afternoon by the emptiness in her life, clasped her hands as if to pray, rose quickly from behind her desk and came round to hold him.

"Please, sir, please," she begged, stooping towards him, "please, don't do that."

She stood, holding his pleading hands in her pleading hands, gazing down at him, looking into those damp but gentle blue eyes, and the ticking of the radiator against the wall became a pounding clamour. Somewhere, down some perfect corridor, a door closed, or opened. The rich smells of the after-dinner hours drifted like an almost visible mist through the hall and out into the darkening day. She grew conscious of her own breathing, of the difficulty of her breathing, of the fact that he seemed not to be breathing at all. Kneeling at her feet. Gazing up at her with a hope as wild as famine in his eyes. His hands were cold, trembling hands.

"Please, Mr, ahm, Mr, please get up. I'll go and see . . ."

He shivered at the hint of promise in her words. He squeezed her hands and tried to rise. But he was tensed now, and his leg hurt. He felt as if his body would knot itself into immobility. But she helped him, taking him under his right arm while he clung to her. She sat him on the wooden bench just inside the door. Murmuring to him, as to a child. He nodded, nodded, breathing heavily and looking up at her with his child's clear eyes.

"There now, there. You sit there. Don't move. I'll have to go and see. I'll be back . . ."

When the woman had gone the silence in the hall thickened. Most people, he thought, are happy people, young and happy, are at home, sitting by a fire, with those they love, contented, at peace. He loosened the thick grey scarf from about his neck and set his brown hat on the bench beside him; he tried to settle himself a little. How cold ageing bones become, how sluggishly the blood dribbles through ageing veins, how heavy the flesh hangs on the weary frame, how the eyes dim, like a blue sky slowly overcome by afternoon, then evening, and soon . . . night. He looked down at his hands, grey, too, almost grey, touched with blue and purple veins, splotched with rust. They were trembling; his whole body trembled, with an excitement that he tried to hold in check.

"Blessed are they who do not expect," he said out loud to the listening world.

The attendant had opened a door to the right off the hallway. It had closed after her by itself. So *she* must be down that way. His eyes lightened. His hands clutched at the scarf. With some difficulty, as if each time he stopped moving his body began to seize up like an engine without oil, he hoisted himself off the bench. If they were only going to send him away again . . . after even this short space of hope, this small, tentative, but urgent, remotest hope . . .

He crossed the foyer to the desk. All was silent. There was a file of cards standing innocently among a jumble of papers, notes, pencils, a plastic ruler, the phone. The TV Guide. As quickly as he could he ran his fingers through the files. He found her almost at once. There. Her name. The date she had entered Abbey View House. November 14th. Then a number: 3G. That must be it! He was shaking now. 3G. *Her room.* Surely her room! Even if he could stand a moment in her fragrances, breathe in her talcs, the echoes of her perfumes, the aura of her past, perhaps see her dressing-gown on the back of a door, her slippers under the bed, flowers in her vase . . . perhaps even *his* flowers, though one of the nurses had told him rudely she did not accept flowers from him. He stopped himself thinking further.

"Battle stations!" he said aloud to the waiting world.

He opened the door off the hallway. 3G. G. Ground floor, room 3? A short, bright corridor ahead of him. Stairs to his left. A door opened down the corridor. He moved, with unexpected agility, to his left. He was climbing the stairs. Everywhere was clean, bright, a world polished to a sheen. Paintings on the wall; reproductions he could see, birds, and clouds, eagles, even a condor!

"In the skies already," he murmured. Anything, anything to keep the courage in the heart, to keep the body moving in its purpose.

He reached the top of the stairs, the first landing. He imagined he heard footsteps. He must not be caught thus. Trespassing. Where he was not wanted. He climbed. He was finding it hard, this climb, carrying up with him his weight of years, of sufferings, of joys, of yearnings. He paused. Near him was a door, the number 1A printed on it. First floor, room A. So! 3G, third floor, top floor, room G. He looked up at the next flight of stairs, he began to climb. *Oh for the wings, for the wings of a dove . . .* But perhaps she was up there, high above, waiting for him, hoping for him, in spite of all that they had said . . . Don't think, man, just don't think. Do, and suffer the consequences.

Pictures, bright reproductions, on this flight of stairs were of mountain chasms, ski-slopes, coloured Swiss chalets nestling among high pastures. He laughed to himself. Coming down are we, coming down; and all the poor old folk being reminded of what they can never have, never did have perhaps, ski holidays, the purity of high snow, dark glasses, exhilarating movement, and the prospect of big fires and warm whiskeys . . .

He began towards the third floor.

"I knew it, I knew it," he chuckled. The reproductions

now were of hares and rabbits sitting perkily on fertile ground, bright meadows where poppies flowed in a scarlet river, forest floors alight with bluebells, a waterfall where three rainbows danced. Make your way upwards, towards the earth! He chuckled, relishing the joke.

The door of room 3A opened right opposite where he stood. After all this, he was caught! There were tears of disappointment, tears of effort, when he looked up. An old woman stood gaping at him. Old, parchment old. Red-eyed. All talced and rouged. For Christmas. She nodded her head gravely at him, up and down, up and down, scolding.

"Wrong floor, you wicked, wicked man!" she cracked at him. Then she grinned hugely.

He watched her. Uncomprehending.

"Women's floor, you wicked person! Up to no good! At Christmas, too! You should be ashamed of yourself. And happy, too!"

She put her clawlike fingers to her lips.

"Ssshhhh!" she chuckled. "If you can get away with it, good luck to you!" She turned and moved away from him along the corridor. He watched her go. She stopped, pressed a button for her lift, turned and looked back at him. She was still grinning, shaking her index finger in admonition. The lift door opened. She disappeared.

Quickly now he found the door. 3G. *Her* room. A plain white-painted door without panels. An ordinary, brass handle. No lock. He stood, still as death. If he could now find the courage . . . He could hardly bear to lift his right hand. He held it, poised. Then he closed his eyes and knocked. Tap, tap, tap. Timidly. Softly. There was no response. No sound from within. He opened his eyes and knocked again. More firmly. There was still no sound. Again he was unsure, very, very unsure. But he had come this far. Up the long climb of all these years, rung after rung along the dreadful ladder, this far. The corridor was lit by a pale light at either end, two dim red lights on either side about half-way along, where the lift doors were. Everything was still. Deathly still. He put his hand on the doorknob and opened the door. Surely this was a criminal act. But he was desperate. And he had come so far, with so much hope ...

If his grandfather's grandfather, and before him *his* grandfather's grandfather, and before that again *his* grandfather's grandfather back to the eighteenth century and beyond, when time would have been on his side had got up every day of his life on the high pier of the farmyard gate and had jumped, and jumped again, and again, and again, flapping his arms vigorously, out through the air to land on the mossy patch of the meadow, by now he, Jack, would have developed wings and would be able to fly. It was a rumour, kept in the heart of the family like a sorrow locked away in an old chest under the stairs, that Peter Edward Golden, an ancestor from the famine times, watching his own wife and son sway backwards and forwards in the silent lunacy of starvation, had climbed onto the highest tree he could find, had waved his arms about and screamed: "Look! Look! Look! I'm a bird! I'm a bird! Watch me fly away south where the potatoes grow big as boulders on every bush and tree and flower . . ." and he had leaped face forward onto the air. Whether it was the delicate canvas of his flesh and the thin fuselage of his bones, after two years of eating little more than birdseed and roasted moths, or whether it was some actual inherent potency in the family towards birdhood, Peter Edward Golden, when he fell, merely broke both arms and legs, and his nose, and lived to tell of his experiences.

John (Jack) Edward Golden was born into the age of flight.

Jack began to learn to fly by leaping from the high pier by the farmyard gate. When he was ten years old he gathered mounds of hay and straw and built them up to form a soft landing area for his jumps. He launched himself outward, spreading his arms wide, trying to land as far out from the pier as he could. For a second and a half he was in the air. Flying.

"Look! Look! Look! I'm a bird! I'm a bird!"

Sometimes his mother, standing at the back door of the house, her hands rubbing idly in the folds of her apron, watched him, delight in the growing maleness of the boy spreading like a ripening flush over the down of her cheeks.

He held on to umbrellas, to blankets, to anything that might delay, even for a moment, the jarring thud back onto the earth. Then he would run, as fast as his youth would take him, along the earth, waving his arms rhythmically, longing to lift up then onto the comforting and supporting breast of the wind.

Gráinne watched him sometimes, and laughed. Gráinne Flannery, neighbour, ten years old too and pretty as a sunlit morning. Once he persuaded her, too, to try and fly, to become a bird, like him, to soar. He helped her up on the bars of the gate, holding her gently about the waist, then pushed her onto the high cement pier. For a moment his hands held her buttocks and something hurt her far away inside. In him, too, something uneasy began to stir, and some tiny flame set itself alight in the palms of his hands. Some urgency towards bearing her weight on his own white flesh took tiny root under his skin. A caring, and a demand for comfort. She stood there for a long time, afraid, and he urged her on, taunting her, cajoling, until she jumped, her hands thrown high before her face, her dress flying up around her, her eyes shut tight. She landed heavily and rolled too far, into a muddy hollow; she was shaken and hobbled about the yard for a while like a heron with an injured leg. Her dress, her hands, her knees were soiled with the glaur; she felt ugly, foolish and angry.

But Jack, Birdman Jack, did not mock her. For a moment the sense of her flesh, secret and hidden, took his breath from him and when she fell, rolling over on the ground, the white flesh of her thighs and the soft primrose mystery of her knickers hit him like a punch to the stomach. He moved forward to gather her up, anxious suddenly lest she had hurt herself. He saw her eyes, then, angry and frustrated, and he stopped.

"Girls!" he muttered, and began to climb back up onto the pier.

There was a grove of pine-trees beside the Goldens' house, great trees planted decades before to provide some shelter against the marauding Atlantic winds. Jack climbed their heights, swayed in the breezes amongst their topmost boughs, held his small body against their hard, soaring limbs, covered his hands with a fragrant, sticky resin, tree-blood, tree-sap, that power that urged them to rise vertically towards the reaches of the sky. He knew the comfort of their presence, the stolid girth and the airy tips, and watched out over a dull and spattered landscape the way a hawk would watch, from on high, pausing before it swooped to bring its power to bear on the weaklings of the earth.

When, in the evening time, his mother came to the back door of the house, the wooden door that scraped over the roughened concrete of the threshold and sent a shudder through Jack's body as it squealed, she would stand there, needing his living presence, loving him, calling him, urging him home to eat, to come in for Rosary, to get ready for Benediction, her hands fretting still against the dry coolness of her apron, calling him down out of the sky to the dull and tasking earth. He would stay still for as long as he dared, absent and distant, high in his world, flying there for as long as her patience allowed him. She would wait, lost in her own heaviness, gazing away to her own grey horizons; she would stand, under the burden of her husband's presence, there, in the house behind her, suffering.

He gathered, raking them together, great piles of pine-needles, forming a mound, decades old and feather-soft. And he would hold to the highest branch he could, hang there and wait, hovering in mid-air. Then he would drop, in flight for a delicious second through the air, the world of branch and pine-cone and bark and needle a blur about him, and lie, cradled in fragrances, watching back up through the wonderful lace-work to the grey sky over the island.

"I come from way up there," he would think. "From away, away, away up there, so high up I am out of sight. And one day, one day I will soar up there, back home, back where I came from." He watched the dark, threatening clouds that moved slowly and sullenly over the island, having gathered their heaviness from the depths and surges of the Atlantic Ocean. How he longed, one day to fly above and beyond such grey heaviness, to be a great bird, an albatross, an eagle, a hawk, even a simple gull, and be able to discover what the world looked like from up there, its small and intrusive presences lost in the view of the whole, and how the sky seemed as he came close to touching its silken skin.

A blackbird whistled from a dark bower at the edge of the wood, somewhere among the big leaves of the rhododendron hedge. Sometimes, if he stayed unbearably still, a fox might come over the ditch from the common ground, slip like an eel through the rhododendron undergrowth and pass along the damp earth floor of the wood as silently as a thought. An orange-red presence just as quickly become an absence. Jack would thrill at the miracle of it, at his presence in a world of otherness, eye to eye with magic.

Once, near dusk, as he sat astride a branch, his arms round the bole of a tree, his chest pressed firmly against the bark, and swayed and swayed, gently, one with tree and breeze, high up and almost invisible, a long-eared owl came silently as a whisper from some hole in the darkening air and flew, slowly, elegantly as a cloistered nun, to perch on a branch nearby. Jack would not breathe as that strange, po-faced creature settled itself, slender, a mottled rusty-brown merging almost at once with the rust-brown of the tree and the grey-feather darkness of the evening. Slowly that quizzical face revolved until the eyes looked into Jack's eyes. For a moment the two creatures gazed at one another, Jack's heart singing with excitement, his fingers stiffened against the tree. And then the bird gradually lifted its ears above its football head in a gesture of cautious alarm, let out a sound that seemed to come from the freckled and mottled feathers of its body, a sound that echoed like a sigh, a long moan in the gathering darkness. "Oooooooo-ooooooh!" Then it allowed itself to fall forward from its branch and elegantly, slowly unfurled its wings and flew, like a barely whispered prayer, away among the trees and disappeared.

Once he persuaded Gráinne to climb the tree with him. She murmured and whimpered as he scolded her, her dress awkward against the lower branches, her body already leaning back from the tree with a consciousness of its own weight. He was strong, this boy, strong in body, in presence, and she feared him even as she longed to be beside him, accepted, part of him. Of his world.

"No, lean into the tree, why don't you? Get your balance. Climb. It's easy."

"I'm scared, Jack. I'll fall. I'll ruin my dress and get killed."

"Girls! You're as soft as jellyfish. You don't let excitement into your lives at all. Who cares about your bloody dress? This is something special I bet no other girl will ever have done."

He climbed ahead of her, aware of his embarrassment should he stand below, and helped to draw her up. Eventually he had her sitting on a branch high over one of his mounds of leaves.

"Now you must let yourself hang from that branch, hold on a while, then drop. It's marvellous. You'll see."

But she was unable to swing her body down so that she could hang by her hands, and she twisted and turned on the branch and complained. She looked up at him and there were already tears in her eyes. That he should take pity on her fears, on her smallness, on their differences.

"I'm scared, Jack," she whimpered. "I don't want to fall."

"Ah just do it for God's sake!" he scolded, and he pushed.

Gráinne fell heavily from the branch, her cry coming to him like that of a hurt kitten, a cry of an earth-vole when the claws of the swooping hawk have grazed it, a cry not high and screaming, but sharp and awestricken and helpless. Surprised. Shocked. She landed on her back among the leaves, unhurt but shaken. He stood on the branch and looked down anxiously at her. Had he killed her? Was she dead? Was she broken? He knew a dread, then, that made his entire body tense with an overwhelming ache and he moved quickly down along the branches of the tree, down, like a squirrel, along the bole.

For some time she lay there, happy in his caring, watching up at him, marvelling that she had fallen, unhurt, from such a height. But she felt angry, too, angry that he could treat her with such carelessness. She crawled off the mound of leaves at last and stood up, brushing the dust and pine-cones from her clothes. Snuffling. Half-afraid in the darkness of the grove. Afraid of his scorn. Of his disgust.

"Girls!" he shouted, relieved, from his perch just above her.

"We're hens," Gráinne thought, "small, fat, silly, heavy hens, that's what we are. We're in a stinking little prison, fenced in by chicken-wire, pecking about on the soiled earth; and sometimes when we're frightened we try to fly, we rush at the chicken wire and bash our bodies against the fence and bounce back in a tumble of feathers. We must just hold on, hold on tightly to what we have and not let go. We're hens, and our wings don't work, they just will not work."

At long last Gráinne had her own room, a tiny attic room high over Flannery's Store. It was small. Very small. But for Gráinne it was Paradise. The ceiling was made of boards nailed up under the rafters, and painted white. During the daytime the nail-heads were black stars in a white sky. At night, with the wind singing and capering like Halloween clowns around the high angles of the store, the gaps between the boards opened onto small cracks in the slates above; Gráinne would admit the angels into her room out of the wearying turmoil of those winds, and talk to them, *oh Angel of God my guardian dear* . . . Sometimes, lying awake and trembling with delight, Gráinne could see a star, her star, its light still and beautiful, trembling and pure, move with infinite slowness across the small square space of her skylight. She knew, then, somehow she knew, that God was there, watching and guarding her, preparing her, and she would prove true.

But she was lonely, Gráinne; she was the only child of Fintan and Nora Flannery, merchants, who had their standing in the small world of the island to maintain. Mr Flannery had plans for his daughter, his only child, and for her he would build up the business, to make her strong and proud in a nation growing powerful. She was urged to come quickly home from school, to take her part in the growing labours of the stores, to help out in the bleak and caterwauling premises of a small but developing commerce.

She got to her room by climbing a narrow, almost vertical, wooden stairs; there was even a trapdoor! Jack had never been in this room, never! And she would not let him, nor anyone else, enter it yet, not yet! It was hers, only hers. You climbed the narrow stair, you were climbing towards Heaven, you pushed at the trapdoor with the top of your head; the door swung back on its hinges and you were in this most special of special spaces. There was one window, a skylight, opening only onto sky, and clouds, and soaring gulls. The moon often hung there, framed, impossible. Often, too, the rains drummed on the skylight with their own, sometimes impatient, sometimes insinuating, messages. The walls of the attic were painted cabbage-green, a colour Gráinne was not too fond of, but it helped her to think of the trees of Paradise, the lush, unspoiled undergrowth, the harmless presence of creeping things, the silence that is the best of companions, the ever-present, living, God.

Gráinne was still an ungainly child. She was tall, carrying her height awkwardly. She was not willowy, she was heavy; she was, as her father would mumble, in no way cherry-blossom. But her hair was long and full and golden, so pure in its honey light that little streams of scarlet seemed to flow through it as she moved. And so her body, growing already towards a young woman's body, yet held and twisted still by her childhood, acquired a grace in movement when she walked, or swam, or danced, that made of her a goldcrest in flight, a house martin, a grebe, or even – though she would have laughed at the thought – even a swan. Poor Gráinne, poor ugly duckling Gráinne. She hid herself away whenever she could, in her green cell, watching the heavy clouds pass above her, hearing the distant rumours of a slow commerce from the world below.

Jack Golden was her neighbour, and her friend. He was the one in school who would always stand by her, loudly, ostentatiously guarding her from the boys. From the other girls. He would push her about, gently, and she sensed an innocent affection in his shoving, how he walked home with her in spite of the mockery of the boys, how he never, among all her classmates and companions, never tugged at her golden hair. And the others, all the others, the boys and the girls, sniggered and squirmed at words like "knickers", or "bum", or "fart", but never, never did Jack Golden speak such words and he cuffed those who used them when Gráinne was about and because Jack Golden was strong and good-looking and intelligent, the others shared out with Gráinne what little human respect they could find within themselves.

But Gráinne Flannery, child, was convinced of sin. "We're hens," she would think, "hens, hens, hens. Pecking in the dirt. Destined for the pot when we have laid our share of eggs." The drag of her own body when she was tired – and she was so often tired – the pains she was getting now, aches and twinges and catches in the strangest, most alarming places of her body, as if she were being pushed, pulled, manipulated, stretched by strong hands within her, all this convinced her of sin. And every evening she knelt with her mother to recite the Rosary – Fintan not wanting any part in such foolishness – words circling and circling in a dizzying cacophony of sound, and almost always her head drooped onto the back of the chair where she was kneeling; her mind strayed often and often from the wonderful mysteries of the finding in the temple, the crucifixion, the ascension into heaven. She would loll instead with Jack Golden along the roads or over the moorland, away from the stores and offices and outhouses, or down along the wet, lush banks of Stony River where she often wandered on her own, sharing the delicious whispering of the water over pebbles, or its more certain gurgle as it was channelled into faster streams around the larger stones – until her mother scolded her for her inattention, for saying nine Hail Marys instead of ten; and she pointed to the picture of the broken-hearted Jesus hanging over the range and accused her of adding always to His pains.

They loved her, yes, they loved her, she knew that, and she loved them. Fintan and Nora Flannery, small merchants, thin and angular people, pencil people, dressed almost always in shopkeepers' smocks, fingers smeared with flour or paraffin oil or the dark dust that came off the islanders' coins, busy about their talk of commerce, competition, growth. But they loved her in that big, distant country way of loving, where all the love is held away in embarrassment at the showing, where it is wrapped in wool and tissue paper and put into a chest and pushed aside as an exotic thing fit for wilder climates and gypsy peoples, not suitable for west of Ireland simple folks who earned their daily bread from weights and measures, buying and selling, fixing and dealing and practical good sense. They directed her, and themselves, down the track of work and service and ritual, the path that led down into the dark and shadowed way but that carried on, ineluctably, up out of the valley of tears into an eternal kingdom of light, psalms and marble halls. But meanwhile and secretly, Gráinne, their ungainly daughter, was wholly convinced of sin.

She watched Jack's body, its supple, exciting powers, its strength, its angular mysteries, its sudden energies, and somewhere within herself she longed to know that body, so different from her own, to know why it drew her so, why sometimes Jack's stirring presence aroused an ache of unease and longing in her own flesh and once, lying awake in the loneliness and pleasure of her attic room, thinking of him and his fine body urging itself to flight, she moved her fingers along her own body and gave herself sensations of pleasure she knew were wicked and evil, but she luxuriated in them, and prayed to God for pardon.

She trudged unhappily to school every day, with all the other girls and boys, trudging there and trudging back. She found school as dull as her own back yard – all that learning by rote, the rattling off of verses, catechisms, bible stories, the sums, the pointless arguing and bullying and boisterous hair-pulling of the school-yard, drudgery, dullness, stone! And in the afternoons she had to help in the store, weighing out tea and sugar and flour, fetching and arranging, dusting and sweeping, growing slow and heavy in her life. Dogged. Taciturn. Determined. Stubborn. Proud. She was in charge of the hens that the Flannerys kept at the far end of the yard, fenced in to their own small world, days spent in the drudgery of pecking about among their own leavings, nights in the coop, offering up their eggs in homage to the overbearing presence and demands of humankind. Gráinne put on her hen-boots, opened the chicken-wire gate, passed in among them, trudging over chicken-shit and mud and famine tufts of struggling grass.

"Here, chuck chuck chuck chuck chuck chuck, here chuck chuck chuck chuck chuck chuck!"

Endlessly. Her right hand scattering meal among the poor, stupid creatures, as they skittered importantly about their drudgery, strutting and pouting and murmuring their platitudes to the air.

Gráinne had become expert, too, in finding their eggs; she was a witch in her knowledge as to which hen was growing ever-so-slightly weary of this world. She could catch one, confidently, by the neck and claws, bring it down behind the turf shed, hold it in her left hand, gather up the axe in the other, lay the squawking, wondering creature over a tree-stump and chop its head off with one perfect, guillotining, swipe. She knew how to hold on to the yellow, gnarled claws while the body fluttered and jerked and the blood spilled out onto the earth. She knew how to avert her face from that small head that lay, separated from its body, on the earth, the eyes holding a startled, accusatory stare that would not go away until she had buried it in the turf-mould graveyard beyond the fence. The breeze blew in across the yard from the distant world, smelling of salt, surging in from the enormous beyond, touched her hair and fingered through the cooling feathers of the hen, then carried on its way, busy and clucking and venturesome. And the young girl, still holding that nerve-live, shivering and headless body in one hand, swayed in the heaviness of her existence, her ungainly body balancing from side to side, death in her hand, and consciousness of weight flooding through her difficult soul.

Out of the bleak grey landscape of her life, her Uncle Jim, ship's engineer, offered some little feathers of colour. Letters came, haphazard, irregular, from remote and unheard-of corners of the world, brown envelopes, white envelopes, packages. Uncle Jim Flannery would write to Gráinne, and to nobody else. All his mail was addressed to her, only to her: to

> Miss Gráinne Flannery,
> Flannery's Stores,
> Bunclabhan,
> Achill Island,
> Co Mayo. Ireland.

Fintan and Nora Flannery knew better than to open Jim's letters to Gráinne. They knew better than to stop her gathering up the letter and climbing at once into her attic room. For she would grow wild and scatterfisted at an invasion of her privacy, scream and scold and clench her fists in ungovernable rage if they tore the string of the little packages to pry into her strange apartness. She was stubborn, they knew it and they knew to wait until she had savoured her moment, examining first the exotic stamps – Australian, Mexican, Brazilian, Canadian, Chinese – imagining the route the letter had taken, the continents it had trekked across, the great rivers it had leapt, the seas it had sailed. She opened each one carefully, so she could keep the envelope intact. Nearly always Jim sent her a gift, a butterfly or a moth, pinned and mounted on cardboard and named, the words carefully inscribed in Jim Flannery's painstaking hand. Gráinne would read the letter; she would sit on the edge of her bed and draw her two knees together, flattening out the paper on her lap; she would bow her head down over the writing, her body swaying slowly, backwards, forwards, backwards, forwards, her tongue out between her lips, her eyes wide in wonder;

Dear Gráinne,

Our ship, called *Wandering Albatross*, docked in Zanzibar last night. We will be here for four days. My work is done for today. I sit in my cabin. The water is slopping against the side of the old tub. I can hear natives calling. They are loud. They are like parrots. I am very well. I hope you, too. And Fintan and Nora. Give them all my wishes. The weather here is awful. Hot. Can you imagine trying to live while you're drowning in hot soup? Or tar? It's like that. Moist and hot and hard to breathe. On Saturday we're off for New Zealand. I don't know exactly where yet. I'll write. Keep this safe. He's a moth. I bought him in a tiny shop this morning. I think it cost me about tuppence. Isn't he beautiful? I love the tiny blue colours, aren't they like the sea in Keem Bay on a warm summer's day? And the little white dots on his wings and back? like tiny stars in a tiny sky. Like the stars over your lovely island. How I miss your island. My island. Keep him safe, Gráinne, with the others. I'm dying to see your collection when I get home. They call him a "polka dot moth", what I have written underneath. I hope you keep well and happy and I'm sure you're growing beautiful and tall. Tell Fintan and Nora I met Doctor Grieves in Hong Kong. We chatted and he remembers them and sends best wishes. I will lie down in the soup now, Gráinne, and see if I can sleep.

Yours faithfully,
Jim.

Pinned carefully to one of the cabbage-green walls were the treasures of colour and pattern Jim had been sending her, little songs of high light, jewels of improbable size and pattern, butterflies and moths from around the world, their wings spread wide and held, their seed-bodies, furred and striped and patterned by a childish God's wild imagination, fixed now forever in their dust by a slender pin. The *clothes moth*, eyes and elfin dancing shoes on its lava-coloured wings; the *gypsy moth*, small and dark, tree-bark patterned; the *imperial moth*, huge and coloured golden iris with small explosions of lilac patterns on its wings; the African Peach Moth, the Giant Hercules, Copiopteryx Derceto; the Blue Mountain Butterfly, coloured dark night with the blue-green sky of intruding day; the Christmas Butterfly, all forest green and forest shade; even the small and incredibly delicate white *cabbage butterfly*, so delicate she feared a too strong sigh of awe before it might blow it away in dust. The cabbage butterfly, as common as midges about the fuchsia hedges near her own house but grown miraculous when pinned and held and mounted for adoration. And they were hers, these caught glories, pinned still and perfect and beautiful, hymns and calls and dreams from around the world, her joy, her secret, her release.

"Sir" faded in and out of Jack's memory as he had faded in and out of his life. "Sir". Edward Ronald Golden. He was a ghost, now, named and heavy and grounded, but a ghost nonetheless. Jack remembered him sitting before the open fire in the kitchen of the old house. The thatched house. The house whose brain was filled with mosses and lichens, with swallows in the summer, and with beetles and cockroaches during the whole of the year. Warm and comforting. And at night sometimes, if you leant a certain way and squinted, you could see tiny holes in the thatch that could have been stars. Moths coming, too, to inquire about the yellow glow of the oil lamp, knocking their strange bodies against the heat of the globe, distant disturbing sounds.

Sir seemed to have been sitting in that cosy chair for years. Often talking to his son about the good years, the long-ago years when the world was ordered and the people were marshalled under certainties. Steady and removed like the oil-lamp before the Sacred Heart, Sir was still tall in those years, and imposing, though he had aged suddenly and grown hard in his flesh and mind as a bog-deal root. Jack had watched that yellowing moustache, how it came down over the mouth, how a mist gathered at the tips of it, sometimes growing into a teasing, hanging droplet. Sir always chewed on the edge of a pipe and – on the mantelpiece over the fire – he kept a collection of them, from foolish old Irish white clay pipes to long, curling pipes to wooden pipes to meerschaums. Tooth-marks on the dark mouthpieces. Dents and dunts on the bowls.

Sir, grown ever more urgent about order in his life, in his family and in the world, turned his pipe upside down and knocked the bowl against the side of the grate. The worn-out ash fell among the embers. Then he reached up and changed pipes. The elaborate and exasperating ritual began. Jack forced to hear the stories of the aging man's history, how small the island was, an island off an island off the great and world-redeeming England. Pipe. Pipe-cleaner. The old chipped tongue curling out between teeth and lips in concentration. Penknife from the darkness of a pocket. The bright tin box of plug from the mantelpiece, the slicing and rubbing, the friction between the two dried palms that sent shivers of physical pain through Jack's body. Until the flakes were placed in the bowl of the pipe and packed down with the stump of the penknife. How Ireland in her foolishness had cast her lot with chaos and black night and thrown herself headlong into anarchy. Jack earned a penny a day by keeping Sir supplied with spills of newspaper, torn and twisted into taper shapes with which he could light his pipe, kept in a heap on the hob beside the cosy chair. An old man already. A man who had given up on ordinary living and who wallowed now in self-pity, making his one child call him "sir", insisting always on due law and regulation within the strict confines of his family where he would live and die. Talking the grey-smoke talk of politics, explaining, gesturing, clogging the young boy's brain with the aging man's view of things.

But the boys in the school had told Jack otherwise, and

the teacher, in her own cautious way, had told him otherwise. And Jack, his eyes cast down on the floor before the loud words of his father, thought his own thoughts within his head and murmured in his brain the word "traitor".

Then one day Jack saw him stand and lean towards the grate. He stopped, half-way. There was a low grunt and a few gasps and he sat back heavily on the chair. The ash fell from the bowl onto his old, soiled lap. The pipe fell from his hand and rolled slowly down his trouser leg and hit the russet flags of the kitchen floor where bowl and stem cracked apart. The old man writhed slowly in his chair, his eyes closed, his head thrown back, sweat already on the dried-up skin, the feet shifting in a slow, slow dance on the floor.

They put him to bed in the tiny back room at the end of the twisting hallway. They gave him a heavy hand-bell which he rang in irritation at the heaviness of his dying. Its dull, demanding peals echoed across the landscape of the young boy's soul. Sometimes, across the rafters of his low room, Sir saw carts go trundling slowly by, the horses drawing them as feeble, fretted and woebegone as the small wide-eyed family cowering together. A skeletal people, the flesh falling from them in clumps, the land behind them burned black with famine, only the rocks of the sea-shore remaining in their dreams. Accusing him, accusing him. At the edge of the ocean they would heel up the cart as a wind-break, gather what periwinkles and barnacles, seaweeds and mosses they could and boil them up to make them palatable. Their silent, white eyes gazed down from the thatch at Sir, accusing him, their clothes hanging about them like leaves on winter trees, accusing him, their hands

29

already crossed over their chests in preparation for corpsehood, and Sir shuddered where he lay, his eyes filled with salt water, his mouth gaping, wishing to sink down through the bed and the floor and hide his unbearable weight in the soft flesh of the earth.

Jack had to touch him sometimes, when he was brought into the presence to pray. Sometimes Sir turned his awful eyes towards the young boy and the long brambles of his hands reached towards him. Jack watched the tiny purple veins that hammered and pulsed through the flesh that crinkled under a weak, grey stubble of beard. He saw the white cloth spread on the little table, the two death-candles, the little jug of death-water. These were the only luggage he was permitted to bring with him on his final journey, his flight towards heaven, away, away up there where the blue sky shaded into silver, where the silver shaded into white like snow and there, on oceans of feathery clouds he would be clothed in garments of eternity and he would sing for ever before his God.

Sir groaned and moaned and suffered. The final order of his flesh was falling apart. He closed his eyes and sweated, soundlessly. And when he died he offered the men a problem; his body stiffened so quickly into such a long, plank-like shape that they could not get him out of the room without breaking him. They laid the coffin in the kitchen, before the dead and empty grate; they lifted the long body, forcing the legs about the knees; there was a muffled crack, the men glanced at each other but made no comment. They heaved him around the corners and up along the stone floor of the hallway, they laid him beside the open, plain-wood coffin. Jack heard the dull thud of his body as they laid him down.

"The dead do be awful heavy, son," Patsy Mulqueen mumbled towards the boy who stood watching at the door. "They do be heavy with the weight of their dyin', heavier lots than they was in life, that's for sure. But maybe it just serves to quicken their sinking into the soft wet of the kind earth when they do get put down."

They put the plain white board on the coffin. Patsy had nails. And a hammer. He put the nails into his mouth. They came out, one by one, like bitter words, long and terrible and definitive, and thudded dull and echoing and with finality into the shivering, stunned soul of the watching boy.

After his father's death Jack found there was nothing now to stop him from doing all the things that came naturally into his mind to do. His mother brought in a maid, Mary Alice MacNamara, to help her with the chores and to run the house when she was away at her teaching job. Mary Alice MacNamara took up her place in the small back room at the end of the twisting hallway. Filling the space of the lank ghost with her full and lovely body. Then Mrs Golden had the men come in and for several weeks they worked at the old house, lifting off its ancient thatch, fitting new and shining rafters, laying on the slates. The Golden household had been dragged through, at last, into the new century.

Jack rooted through the old trunk that had belonged to his father. It was big and humped, hooped and clasped. And it had always been locked during his father's lifetime, a big mortise lock with a big key the old man had always kept in the fob pocket of his waistcoat. That trunk, just lying there, a temptation and a thwart to a young boy, in the dim recess of the twisting hallway. His mother had left the key in the lock. As if she wished him to find out for himself who his father was.

Jack lifted back the lid.

There were books, Moore's Almanacs, bible histories, an edition of Tennyson's *In Memoriam*, Dickens's *Little*

Dorrit and *The Old Curiosity Shop*. There was a big leather belt with an empty holster. There was a fat fob watch with an inscription on the back: *To Ted Golden on the occasion of his 25th year with the RIC*. The watch was dead, as silent as its master.

Jack strutted the length of the twisting hallway, up and down, up and down, dressed in the dark jacket of the uniform, wearing the peaked cap that came down over half his face, bumping into the hallstand because he could not see out from under the cap, the jacket on him big as an overcoat, the dark trousers trailing on the ground and tripping him up as he strutted, the sleeves down over his hands. His mother laughed to see him, laughed also with a sense of ease and freedom now that Sir had released her, too, from himself and the awful burden of his righteousness.

"You're a right-looking constable, Jack," his mother said. "You look good and handsome in a uniform. But fold it up neatly and put it back when you're finished. The way he would have wanted it."

When she had left him he strutted some more, up and down, up and down, this time hoping, in a ghostly way, that his taunts might reach out and touch the man whose orders and discipline had kept Jack's childhood tightly tethered to this old house.

"I'm a constable," he intoned, "a constable, of the RIC. I am a traitor to my country. I fought on the side of the invader. I am a constable, a constable, of the RIC. I am an Irish man but I upheld the laws of the English. I am a constable, a constable, of the RIC."

From her own place in the kitchen his mother heard him and suffered her own small deaths.

Jack knelt, quietly fingering the crown embossed on the buttons of jacket, sleeve and cap; the brass was cool although it was already beginning to tarnish. Every week, even after his inglorious retirement, Sir had cleaned and shone the buttons, refolded the jacket and trousers, fingered the empty holster. Jack lifted a sleeve close to his mouth and hawed over the button; then he watched the dulled brass gradually brighten again as his breath faded away. It was a sun coming back out of the clouds. It was a boy surfacing from the lake after a dive. He licked the button, he chewed it, feeling the rough texture of the jacket against his lips. There was a faint musty smell, a mixture of office papers and pipe-smoke and man-smell.

When he was putting back the uniform Jack's hand touched something cold and hard, hidden within the cotton lining of the trunk. Cautiously he drew it out; it was a gun, a small, black pistol that felt hard and ugly and dangerous in Jack's hand. There was a small cardboard box, too, without markings, like a big matchbox, and when he opened it he saw the six small, shining bullets. He was scared. He put them back, gun and bullets, quickly, in their place, resolving never to tell his mother, or anyone else, about them. The adults never spoke about the crown, they never spoke about the pistol, they never spoke now of the RIC; that was something they hated, and still feared, something the adults kept to themselves, like the truth about sex, but the children round about him knew, and the teacher knew, Jack knew, and he exulted in his knowledge.

They often met after school, Jack and Gráinne, being neighbours, Jack being sent for messages to Flannery's store, Gráinne coming to the Golden's house with eggs. They were friends but they held their ground. They defended their territories. Their wondering, vulnerable children's acres. There were distances; they were boy and girl, after all, they were adolescents, in an adolescent country. And all about them the talk of the young country, the new freedom, the hope . . . There was closeness, too, closeness they both cherished without being conscious of their cherishing. She was the only one he allowed into his space, onto his pier, into his wood, into his dreams of flight. But he kept away from her his growing awareness of Mary Alice MacNamara. His secret. And his alone. And Gráinne admitted him into her chicken-yard, behind the counter in the stores, into her distresses and disappointments. But not into her attic room, not up there, nor did she mention the butterflies and moths on the cabbage-green wall. Her secret. And hers alone.

In every life there are many deaths, her Uncle Jim knew that, in the dark engine-room of his freighter; he lived his working days covered in oil and sweat while above him the sky would be clean and blue; as if it were built into the energies of growth that every human urge and effort be countered by a heavier weight, as if each lift and cheer of the human heart be brought back to earth with a harsh, defeating bump. Uncle Jim pondered all of that, hearing now and then from Gráinne, all her small stories, her news, the name of Jack Golden she allowed slip into her letters every now and then. He feared for her, too, for her innocence. And he feared for the young country, for the young world teetering along a slippery path of speed and experiment and commerce. He sat, Jim Flannery, in the engine-room, the old engine coughing back into effort. And he sighed. As if the life a human soul strains desperately to create must be continually de-created so that the human mind be never allowed to turn fully upon itself for comfort but be wrested constantly back towards its origins in death. And every little death is countered by a weak rebirth, a resurrection, until the final death, the ultimate victory that is gravity's alone.

Gráinne found him. Jack was swinging, as usual, among the high branches of a tree. She was breathless, urgent, her face flushed with excitement.

"Jack! Jack!" she yelled. "Come down! At once! There's something special I must show you."

And he came down, making a show of his reluctance, of his favour. Together they walked the short distance from the Golden home to the Flannery stores, keeping apart, he quizzing her impatiently, she laughing and holding back her surprise.

And there, in a small nest of dry, yellow grass under a fuchsia hedge beyond the chicken-wire, she showed him.

"Christ!" he hissed, and fell on his knees with delight.

There were six kittens in the nest, all but one the colour and texture of marmalade, the sixth being black, a sheer, wet black that gleamed in the dusk of the shade.

"Aren't they gorgeous?" she asked. "Absolutely gorgeous. And listen! I've given them names." She pointed, touching them, one by one. "This one's Ginger, and this one's Blackie, that little one there is Kitty, that one Jane . . ."

She paused to look at him, her face aflame with gladness.

"And this little one here, beside Blackie, I've called her Gráinne."

She looked up at him, and he smiled, and she was content.

Then she took one of the marmalade kittens in her arms and stood up straight, stroking it.

"This one is Jack," she announced determinedly, "and he's yours."

He was nonplussed. Stricken, pleased, and on the defensive.

"How do you know if they're . . . you know, if they're male or female?" he countered. "I mean, men or women cats, how do you know, so that you give them those names?"

She stopped. Now she was nonplussed. The five kittens in the nest squirmed like worms, they were blind, mewling, scrabbling feebly and climbing over one another. They were falling and rolling and squinting and Jack chuckled with delight. She turned from him and laughed down at them, too, hoping to avoid his question. Hoping.

"How do you know?" he repeated.

"I don't know, Jack," she admitted. "They're just kittens, now, let them be just kittens, Jack, let them be small and free and . . . and kittens, just for a while."

He laughed again. On a footing now, and more relaxed. He bent down and picked up the tiny black one from the nest into his two hands and felt its birth-dampness, saw the squingeing of its tiny snout, the effort of the locked-closed eyes to open.

"Aaaaaaggghhh!" he sighed, delighted.

And suddenly Mr Flannery was there, in his brown store apron, a hessian bag in his big, red fist.

"So!" he said, loudly, with authority. "You found them."

He stooped quickly and picked one of them up and dropped it into the hessian bag. He gathered the one Gráinne held and dropped it in, too. Then he reached down for another.

"What are you doing?" Gráinne shrieked at him.

"I'm doing the best for them, Gráinne," he said to her, dropping the third kitten in the bag. Then the fourth. Gráinne could see the coarse material of the bag, how it squirmed and shook and lived with the sorry scrabbling of the tiny creatures inside. Tiny bodies dropped back into a darkness more hostile than the one they had recently emerged from.

"What are you doing? What are you doing?"

"This is too many kittens, Gráinne, we can't keep them, we simply can not keep them."

He picked up the fifth kitten and dropped it in the bag. Jack had slipped the tiny black one inside his jumper and kept his arms folded over his chest, hiding it.

"But what are you going to do with them? What will you do . . . ?"

"Now believe me, Gráinne," Mr Flannery reasoned, "believe me, what I'm doing is for the best. They just cannot stay here, they'll cause havoc, we've too many cats about the place already. We need a few to keep the mice and rats out of the stores, yes, but we have enough now, too many." The big store-keeper was already walking slowly out through the yard, the two young people following. "And nobody wants more kittens now. Nobody. So the simplest and fairest thing, fair to us and fair to them, is to get rid of them now, at once, before they even really begin to live. Believe me, it's for the best. They'll only suffer if they live, they'll starve, they'll be kicked about the place, they'll become scrawny and weak and the foxes will tear them to shreds. So it's the humane thing to get rid of them now, before they know life, before we get to know them."

As he spoke he moved swiftly and determinedly up along the chicken-wire fence, down by the back ditch and over the drain into the commonage beyond the yard. Gráinne followed close, appalled, clinging to him, tears already running on her face, the words stuck somewhere in the heavy mud of her sorrow. Fintan Flannery bent then and gathered up several big stones from the ground; he dropped them in with the shifting creatures in the sack and gathered the neck of it into a knot. The kittens within seemed to have quietened already as if, with the stones as their travelling companions, they had already been returned to the womb from which they had just now come.

"Stones!" she sobbed. "It'll hurt them. Don't hurt them. The poor, poor creatures."

"It's for the best, Gráinne, I'm telling you."

Behind them Jack walked, surly and quiet, knowing the horror of it, knowing, too, it was not his place to interfere. They came to the edge of the small lake that had filled up an old, abandoned quarry. The water here was black, the bottom soft and oozing and muddy, the children always warned to stay well away from here, it was a trap, a danger, it was bottomless.

Without another word Mr Flannery grasped the sack about the neck and swung and swung it in the air, round and round three times. As it swirled about his head Gráinne could hear a low-toned humming chorus from the sack as if the living souls within had begun a hymn of praise to stones and darkness and hempen threads, a sound, too, like that of a woman's voice humming to itself, an echo from a sound that had not been made. Gráinne could see the hard edges where the stones were, she could hear the whistle of the bag as it hurtled through the air and then it was flying, high and out over the centre of the lake.

The sack made only a small splash, only a moment's effort on the surface of the lake, then it was gone, down to the black sodden depths of silt and mud to which, she thought for a moment, we must all return. Mr Flannery's shoulder hurt. There was some gnawing pain beginning deep within him as he saw his daughter's face grow pale as putty. He would have to answer for this. At whatever court . . .

"Believe me, you must believe me, Gráinne, what future would the poor things have had? What future . . . ?"

Gráinne said nothing. She watched to see if there were bubbles on the surface of the lake. There was nothing. No sign. Mr. Flannery turned away, back towards the store. Gráinne sat down heavily on the damp earth. Jack sat with her.

They were silent for a time. The black depths of the lake were silent, too. As if the world should split apart and reveal a scarlet core of resentment, or of explanation.

"I hate him!" Gráinne hissed then. "I hate him! It's a sin, that's what it is! A mortal sin!"

For answer Jack drew the tiny black kitten from inside his jumper. It made a pathetic mewling sound, scrabbling to get back to the warmth and darkness inside the jumper.

Gráinne was filled with delight.

"Jack!" she whispered. "You saved him! Oh thank God! thank God! We'll really have to mind him. Well done, Jack, well done! That was clever, oh bless you, bless you, bless you!"

And she reached her awkward body awkwardly towards his and kissed him suddenly on his cheek. He was startled. He looked quickly towards her and was amazed and moved to see the brightness in her eyes and the fond gaze with which she looked into his. He wanted, then, to hold her, to tell her that it was going to be all right, that the kittens couldn't have known anything, couldn't have suffered . . . but it was confusion that had him reaching for her, and of course the kittens must have suffered, of course he could not pretend . . .

"I hated my father, too, Gráinne," he offered instead. "He was always going on at me, making me do things, orders, always giving orders, as if only he knew how the whole world was to be ruled. And we had to call him 'sir', can I go to the shops, 'sir', would you like a cup of tea, 'sir', I hated him, Gráinne, I hated him. And everybody says he fought for England when Ireland should have been free. So your father isn't all that bad. I mean, he didn't mean any harm. And we've got this little black one. We'll share him. I'll mind him up at our place where he'll be safe. My mother is kind, well, she's not really aware . . . And you can come and play with him whenever you want. He's our kitten, Gráinne, our secret. We'll have a secret that only you and I will share. Our own, special, secret."

She smiled up at him and her heart was never so warm as at that moment.

"His name is Jack," she said, "but maybe we'll give him

just a slightly different name, so that when I say, *I want Jack*, or *where's Jack?* or something like that we'll know that I'm talking about the kitten, or about you. Whichever. We'll call him Jackie. And that way, too," and she grew excited at the new idea, "he can be either a woman or a man cat, I mean a Jackie can be a man or a woman, can't he? She . . . ?"

Jack laughed and took Gráinne by the arm. Her flesh was warm and firm to his touch. The kitten slipped and squirmed in his other hand. The day was mild again, the lake sparkled with original beauty. They smiled at one another. And far away, in the dim, dark hold of his freighter, Uncle Jim stood, rubbing his hands with a dirty rag, gazing abstractedly at the round faces of the instruments before him, the old engine grumbling away, and dreamed his own, distant dreams.

It was a dead, dark evening. The barracks backed onto the low sand-hills that gave minimal protection from the winds that came cursing and clawing down the long curve from Siberia. Between the dunes and the barracks there were only flat sandy acres with bushes of marram grass scattered, shivering, here and there. There were the cold winds. The blown sand. The little spits of rain. And seven men.

The men were crawling through the darkness, now – as they came nearer the barracks – they were on their hands and knees, crawling like sheep from wet grass-clump to wet grass-clump. Any noises they made, the scrape of a rifle off a stone, grunts of effort, curses at the difficulty of the weather, the occasional muffled sneeze, were covered by the whistling, shrieking, burning-cold winds. They moved slowly. With extreme care. This was serious work. This was insurrection! Against the forces of the crown.

"An army marching on its knees, what, lads?" hissed Patsy Mulqueen, and his low chuckle did not impress his fellows.

There were two men on duty that evening in the RIC barracks. Edward (Ted) Golden and John Albert Quinn. Ted was walking restlessly up and down the main room of the building. John Albert sat at the table, chair slightly tilted back, leaning on air. He was looking vacantly at

43

sheets of paper on the desk in front of him, at his long, thin pen with its rusted nib; in his head he was hunting for elusive words, words that raced from his grasp the way sprat will leap before a marauding mackerel shoal. He watched Ted's shadow swell and diminish along the wall from the single oil-lamp. A fire of turf and driftwood did little to warm the stone hull of the two-room barracks. An occasional, rare, flame from the fire gleamed softly on the brass buttons of Ted's uniform. He always wore full uniform on duty, even when there had been nothing to do for days. One does what one has to do to order one's life, to place one's living in some focus, to locate it in some place, Ted thought. One does what one has to do. He had nothing special on hand. Nothing but order his subordinate to fill out the requisite report forms; nothing but count the sharp calls of the curlew or snipe from the wetlands beyond the barracks; nothing but fetch damp sods from the clamp out at the gable wall. Behind the small and rapidly diminishing clamp, two bicycles rested against the wall, solid and dependable as the British presence in Ireland.

Two men. Islanders. On a war footing. Expecting islanders.

The invading men of the IRA knew Ted and John Albert well. Were fond of them. Drank with them sometimes out of the worrying rain. And would be known to them. They had rough clothes, boots, belts; in their pockets they had scarves and woollen caps to tie about their faces during the final assault. Soon, Pat Seán Joe would come to the front door of the barracks to capture the constables' attention. Soon. If they could get their timing right. Striking a blow for freedom. After so many centuries.

One of the men, crawling still on hands and knees, slipped and fell forward onto the wet sand.

"Shite!"

"SSShhhhh!"

Like the Siberian winds on their sleds of ice.

"I feel like a bloody fool!" muttered Wheezy (the Wheeler) Wheelan. A huge man, strong as a carthorse, face down now in the sand. His chest loud with effort as the ailing engine of a half-decker. "Like one of the Tuatha Dé Danaan, creeping about in the underworld."

Ted's gun was loaded. Ready. There was unrest in the country. Other barracks had been attacked. There had been murders. Atrocities. Reprisals. Here, among their own, at the windy edge of the world, it was unlikely there would be deaths. Still, when a disordered rabble high on porter took it into their heads to carry out a dream, anything could happen.

"It's awful quiet, John Albert," Ted said, peering through the window into the darkness.

"Sure isn't it forever quiet, sir?"

"Not this quiet, man, this is an unnatural quiet. Can't you sense it, behind the wind? Everything's not in order, I tell you, the world is crumbling into pieces."

Order again, that word; and how could the world be forever in order if any move forward was to be made?

"Times are awry, John Albert. The edges have frayed. The country's falling out of kilter. Can't survive without the steadying hand of England about its waist."

"Up its arse, you mean," John Albert thought. To himself. To himself. Right time now to be a patriot. Time to get out of this. With honour. With all your limbs intact!

Ted was pacing again, irritating, disturbing any hope of ease.

"Please, John Albert, please! Your jacket, man. Put on your jacket. We're on duty now, you know, we're on duty!"

John Albert stood up slowly and sighed. He took his jacket from the back of the chair and put it on. Ted had paused again before the window. A tiny white light was approaching down the road from the left, swaying and flickering. Ted watched it, indifferently.

The seven men had stopped. Between them and the yard-space behind the barracks was a swiftly-flowing river. They had forgotten about the river. In the large darkness they still could see the powerful surge the swollen water made . . .

"Mick!" someone hissed. "Mick! You're the tallest. You'd better wade in, carefully mind, and see can we get across."

All this in a loud whisper. There was shuffling. More whispers. Then one of the men stood up. Mick Mulvanny. Labourer. Roadmender. He moved into the water. He held a rifle high above his head. He stepped gingerly forward. At once he was up to his knees. Soaked. The force of the flood pounded against him. He leaned against it and carried on.

"It's fierce fuckin' cold!" he hissed over his shoulder.

There was no response. The men could see the small lamp on the bicycle of their companion as he approached the front of the barracks. Right on time. Good man. Good man. Distract the buckos. Mick Mulvanny was in the centre of the river. The water reached his belly. The ground under his feet was soft, like sand, and almost flowing, like the water. His coat lifted and floated about him. He went deeper. The water touched his chest. He clenched his teeth tightly against the cold. Then he was near the opposite bank. The ground shelved steeply again. He was across. Wet, cold. Shivering.

"Right men! It's deep. But we can make it. One by one now. And wait at the other side."

Another shadow lifted from the sand-dunes.

At the front of the barracks the man on his bicycle had come to a halt and leaned his bike against the front wall. He switched off his lamp. He tried to whistle. A heavy, hissing sound escaped him. He could see nothing in the dark world behind the barracks. He moistened his lips and tried again. Only a heavy, puffing sound. Fuck! And he had whistled so well all his life! Till now. Fuck! He knocked at the door.

"Evening, Ted," he began.

"Evening, Pat. Anything amiss?"

"No, no, no, just wondering like . . ."

"Wondering?"

"Yes, I was just wondering . . . I'm off over to Lynchehaun's like. You know. To see. And I was wondering . . ."

"What is it, Pat? What were you wondering?"

"Is, ah, is John Albert within?"

"Yes, he's inside."

"Can I speak to him a minute, Ted? You see, I was wondering . . . you know, I was wondering if the missus, John Albert's missus, wanted any turf or sticks or that. Brang up?"

Ted looked back into the lit room. John Albert was bent over his papers, the tip of the pen in his mouth. He was chewing.

Out in the back yard six men stood on the near side of the river. They were all shivering violently with the cold and the wetness. The seventh man was in the water. He stood, near the middle, petrified. He was shorter than the others; the water already touched his chest. He was scared, too, to turn back. It was difficult to turn on the shifting bottom of the river. The man's eyes were wide open, the whites of them visible like two stars in the darkness.

"Come on man, get a jerk into yourself!" from the near bank.

Ted called out:

"John Albert! Pat Seán Joe here wants a word."

John Albert looked up from his work. He glanced quickly at the old clock over the mantelpiece. He glanced at Ted.

"There's, ah, something strange here, Ted, in these forms, I mean. Maybe you'd come and have a look. I'll talk to Pat Seán Joe."

Out at the river the seventh man had let his rifle fall into the water. He still stood, motionless, half-frozen in the flow of the river. Someone whispered: "There's a war on! We'll have to leave him!"

As John Albert came to the door and stepped outside the barracks to deal with Pat Seán Joe, six wet and shivering men came round the gable of the building. Immediately John Albert's hands shot up into the air. Pat nodded at the men, and pointed sheepishly towards the open door. The leader moved cautiously to the light and looked in. Ted Golden was hunched over the forms on the table.

"Right! Ted, sir!" the man shouted suddenly as he jumped forward into the barracks. "Hands up, there's a man, we're taking over this barracks in the name of Ireland."

Ted looked up. He smiled, sardonically.

"Hello, Seamus," he said, casually. "I've been expecting you this few days. Do you think you can just . . . ?"

They had forgotten to put on their scarves, their masks. Five other men, all wet and shivering, their rifles and hand-guns shaking in their hands, pushed their way into the room. Outside, John Albert and Pat Seán Joe had gone to the assistance of the man in the river. They reached forward the handle of a spade and helped draw him across. In the room, Ted raised his hands slowly into the air. One of the men moved forward and took the gun from Ted's holster. Another picked up John Albert's gun from the edge of the table. There was an audible sigh of relief.

"Right, lads, that's done!" Seamus announced, and they pushed forward across the room towards the struggling fire.

"Any chance of a cup of tea, Ted?" Seamus Sweeney asked. "We're fuckin' frozen solid."

That night, Pat Seán Joe, the only dry man among them, spent the night in the barracks, taking possession for the newborn country. The other men went home, quickly, to dry off. John Albert took his bike and cycled home, indifferently. Ted was sent home, too, mumbling and complaining to the world. They had given him back his pistol. He had promised . . . given his word . . . He felt cheated. He had given his life to patrolling the world for these men, his neighbours, his friends. They had broken his life open, like an egg, had left him spilled across the floor. He could not accept it. When had he become the enemy? When had his neighbours become his enemies? The world was a tall building, high as the clouds; now the foundations had been rattled, the building was shaking, he was cast out, how could he carry on?

When he reached his old, thatched house, he left his bicycle in the stable outside. He stomped in the back door without a word to his wife or his young son, Jack. He went quickly to his bedroom and changed out of his uniform, bundling it, his cap, his leathers, his holster, his pistol, into the old trunk, locking the trunk, putting the key high on a rafter. Then he ate his evening meal without a word. When he was finished he sat in his usual corner by the fire, took down a pipe, tobacco, a spill, and set to. Just as usual. Just as always before. He was not aware of the small child sitting in a far corner of the kitchen. Still. About to be told the ways of history, the ways of the world. Watching him. Feeling the awful heaviness that had come in as his companion from the black night outside. Feeling the chill in the air. Afraid to approach anywhere near the warming sods in the fire.

Since his father's death, Jack had grown quickly, inch upon inch upon inch, his mother imagined, as if his body were responding to the sun after the darkness had lifted away. He would be tall. He was good-looking already, his features strong, his hair as black as the chough, his skin bronzed by the high winds of the island. And already things strained and shifted inside him, disturbing things, things that left him breathless and flushed, that weighed down the urge to fly that his body knew.

At night, sometimes, when Mary Alice MacNamara had settled herself into the back room and his mother had finished shuffling about in the kitchen, when he had heard the door of his mother's room close softly behind her and the silence came down heavily upon him, from the walls of the room, from the roof of the black world outside, he shivered and trembled with his growing. He would take the old lamp from his father's forgotten bicycle and travel down under the sheet, the blankets, the eiderdown, to explore the frightening wood of his body. He touched the dark, small hairs beginning to grow in strange places, he touched the soft flesh of his penis, watching it swell, and stiffen, and excite him.

He was afraid of this new body, his and not yet his. He had no-one to talk to about these changes in himself, his mother away schooling, tired in the evenings and often abstracted, and he climbed more often than before into the dark and comforting nest of branches high on his favourite tree. Now, too, he was more aloof and surly in Gráinne's company, too aware of her body near his own, longing and scared of his longing, scared of what would appear in Gráinne's eyes should he begin to speak.

One day he was standing in the angle the stable wall made with the gable of the house, a dark dank corridor that led to a blank patch of wall; it was a place out of harmony with the world and he had brought himself there by the calls of his own dying childhood, his instinct to hide, his need for caverns where he could stand and wonder. He stood there, a patch of sky in the shape of a grey ruler high above him. Sheltered from the breeze. Invisible to the world.

Mary Alice MacNamara was at the turf-shed, taking sods from the tipped-up cart and flinging them into the shed. He watched her. It was heavy, tedious work and he was glad she was there to do it. Mary Alice was strong. She was big and she commanded the world. She bent and swayed and swivelled to her task.

The breeze played eagerly about her and she welcomed its embraces. It pulled her long black hair about her face and she flicked it back again. It swung her skirt and blew it tight against her limbs. She relished its grasp. She was pretty, too, she knew it, and she knew that Jack was there, standing in the angle that the stable wall made with the gable of the house. Jack. Young and handsome and adolescent Jack. Alone and silent. A toy.

Then the breeze lifted her skirt so high about her that she had to stand erect and push it down again. Her red skirt, flannel and heavy and safe. But Jack had seen her, and he had seen that she wore nothing underneath. The flesh was white, white and full and deeply disturbing in its shadows, gleaming and wonderful against the dark red world of the uplifted skirt. Something slipped heavily from his chest where he was breathing and landed on the bottom of his stomach; he could not breathe and he lifted his hands to his throat.

Mary Alice had turned and looked at him. He had stepped out, involuntarily, into the day. Now she stood there. Watching him. She was several years older than him and filled with the wisdom of those extra years, alert to the glory of her own body and the power to soar over men that she had already begun to know. Now she looked across the space of the back yard into Jack Golden's face. She looked into his eyes. She looked across the terrible distances between them, between their sexes, between their ages, between their positions in a young, immature country. And she smiled at him, gently. She was – beautiful. He said the word to himself and knew, at last, something of what it meant. But he could not look back at her, not now, not now. He coughed, lightly, breathed in a great gulp of nonchalance and moved out into the flowing river of sunlight and wind that was the afternoon.

When he took the torch under the bedclothes that night she was there, in the wood with him, frightening and irresistible, a strange glow about her terrifying body, a smile on her face. And Gráinne was there, too, a quieter presence, just as beautiful. And Jack pushed and pulled at his risen penis until a great wave of pleasure broke over him and he cried out into the darkness of the night.

"Bless me Father, for I have sinned."

The dark box, the anonymity, the armour of daily living thrown off before the all-seeing power of God, the naked soul left prostrate under the weight of sin, at God's feet.

"Yes, Jack, how many days . . ."

Father Wall, too small an island, too intimate a place.

"It's not days, Father, it's five weeks since . . ."

"Don't slip, Jack, don't slip, man, now that poor Ted is no longer with us. Don't slip. A man can fall, you know, fall quickly and forever, down, down, down under the weight of his sin."

"Yes, Father. Father, I touched myself . . ."

A pause.

"Yes, Jack. Go on. Did you cause seed to spill?"

A pause. Jack considered.

"Yes, Father, yes."

"I see. How many times, Jack?"

"Often, Father, maybe . . . every night."

"Jack, boy, Jack, that's not good. And did you bring the image of a woman into your mind while this was happening?"

"Yes, Father."

"I see. I see. You must avoid this, Jack. You must avoid it. It's a habit, boy, a habit, a terrible sinful habit that will grow on you until you cannot control it. It is Satan taking control of your soul. You will go blind, Jack, you will go blind. You will go blind to the higher things of life to which you are undoubtedly called. It wearies you, you cannot live properly. You will be dragged down and down and down into the deep sump of Hell. It's the imagination, you see, the imagination that is the great curse of man; we can bring into our imagination any level of evil thing and play with it until it has become as real to us as our own lives. And that is the end of truth, Jack, all truth and integrity and honesty goes out the door and there is nothing in our life that we can trust after that. For the imagination is a lie, Jack, it is a lie. And I know you are called to the highest things. The highest. The priesthood, now . . . Promise me, Jack, this terrible, terrible sin . . ."

As he knelt, fervent for a while at the top of the small church, Jack promised, faithfully, and his soul sang again at the knowledge of his purity, of how high his soul could fly. He looked up at the face of the Christ standing in the niche on the chapel wall; he saw His curls, long and brown and perfect, he saw the beard, trim and brown and perfect, the long, unsexing, red gown, red and flowing and perfect. His eyes, almost squinting, were turned from the young boy and gazing towards the high rafters of the church.

Early in Summer, one of those days that come out of nowhere, a still, bright day, filled with warmth, Jack had decided to head down to the shore to swim. At the same time his mother had called Mary Alice MacNamara and asked her to cycle down to the pier to buy some fresh salmon. *The Star of the Sea* would be coming in after a night's fishing; if she was on time she could buy a salmon from Leo. When Mary Alice reached the shed she could see that Jack, young Jack, was distraught. Sir's bike was flat! The front wheel was hopelessly down and when Jack pumped it up it went flat immediately. He cursed. Loudly.

"What's wrong, Jack?" It was Mary Alice's sunshine voice.

"My bloody bike is flat and I want to go swimming down at the shore."

"You can come with me, then, you can hitch a ride on the carrier of my bike."

Mary Alice was pert today, she was glowing in the rare embraces of the sun, she was big and tall and pretty, she was strong and determined in her mind.

Her bike was a woman's bike, without crossbar, with a fine wicker basket fixed to the handlebars and a strong carrier fixed over the back wheel. She wheeled the bike from the shed and straddled it.

"Now," she called to him, "you get on the carrier and balance yourself carefully. Hold on to me."

Jack climbed on the carrier, she pushed the bike off powerfully and sat up on the saddle. Jack clasped her tightly around the waist. His hands glowed with a special warmth at the sense of her flesh underneath her blouse. The road to the shore was a poor one, the surface sandy and littered with stones, but it was downhill and they sailed along smoothly enough under the warm sky. Jack closed his eyes, his head touching Mary Alice's back; he inhaled the fragrance from her clothes, his arms knew the feel of her waist; he wondered if today she was wearing anything under her dress . . .

They arrived at the pier. There was no sign yet of the *Star Of The Sea*. Mary Alice left the bike leaning against the wall and she sat on the end of the pier, her legs hanging over the water. The tide was high. A current ran by some hundred yards offshore.

Jack moved along the small strand to the right of the pier. He went in behind some rocks and changed into his togs, keeping an eye to where Mary Alice was sitting. Quickly he was in the water, swimming strongly, relishing the coldness that brought a rush of life and blood to his flesh. He could see Mary Alice in the distance. Once she waved to him and he waved back out of the water.

As he got out to dry himself off he could see the *Star Of The Sea* rounding the point and heading in for the pier. Jack ran quickly up and down the strand to dry himself off and warm up again. Mary Alice watched him, her legs swinging slowly, her hands holding the rough edge of the pier. His body was fine, she thought, fresh and filling and golden fair. A pity he was so young. She would like to find

. . . love. She would like to find love and freshness and a body fine like that. But he was young, too young. A toy. She smiled softly to herself. Her imagination pictured him, naked in the water, floundering in the overwhelming embrace of the ocean, a fish, a salmon, an eel. She laughed aloud and waved to him once again.

Jack towelled his body fiercely behind his rock. He took off his togs and saw how his flesh was red and blue from the cold of the sea. He stood longer than he needed to, allowing the sunshine and the fingering winds of the island to examine him. He relished standing naked in the world, all burdens shed, for the moment. When he got back to the pier, Mary Alice had a fish wrapped tightly in newspaper and she was talking to Leo at the edge of the trawler. Then she waved goodbye and came to the end of the pier. Jack was waiting.

"You want to get a lift back, too?" she asked him, smiling.

"Yes, please, if you can manage?"

"Of course I can manage, Jack, of course I can manage."

She put the fish into the basket of the bike and wheeled the bike out onto the pier.

"This time, though, you mustn't hold me round the waist," she smiled at him. "I found it hard to pedal that way and it's mostly up hill now. I'll have to feel free to move more."

"I'll hold onto the edge of the carrier, then."

"No. I want you to hold onto the saddle." She watched him closely. She was smiling, a curious light in her eyes.

"But . . . you'll be on the saddle."

"Yes," she said, laughing, and the sound was a soft stream bubbling over pebbles, "yes, you put your two hands on the top of the saddle and hold on and I'll sit up on your hands. That way you'll not fall off and I won't have you draggin' off my waist."

Jack's body heaved with wonder and anticipation. He put his towel and togs inside his jacket and climbed onto the carrier of the bike. Then he placed his hands on the top of the saddle, one on top of the other, and looked at her. He was frightened, too. He could feel his penis stir. His whole body tingled from the sea; now it trembled, too, in anticipation.

Slowly Mary Alice wheeled the bike onto the sandy road. Then she straddled it. She pushed off with her right foot and for a few yards pedalled upright. When the bicycle had gathered some momentum she lifted her body backwards and sat down carefully on the saddle. Jack felt the fine stuff of her dress caress his hands, then her weight descended on him and he knew the firmness of her buttocks, felt the flesh work rhythmically against his hands, and knew that underneath her dress she was naked.

Jack closed his eyes and concentrated all his living on his hands. Mary Alice was heavy but as she moved on his hands Jack was all pleasure, his heart thudded with fear, with wonder, with delight. Mary Alice had to work hard to make her way up the long slope of the hill and she shifted her body about for greater purchase. Jack was in ecstasy. Neither of them spoke. He could feel her breathing, he was aware of the effort she had to make as she climbed. Then at last she topped the rise. The rest of the way home was gentle.

Mary Alice seemed to relax now and settled more cautiously on Jack's hands. He could feel the wonderful parting between her legs, the firm and softly-rounded flesh of her buttocks. Quickly, now, his penis exploded inside his trousers and he felt the wetness spread about his flesh. Mary Alice was breathing harder, too, small gasps as she shifted slowly on his hands. Then suddenly she let out a small, animal cry and stopped pedalling. She went very quiet. For some time the bicycle flowed like a silent stream down the gentle gradient towards home. She stopped the bicycle and said to him, gently lifting herself from his hands:

"Maybe it's best if you walk the rest of the way, now, Jack. Maybe it's best . . ."

As he walked home, Jack felt as if he had travelled for miles; he was weary; the excitement had been too much for him. He felt heavy and grown-up, embarrassed at himself, happy beyond belief. But this would be a secret he could not tell, not to anyone, especially not to Gráinne who came into his mind at once, Gráinne who would not understand, who would be angry with him, not to his mother, not to any of his friends at school . . . But Father Wall . . . ?

"Bless me, Father, for I have sinned. It's one week . . ."

"And you say it was she who urged you to do that, Jack?"

"Yes, Father, but I don't think she meant any harm."

"No, of course not, Jack, but you should not lend yourself to anything like that. That's a serious sin, Jack, touching a woman's private parts like that, even if you did not set out to do it. That's a mortal sin, Jack, a mortal sin. And you must promise me never, never, do you hear me, Jack, never . . . For what is your soul worth, Jack, your immortal soul to burn for ever in the awful furnaces of Hell? All for a few minutes' pleasure with the flesh of a woman. Jack, you must avoid her, you must keep far away from this woman's presence . . ."

If only he could fly, if only he could leave this sodden, heavy earth and soar. Jack imagined himself running along the ground, running, running, running, then letting go of the earth, leaping and falling forward the way you fall forward into a dive, but not falling, not falling, rising rapidly on the currents of air, rising high over the garden wall, higher than the lower branches of the trees, coming out over the tops of the highest pines, knowing then the sudden expanse of heath and lake and field and meadow as he rose higher, knowing the coolness of the rich breezes against his face, rising higher and higher, soaring then, like

62

the hawk soars, like the gulls that circle in the sky so high and pure that they look like a mirage, their salt-caked, their guano-hardened, their scavenger-filthy bodies, purified and beautified in the height of the sky, until he soared away, away, away into the clouds, higher than the sight of man could follow him, higher and higher and higher, until the earth itself became a nothing far below him, and he was indifferent to it, indifferent as he floated and dived and soared in the infinite kindness of the sky. Oh the imagination! Its lift, its passion and its hope! The imagination, it is a lie, young man, remember, the imagination is a lie!

Cornelius Griffin was burly; he was tough as a knot in wood. Some years older than Gráinne he helped in Flannery's store, doing the heavy work, the hoisting, the heaving, picking up a few pounds each week that kept his slack mind at peace. He was built like one of the sacks of meal he hoisted from floor to low loft, except that inside the flabbiness was a barrel frame, hooped and solid and hard. His mind, too, was hooped and solid and hard, his eyes black and slightly twisted, his fists were knotted timber and his flesh was bark.

Gráinne, from the shadows of a storeroom doorway, or through the dust-dimmed window of the snug, sometimes watched that great body as Cornelius, stripped to the waist, his muscles and veins standing out in sweat, his great chest covered in a golden, feathery down, his back with the shoulder-muscles straining, worked at his tasks about the yard. She was stirred and fascinated by his body, hurt and tangled by her own shifting and stirring emotions. Revolted by her own longings and irked by the obtuse stare of the big man's eyes. Quickly then she would turn away, breathing a short prayer of contrition to her ever-watchful, scolding God and carry on about her own chores in store or pub.

He was shifting a great box of tea from the doorway of the storerooms to the furthest, dry corner, a corner rich with the scents of years, dark and fusty, protected with a layer of spiders' webs. As he passed the window, the box keeled on one corner, he saw Gráinne in the chicken-yard, fumbling for eggs in a grassy corner. He watched her for a while. She moved about, a little awkwardly, stooping, stretching, gathering her eggs. She was a quiet girl, he thought, reserved. A bit simple, perhaps. But that was nice. No fancy airs. But then, she was the only child. And there was the store. He went to the door of the shed. She was young yet, and gangly, but she was growing, she would very soon fill out, and then she could be lovely. Her breasts already . . . And her hair – Cornelius imagined himself bathing his hands in that hair, burying his face in it and breathing in its beauty. Almost as if she was aware he had been watching her she turned, embarrassed.

He nodded over at her.

"Afternoon, Gráinne."

"Hello, Cornelius."

"There's a thing in the shed. Would you look?"

She looked at him for a moment. He was a simple young man, she thought. Simple, and quiet. She walked slowly towards the shed.

He brought her over to the window and showed her the great foil wrapping on the chest of tea.

"That's foil," he said. "Isn't it lovely?"

"Yes, it is nice."

"I'm gatherin' foil, you know. Off the chests. Off chocolate. Off the cigarette packets."

"What for?"

"Oh, I do make big silver balls out of it, hard and silver, all wrapped tight as a football. Big ones. And sometimes I do make shapes, at home in the evening, shapes like chalices, cups, that kind of thing. They do shine lovely in the light."

She was silent. He was ripping the foil from the inside of the tea-chest. There was a pleasant coolness in the store. It was well stocked with grain, tea, bags of sugar, flour. Cans of syrup, jams, fruit . . . and upstairs, on the small loft, even more stuff, fertilizers, sacks of grain, tins of paint. He was rolling and shaping the foil between his great hands, grinning at her, his tongue protruding through the left corner of his mouth, and she could see the soft hairs at the top of his chest, the firm flesh of his neck. Through a small doorway at the end of the store was the public bar; the grocery boasted it was *licensed to sell wines, spirits, beers, to be consumed on the premises*, and in the pub-store were many barrels of stout, cases of spirits, bottles of beer. Here, too, was Cornelius's domain; he was expert at the rolling of a barrel of stout, at standing it on its rim and rolling it further, and of heisting it with one quick swoop onto his shoulder.

"There!" he announced with pride, holding up a finely-shaped tinfoil chalice in the dim air of the shed. It glistered and shone in the little light that came in from outside.

They were silent for a while, the dust-motes settling on the air about them. Gráinne looked at him and nodded, smiling a little in acknowledgement and farewell. She was slightly scared of him in this confined space, the bulk, the strength, the squint . . . and that powerful man-smell, sweat and aggression and dominance that seemed to ooze from him.

"It's for you," he managed.

"Thanks, Cornelius." She took it, reluctantly, holding it carefully before her eyes.

"Are you walkin' out?" he asked her suddenly.

"What?"

He looked down at the floor and sniffled. It had been hard to build himself to this.

"Are you walkin' out with anyone?"

"What do you mean, Cornelius?"

He squinted away at a high corner of the store and seemed to examine it closely.

"I mean, are you great with anyone? Are you seein' any man regular, like? Are you walkin' out with anyone? Have you a . . . a friend? I mean, a boyfriend?"

"No. I haven't."

He was silent for a while, unconvinced.

"But what about Jack Golden?"

"What about Jack?"

"Aren't you great with him?"

"We're good friends, if that's what you mean. We pal around together a lot."

"No. I don't mean that. I mean, like, like girlfriend and boyfriend. I mean . . . oh Christ! you know what I mean!"

She looked up at him. She was more scared than ever.

"No. Not like that. We're . . . we're just great friends. Jack and I. Just great friends."

He smiled at her. He swaggered a little before her. She was moving slowly towards the door.

"Well. There's a kind of social down at the valley on Friday night. There's dancin', ceilidh dancin', the stuff Father Wall thinks is good, an' there's a bit of food, an' minerals, an' there's supposed to be a big raffle, for somethin'."

She looked at him. She was holding the eggs she had gathered in a scarf against her breast. The foil chalice in her left hand. She waited. Anxiously.

"I wondered if you might come with me? I mean, on Friday. I'd walk you there, an' I'd walk you back. An' I'd pay for you. In, I mean, an' whatever food an' drink you'd be after. What do you think?"

"Oh no, Cornelius," she blurted it out, too quickly. He jerked back a little from her, as if she had struck him. "I mean, I don't want to go to that kind of thing. I've no interest in that. No interest at all. Thanks though. Thanks."

He watched her. She moved quickly away from him, out into the sunshine. He didn't know what to do or say next. He scrunged his foot against the rough floor of the stores. He rubbed his hands hard against his trouser legs, he spat on them and rubbed them again. As if he had washed them in nettles and needed to dry the stinging out of them. She was gone, in through the back door of the house.

Gráinne squeezed the chalice violently in her hand and flung it away into a corner of the kitchen; she ran all the way up to her attic. She sat down heavily on the side of her bed, the eggs still clutched in her scarf. She was breathing hard, as if she had just escaped a dreadful blow. The sight of the moths and butterflies peaceful and still on the cabbage-green ground of the wall brought her peace and some reassurance. She sat a while, gathering herself back into the world. Then she began to think on what Cornelius had said. Not about himself. Not about the social. Not about that. She began to think about – Jack. About their special secret. About the words Cornelius had used, *boyfriend, girlfriend*. She liked the feel of the words in her brain when she thought of Jack and herself. Together. She smiled softly to herself. Perhaps Cornelius had taught her something. Poor Cornelius. How could he even imagine . . .

Poor, foolish, Cornelius. And she knew that with Jack she did not have those feelings of constraint and isolation she had when she was with other people, she could talk to Jack, she could trust him.

She was happy, suddenly, very happy. She sat over to the small desk against the wall and began to write a letter to Uncle Jim . . .

They were on the lake together, on a boat Jack had constructed from planks and boxes he had gathered at the Flannery store. He had worked on it for weeks, nailing and planing the timbers, soaking them, fastening them into shape. He covered the boat with sacking from the store, layer upon layer, and he daubed each layer over with pitch, black, clinging pitch. They launched it together at the edge of the lake and christened it – *The Half Safe*. They laughed together as they moved, cautiously, out a little from the shore. As Gráinne bent low over the timbers of the boat to push it forward, Jack glimpsed the filling beauty of her breasts and he swallowed hard. He must not think of her like that, not like that. He tried the makeshift oars; they grated hugely against the six-inch nails he had hammered in for rowlocks. The noise echoed across the lake and bounced against the hillocks and heathers of the hills. But it worked, the small boat worked, at least it stayed afloat, Gráinne sitting a little to the right to give it balance. Slowly Jack rowed it, keeping close to the shore. A tiny trickle of water was seeping through from somewhere. Gráinne had brought an empty tin can. Soon enough she would bale it out.

"Maybe we should give it the same name as the cat, all the same, we could call it *Jackie*," Gráinne suggested, teasingly, her right hand trailing in the black water.

Through the quiet elation of her happiness she remembered the small hessian sack her father had flung out through the air and that had fallen down into the terrors underneath her. She jerked her hand out of the water.

Jack was laughing with pleasure. The afternoon was grey but still. The boat worked. It was his. He had made it. It wobbled a little. But it left a lovely wake and he felt good, leaning back against the oars, leaning forward then, and Gráinne in the stern, happy too, watching him. They were together, cocooned, without test or target on each other, innocent in each other's presence, grounded in each other's interests.

"I wonder what Uncle Jim will think of this ship," Gráinne laughed.

"We'll let him come out in her," Jack answered. "Ship's engineer. He can bale us out."

Jack was rowing more quickly now. They were passing about six yards off shore. Then Jack turned the boat to face out across the lake, hauling heavily on his left-hand oar.

"Right," he announced, "let's cross the Atlantic."

Gráinne was nervous. She clutched the side of the little boat with both hands.

"It's deep, Jack," she said. "It's a bottomless lake."

"Nah!" he answered, "sure the boat is safe, and it's only a small lake anyway."

Gráinne brought her teeth together to stop herself saying anything further. Quickly they were in the middle of the lake and she remembered again the hessian bag, the stones, the kittens . . .

"Let's call the boat *Lucky*," she said suddenly.

"Right," Jack chuckled. "And this will be a lucky boat, she'll never come to harm."

Already they were across the lake and Jack pulled hard on his right oar to bring the craft along the opposite shore. He let the boat drift, then, and held the blades of his oars over the water, watching them bleed onto the surface of the lake, watching the drops of water create tiny little pools where they fell.

"It's wonderful to be able to master another element," he said. "Like the water, it's wonderful to be able to go out on it, in this boat. It must be even more wonderful to fly. In an aeroplane, I mean. That must be sheer magic."

He looked at her. Her features had relaxed again and she was smiling at him. Something struck him then, about her, about how good it was to be with her, how much he liked that smile, those light green eyes watching him. He saw her knees, he could even see, from where he was sitting, beyond her knees, in to the dark shadow of her flesh. He remembered her climbing onto the pier, years ago, the pressure of her buttocks as he helped her up. The memory of Mary Alice MacNamara came back to him. At once he felt his penis move again. He raised his eyes and looked directly into the soft eyes of Gráinne Flannery. He must never think of Gráinne like that, he thought again, he must never spoil it like that. That was wrong, sinful, selfish. For a while they watched each other, without speaking. She thought of Cornelius, then, the slight squint in those black eyes, black and threatening as the lake, and she shuddered suddenly.

"Are you cold?"

"No, no, I suddenly remembered Cornelius. He asked me to go with him to the social Friday. He bothers me."

Jack was silent. Something else stirred in him. Something cold and disturbing.

"Are you going with him?"

"No! Not likely. He scares me, Jack. He's rough."

Jack grinned at her. His eyes were bright, a light blue, she noticed, like the noon-day summer sky, hazy and soft and warm. She saw his lips, moist and shapely. Her tongue softly tipped her own lips. She smiled at him.

"It's good to be with you, Jack," she said then.

He smiled at her; he felt embarrassed, suddenly, and lost.

He dropped the oars in the water again and began to row, slowly turning the boat back towards the middle, back towards the shore. His hands were burning again, the backs of his hands were hot still with the memory of Mary Alice MacNamara. There was a sudden longing, too, stirring his soul and his body, a longing for Gráinne, to be more fully with her, to know her body, too, to have her weight on him, to know, to know, to know . . .

Every Monday afternoon Gráinne Flannery brought a dozen eggs to the presbytery. She walked slowly, always enjoying the long walk up the rhododendron-lined avenue to the priest's house. There were wrens, singing and scolding invisibly in the depths of the bushes; an occasional thrush stood on a high branch and sang its delight in living. If it rained, Gráinne simply ducked in to one of the caves of shadow the old bushes made; if the sun shone, there was a gleam off the dark green leaves that she loved, and every May and June the rhododendrons blossomed into great hymns of flowers that took her breath away; then she would carry bundles of them in the processions when Father Wall, dressed in white and gold, carried the monstrance high around the Church and up as far as the river, then back again, around the Church once more, and in for a wonderful Benediction.

She rapped on the back door of the presbytery. Old Hanna Masterson was priest's housekeeper and she would take Gráinne inside, offer her a newly baked scone with the butter embarrassing itself all over it, she would pay her the money, and Gráinne would set off again, back down the avenue. But today she had to rap a few times, louder and louder, before the door opened. It was Father Wall himself.

"Gráinne Flannery! How are you, girl? Come with the eggs, have you? Come on inside, come on inside!"

She followed him in to the kitchen. It was warm and fragrant in there. She said nothing to the big priest.

"There, put them on the dresser, there's a girl, and come on down to the study and I'll give you the money. Poor old Hanna's gone. She was getting old, you know, getting old, not up to it any more. She wanted to go to the County Home, she was alone in life apart from myself, you see. She'll be happy in there. They'll look after her well."

He opened the kitchen door onto the long hallway. Gráinne followed him reluctantly. She had never been inside the presbytery. It seemed dark, the walls panelled in dark wood, a faint, unholy light coming through the coloured glass diamonds in the front door. There was a smell of polish, and of age, of dankness, of – of – of priests, she decided, a smell of priests, musty, and dark, and lonely.

"Do you know the *Song of Solomon*, Gráinne?" he called to her as he went along the corridor. "The Canticle of Canticles. *Let him kiss me with the kiss of his mouth, for thy breasts are better than wine, smelling sweet of the best ointments.* Isn't that beautiful, Gráinne? A song the angels sing, prostrate before the throne of our Blessed Mother."

Father Wall opened a door off the hallway and Gráinne followed him into a big, bright room. The floor was polished wood, there were rugs and mats here and there, a big mahogany table in the centre with six big chairs about it. The walls were cluttered with bookshelves and prints, there was a fire burning in the fireplace although the day was good outside. On either side of the fire there was a big black armchair, the backs oily and grey from years of use, the cushions thrown higgledy-piggledy on seat and arm-rest. Father Wall sat down in one of them and looked up at her.

"Yes, yes," he enthused, "poor old Hanna was a good

one, a good one. And now I'll have to find me another housekeeper. Yes indeedy, yes indeedy, another housekeeper. I have one in mind, though, Gráinne, I have one in mind." His hands gestured grandly again. *"I am black but beautiful, O daughters of Jerusalem, as the tents of Cedar, as the curtains of Solomon.* Come on over here, Gráinne, till I see how you've grown."

She moved reluctantly towards the priest. He was sitting back in the armchair, beaming up at her, his big round face red and clean-shaven, like a baby's face, she thought, though too plump and old. He had his collar off and the hanging folds of his chin and neck were visible under the top of the open shirt, along with a few tufts of feathery white hair on his chest. His stomach protruded and Gráinne could see, and would not look, where a small line of his stomach-flesh showed above his black trousers.

"You're growing into quite a woman, Gráinne Flannery, quite a woman. I'll bet Fintan and Nora are proud of you. I'll bet."

He was leering up at her, his eyes wandering over her body, his hands folded now, making an upside-down V, touching the tips of the V to his lips, nodding, nodding.

"What age would you be now, Gráinne? What age?"

"I'm just gone nineteen, Father."

He feigned exceptional surprise.

"Nineteen! Well now, a proper young woman you are, a proper, comely young woman. Come now, and sit down here on my knee for a minute until I have a good look at you. Come on now, don't be bashful. Amn't I your priest, amn't I Father Wall?"

She was hurt and astonished. She stood, confused, awkward, like one of her hens about to be snatched for the slaughter.

"I – I'll just put the money in the book, Father . . ."

"Nonsense, child, nonsense, sure I have the money here in my pocket. And a shilling extra for yourself, too. Come on now, let me see how you've grown."

He was reaching his arms up to her, urging her, and she moved to him and sat down awkwardly on his lap. He held her there, perched like a crow, and put his hands on her shoulders.

"There now, isn't that grand? Gráinne Flannery. Growing to be a fine woman, a fine woman!"

His hands were moving now, slowly, down from her shoulders, down along her arms, palping her, touching carefully, feeling the flesh inside the cotton of the dress. His mouth was open and she could see tiny threads of saliva shimmering between his lips; the tip of his tongue curled inside his mouth; his lower teeth were yellow and ugly.

"You're going to be a wonderful woman, Gráinne, a wonderful woman. You'll be a credit to your family. Shift yourself around there now on my knees, there's a girl, till I get my hand into my pocket for the money."

She lifted herself gratefully off his lap but his hands held her, turning her until her back was to him; then he drew her down onto his knees again.

"That's it, that's it – you're heavy mind you, but you're a fine girl. Will make some fella a fine wife, God be good to you." His voice became low and theatrical. *"Who is she that goeth up by the desert, as a pillar of smoke . . . How beautiful art thou, my love, how beautiful art thou! thy eyes are doves' eyes . . .* Oh yes, indeedy, a beautiful song, a song for the angels. Not for us poor old fools of human beings. Not yet anyway, no, not until we've dropped our load of flesh into the kind, wet earth."

He was searching with one hand in a pocket and she

could hear the jingle of coins; the other hand held her left shoulder, keeping her on his knee. Then both hands were about her, moving down from her shoulders, down her neck, and then they were touching her breasts, her firm, significant breasts, naked yet under her dress, and she could hear the heaviness of his breathing as his hands felt and fondled her, gently, carefully, surely; under her, too, she could feel his knees, moving so that she had to move, shift her weight from buttock to buttock on his knees. He began to murmur, like a sickly child, muttering through his breathing, softly, softly, "Gráinne, Gráinne, a fine girl, fine girl, wonderful girl, wonderful, oh yes indeed, Gráinne Flannery, a fine girl."

She jumped up from his knees, suddenly, taking him by surprise and the coins fell from his hand and rolled away on the wooden floor.

"I'll have to be getting back, Father, I'll have to go – " and before he could recover she was gone, out the door of the study, down the hallway and through the kitchen. Somewhere in a corner under a sideboard a coin twirled and twirled noisily. She pulled open the back door and ran quickly across the gravel driveway, down the avenue, great sobs shaking her, the tunnel of the rhododendron bushes nothing more now than a threat, dark and skulking and hiding its horrors, waiting to pounce. She stopped at the end of the avenue and looked back; the presbytery stood squat in the afternoon sunshine, innocent, well-kept, even luxurious. She shivered. Where was her God? She could not turn to her God. Not now. Whom could she tell? There was nobody, nobody, especially not Jack, she could not tell Jack, not Jack, not him above all, it must be her secret, it must be her own dark and burning secret.

They were sitting quietly together under a spotlight of sunshine, against the wall at the back of the Golden home. The grass in the small orchard was dry. Gráinne sat, her hands folded over her shins, holding her dress in against her legs. Her dress was a blue meadow with a myriad tiny white flowers growing all over it. Jack leaned back against the wall, his eyes closing dreamily in the warmth. A rosebush, heavy with its pink roses, grew wild against the wall, there was a rich, luscious scent wrapping them around. Stretched out at their feet was the cat, black as wet tar, a silver sheen on his fur, loved and cared-for over years, lazy as death. Gráinne gazed into the distance, across the old moss-covered apple-trees, towards the hedge.

"Cornelius frightened me the other day, Jack."

"Did he?"

"He said he saw us out on the lake in the boat."

"What's wrong with that?"

She hesitated, glancing up at him.

"I think he might be – jealous."

The word was soft and resonant and hung between them like a moth, fragile, sensitive, living. Jack hesitated.

"Why would he be jealous?"

"Because of what we have, Jack, you and me, and what he doesn't have. He's suffering, Jack, I think his life is in pain. He's alone in the world, and empty. Like an empty – barrel."

He glanced at her, surprised. There was a passion in her voice and she had sprung a small torrent of words.

"He's big and ugly and awkward and a bit stupid and I think he knows that. His father just bullies him and his mother doesn't seem to care. I've seen him thumping sacks of flour as if he wanted to burst them open. And I've heard him scream in frustration from the darkness of the store. He wants others to share his suffering, it lessens the suffering, by sharing it. It lessens the – loneliness. It's not pity he wants, that would make him feel we were somehow better than him. He wants to make us suffer, I think, you and me, Jack, and if he knows we're suffering then he won't suffer as much. If all that pain and anger doesn't come out of him some way, it'll just grow and grow inside him, spreading like a poison. And I don't want that poison to touch us. You and me."

Jack was quiet, watching her. He was smitten by her wisdom, and by her concern.

"But what can we do about it? We can't just stop being happy because he's not happy."

"No, I know that, it's just that he's jealous of our happiness and, I think, he's jealous of – of – well, of you and me."

She spoke quietly but emphatically, nodding her head gravely with the words. She was a small moth, too, fluttering in a dim gauze of hesitation.

"I think he's going to cause trouble, Jack. He wants to spread his misery beyond himself. He wants to destroy what we have between us."

"But I've never done anything to bother Cornelius Griffin," Jack insisted.

She hesitated. She looked away from him again, towards

the low hedge, beyond the hedge towards the dull fields and the rough wet foreshore that fell down towards the sea. It seemed that an almost visible pall of heaviness had settled over the distance before her. It's in my head, she thought, only in my head. Her right hand reached towards the cat and she stroked him, softly, softly, as if she were trying to ease her thoughts into the sunlight. The cat stretched himself luxuriously and began to purr.

"He sees me with you, Jack. And he's jealous of our – friendship. I think he – I think he sort of – likes me. Or thinks he does. He keeps asking me to go with him, to dances, socials, places, for walks. And I don't want to. And sometimes he follows me about, in the hen-run, when I'm gathering eggs, sometimes even I think I sense him following me when I'm delivering eggs. Oh Jack, he scares me, he's so big and aggressive-looking."

Jack was silent. The insects about the roses made a low, pleasing hum. Jack felt himself incapable of putting words on the strange mixture of emotions he was feeling.

"And he said, Jack, he said something nasty about you, about your father, Ted, Lord have mercy on him."

"What did he say, Gráinne? Tell me."

"He said, well, he said your father took the Crown's money, the Saxon shilling, that he was a traitor to Ireland, and that your mother has a pension, from the Crown, an RIC pension, and that your whole family were – traitors."

Jack thumped his fist violently against the earth.

"Of course she has a pension! Doesn't she have to live, too?"

"I know that, Jack. But don't you see, what he's doing is trying to anger us. That's why I told you what he said. You must know so that you can see what he's trying to do. He'll

81

hate you because he thinks you're – going to take me from him. That's all."

Some day, she thought, some day perhaps Jack will find the words I need him to find.

He stood up, angrily.

"I don't want him to annoy you, Gráinne. I won't let him do that. There's many people blind enough to the way history runs, stupid enough to accuse people in the wrong. I know there's still people who resent the RIC. I wasn't fond of him but my father did good service on this island and never did harm to anyone. He was respected. It hurt him, the way they threw him out. It hurt him a lot, I think it killed him. His friends dumped him out of a job and he resented it. It's history, Gráinne, you get caught up in the flow of it, like in a current in the river. You feel like a small piece of wood, caught in a torrent, and you grow heavy, and you drown. You never know what forces will take you and turn you into something you never thought you'd be. He often said those things to me, explaining things. It could happen you and me, Gráinne, it could happen Cornelius, it could happen anyone. To be caught up, even in spite of yourself, in the surge of history. But I'll not have Cornelius bad-mouthing my mother. She's too quiet and kind and gentle. And trusting. Or annoying you."

"He's rough, Jack, and dangerous. I don't want you involved with him. I'll be able to look after myself. He'll not do anything to me. He dare not. But, do you see? he's trying to take me from you, as if I – belonged to you."

She was standing now, too. They stood together, in a net of sunshine. She reached her hand to him and touched his arm, gently.

"He's jealous of our – our happiness, Jack, our being – together."

Her hand moved softly down along his arm. She took his hand in hers. She had pushed and prodded him and he was still looking at her as if he had not understood what she was saying to him. And perhaps she, too, was not aware of what she was saying.

"We're lucky, Jack, we're lucky, we have each other, he has no one. By challenging him you'll only give what he says importance. That's all. And what matters is – you and me, Jack, you and me, and that we do not let anyone come between us. Or anything."

For a moment Jack watched her lips, their pink, moist softness, the perfect whiteness and symmetry of her teeth; he could see, too, the delicate beauty of the flesh of her neck, shadowed and lit by the sun, and how beautiful her skin seemed under the open top button of her blouse. He wanted to lean forward and kiss her on the lips, but he was afraid to, he did not know what it would mean, what it might bring with it. He felt she would not be able to accept that, she might think – he was evil. He drew back at once, startled at himself, yet pleased at his desire, and at his control of that desire. She smiled, sensing his concern, and squeezed his hand in hers. He knew the warmth of her hand, her fingers. He remembered the day she had jumped from the gatepost and had fallen, how gangly and awkward she had been, and how he had been stung by a glimpse of her flesh. And now how sure and firm she seemed, how lovely and serene in spite of Cornelius Griffin.

And then he remembered how his hands had trembled and burned under the weight and stirring of Mary Alice's body and he looked away, quickly from Gráinne's moist green eyes lest she see something in his own eyes that would drive her from him. She would not understand, he felt, the strain of his flesh, it would be a rupture between them . . . There was something in her, he imagined, something soft and infinitely frail, like the dust on the wing of a butterfly, that dust that seemed to be the butterfly's life, and all its beauty. He let go her hand, too, and bent to hide his confusion; he gathered up the simple, unresisting, unquestioning body of the cat, warm and sleepy in the sunshine. He would not soil the clean beauty of this young woman with the heavy demands of his own, dragging flesh, he must not, must not, fling her down from the high, bright cliff-top of his hopes and see her fall, screaming and broken, onto the sharp rocks below.

A robin landed on the wall near them. It gave Jack the excuse he hoped for and he turned all his attention, and directed hers, towards the bird. In his arms the cat stiffened in anticipation. For a while the bird watched them, its tiny eye pert, its head turned quizzically to one side. Suddenly the cat sprang from Jack's arms and leaped towards the wall. With perfect nonchalance the robin flew off the wall, going only a little distance to perch once again on a high branch of one of the old apple trees.

"It must be wonderful to be able to fly!" Jack sighed.

Jack pushed the boat out from its hiding-place in the furze bushes and set it on the water of the lake. He took Gráinne's hand and she stepped in, ever so cautiously, and sat down. The day was a hymn in her heart, her whole body restless in the urge to exist, to respond to the joy and beauty of creation. They said little to one another, but they were at peace in one another's company, and words between them were unnecessary. Further along the shore of the lake a small flock of mallard swam, busy and splashing, turning their tails to the sky, feeding off the weeds at the bottom of the lake. Jack took out the oars from under the furze, holding the bow of the boat by a rope.

There was a quick cry of alarm from Gráinne.

"It's filling with water, Jack, there's a leak!"

The golden brown water was bubbling quickly into the bottom of the boat. Already Gráinne's shoes were getting wet. He took her hand and she stepped out, the boat rocking under her haste. Jack drew it back onto the grassy shore. He turned it over and it lay, a black carapace, wet and hurt and shivering under the sun. There was a long narrow gash almost the length of the hull.

"Must have snagged along rocks somewhere," Jack said. "Easy enough to put it right; more canvas, more pitch, a lot more."

Cornelius was watching from the open door of the shed as they came back into the yard. When she saw him,

Gráinne took Jack's hand, for comfort. Cornelius was grinning at them, an ugly, iron grin.

"Titanic hit an iceberg or somethin'?" He laughed, but his face was red and angry-looking.

Jack stopped. He remembered the clean cut on the flesh of the boat.

"You did it!" he said suddenly. "A blade or something. You cut along the bottom of the boat."

Cornelius grinned, a bitter, challenging grin.

"You accusin' me of somethin'?" he asked. He stepped from the black shadow of the doorway into the grey shadow the store cast onto the yard.

"Come on, Jack," Gráinne urged, drawing him by the arm.

Jack looked at the great boulder of a man before him, the red face, the turnip-flesh-coloured hair, the near-squinting black eyes, the leering mouth; Cornelius had his sleeves rolled up over thick, white arms, the collarless shirt open on a buttermilk-dirty vest; the man had a neck strong and squat as a tree-stump.

"I said, are you accusin' me of somethin'?"

Jack hesitated. He was a willow compared to Cornelius. He could feel the warmth of Gráinne's hand in his. She was trembling. Pulling him away.

"Yes I am!" Jack said then, something breaking in him at the memory of his father who had sat hooped into himself over the kitchen fire. "I think you slashed our boat, deliberately, because you're jealous of me and Gráinne. That's what I think."

"Jack! Jack!" Gráinne urged. "If you yield to his ways you're only taking his wickedness on yourself."

Cornelius snarled.

"Wickedness is it? Is that it? By Christ I'm not wicked.

Tellin' you I care is not bein' wicked. But what about this one, livin' off the traitorin' ways of his father! What about that, then? Them that helps the English is themselves English!"

Cornelius had advanced into the yard, his jaw thrust forward, like a bull-dog's.

"An' that oul' boat of yours isn't worth a tinker's fart. You'd only drown herself out of it . . ."

Jack withdrew his hand from that of Gráinne. He knew what he had to do. Flesh was weak, it would have to suffer the consequences of a lively spirit. He stepped back and began to pull up the sleeves of his shirt . . .

Gráinne stepped between them.

"Jack," she said with great determination. "You are not going to fight. I won't let you. It's not worth it. It's only a boat. And can't you see he just wants you to fight him. And this is the store yard, and he's supposed to be working." She turned to Cornelius who was grinning foolishly at her. "If you fight, Cornelius, I'll have my father turn you out of the yard and you'll never work here again. I promise you that."

She stepped away from them, a fine pride in her bearing as she walked from them. Both young men gazed after her in admiration. She did not turn to look at them. She went in the back door of the house.

"Your type was always yellow," Cornelius hissed at Jack, "hidin' behind the wimin. Yellow. Hidin' behind the Saxon invaders. Hidin' behind the wimin."

Jack was fastening the sleeves of his shirt again. His heart was light, suddenly. He had seen Gráinne as he had never seen her before, beautiful, strong, determined, a desirable woman; and he was proud of her company, of her choice of him; suddenly he knew that with her at his side he could transcend the smallness of this yard, the density of

Cornelius, the long dark night of the flesh. He could ride the air! He could fly! He could soar!

"Do you know what it is, Cornelius, poor, poor Cornelius?"

"What?"

"I think I'm in love. And it took you to show me . . ."

"You stupid fuckin' bastard!" Cornelius spat the words at him. He bunched his fist. And remembered . . . He stood still, his great bulk trembling with anger and frustration. Then his features eased. He put the index finger of his right hand to his mouth, licked it, then reached and rubbed it on Jack's cheek.

"Now!" he said with some satisfaction. "I've laid the wet finger on you. You can't ignore the wet finger, unless you're a total weepin' yellow-bellied toad of a cowardly bastard of a fuckin' Saxon-lovin' oul' RIC man. You're challenged. You'll have to fight me. You'll have to."

Jack rubbed his cheek. He laughed.

"I'll not fight you, Cornelius Griffin," he said, quietly. "You and I ought to be friends. Life is too good to be fighting. I'm not a fighter. And I don't believe in that wet finger story. That's childish."

Jack turned and began to walk out of the yard.

"You're a coward," Cornelius called after him. "You're a coward, like your father before you, a yellow, good-for-nothin' coward. An' I'll get you, wait and see. I'll get you!"

But Jack was floating on a cushion of joy. Around him the island fields, small and sparse in their growing, seemed meadows alight with flowers, the hills and hillocks were carpets of purple, mauve and golden patterns, flying carpets from the magic corners of the world. And in this world of rocks and mud and gravity, grace was possible, to lift the human flesh out of the mire of its living.

Often now, about the house and farm, Jack watched the movements of Mary Alice MacNamara. They scarcely spoke to one another, Jack was about the work of the small stables, meadows and gardens, Mary Alice was about the housework. At times he stopped to watch her, fascinated, frightened still, and wondering, while often a strong physical longing came over him. He thought of her in ways he would not allow himself to think of Gráinne. He thought of her at night, there in the bed, downstairs from him, down the long and turning tiled hallway. Alone. Beautiful. Half-naked in her night attire. And he wondered. He hurt and longed and wondered.

She was out in the field one day, in the small kitchen garden Ted had developed and Jack kept alive, up the rough road to the turf-bog, in the small wooden gate to the right. The garden bordered on the grove of pine-trees, it was sheltered, warm and dry. Jack was digging in a corner of the field, near the wood, his chest and back bare to the sunshine that occasionally touched the island from its great distance. He was clearing a patch to sow winter cabbage; he stooped and gathered away old roots, grasses, weeds. Then he dug again, turning the soil, content in the pleasure of the physical activity. Content in the gentle warmth of the day, its embrace, its physical, cajoling contact.

When Mary Alice came into the field she paused, to

watch him. Jack knew she was there, and he watched her, too, out of his awe and longing, working still, bending and digging. She went over to a small ridge of carrots, bent, pulling them by their light feathery stalks, laying their bright orange flesh on the dark soil of the ridge. Jack watched her, his heart thudding at the wonder of her physical presence. Somewhere within the grove a bird called. The world seemed to stand still about them; they were hawks, poised on the apex of an invisible spiralling updraught. Wary. Watchful.

Mary Alice put the carrots into a basin and stood up. She rubbed her hands free of the dry soil and looked towards the young man. He was a young man now, but beautiful, innocent, shy, attractive. She knew her power over him, she knew ease in the gentle warmth of mid-afternoon. In the physical glory of her body remote unknown and unquestioned impulses stirred and surged, and she knew she could answer them any time, in her power over the flesh of this fine young man. It would be pleasure, delight, and she would know the authority of her flesh over his flesh, over his mind. She watched him.

Tiny beads of perspiration stood out on his chest, and his shoulder muscles seemed to gleam with the activity of the digging. She left her basin on the soil and moved towards him. He watched her come. The world was silent. Wholly silent. Soon he would be as wise as she was, soon. Soon he would know more about the forces that stir to draw men and women together. Soon. But as yet it must be she who was in command, she who could control and order the world that set such contradictory feelings pounding within him.

He stopped his work. She smiled at him. She wore a bright yellow cotton dress, short-sleeved. She came close to him and stopped, smiling towards him. Her breasts, full and tingling, rose and fell with her soft excitement. She reached out her hand and touched him on his naked shoulder. He trembled at the touch. The top of her dress was open, he could see the lovely gleam of her flesh, the swelling of the top of her breasts, the cool darkness plunging between her breasts, the lace frill-work of her bra. Her fingers moved gently down his arm, sending shivers of pleasure through his body. He saw the delicate fuzz of golden hairs on her arm, how soft and tender they looked. She was smiling at him. Drawing closer. The world was breathlessly still. This was a hidden corner of warmth and growth. The grove behind them was dark, fragrant, cool; a world of silence, of pine needles and of darkness. Moist. Fragrant. Waiting.

She raised her left arm and placed her palm flat on his naked chest. He loved the touch, the firmness and decision of her hand, its coolness against his heat, the certainty in every move she made. His whole body seemed to be sounding like a bell across the air yet he hardly dared breathe; watching her. He saw her fine mouth open, her tongue licking the insides of her lips, a tiny froth of spittle on the tip of her tongue. Her breasts brushed against his arm. And then she gripped him, gently but firmly, and began to draw him after her, smiling, unspeaking, towards the darkness of the grove. The spade dropped from his hands. He followed, his whole body burning, an excitement like he had never known shaking him to the very depths of his soul.

From the wood came the sudden alarm call of a blackbird. They knew the fragrance of the dark place, the rich intoxicating fragrance of pine, the disturbing scent of decay from the layers of pine-needles and pine-cones, of branches and leaves beneath their feet. It was a sweet decay, still and moist and soft, it was a secret world, as old as time itself, and he heard the small teasing mockery of her laughter before she turned to him, lifted his arm and held his hand tightly against her breast. He gasped, sensing the fullness of her flesh, knowing the great giving and taking that was hers and would be his. Her eyes were alert with joy, her fine face lovely in its smiling, its welcome. She took his other hand, too, and held it against her other breast. Then she allowed herself to lean her weight against his hands, all her virtue concentrated in her wondrous breasts, depending on his hands to support her. He held his hands firmly against her breasts as he took her weight. She closed her eyes in the pleasure of it. He shuddered, frozen beyond delight.

She sighed, deeply, then lifted herself back from him. Taking his hand again she began to draw him further in to the secrecy of the wood, in where he had hoped to find some moments of flight, some moments free of the drag of earth, suspended high in the wind-caressed branches of the trees. He followed her, knowing now that this was to be his time of unexpected, almost insupportable, joy and knowledge, here, with this wonderful woman, a full-bodied generous woman, years older and wiser than he was, who would . . .

She walked in front of him, luxuriating in the coolness of the wood, in the sound of his breathing, in the warmth of his strong hand. He watched the fullness of her buttocks under the yellow cotton of the dress, how they seemed to swell and waltz with her movements, he remembered their pressure on his hands, wondered if now, if now at last . . .

And then she screamed, dropping his hand to raise both of hers to her face, to hide from herself what she had seen. How she screamed and screamed then, staggering against him, and how she turned, as if terrified, and ran from him, ran back out of the grove, out into the sunshine of the garden. Away past the fence and away from his aching body. She was gone, leaving him lost, spent, bereft, in an agony of frustration and despair.

Hanging from a branch of one of the pine-trees was the cat, a long piece of fishing-gut tied so tightly about its throat it had cut deeply in through the black fur; the small, pink tongue protruded and the teeth had bitten it through. But worst of all, worst of all, there as it swung slowly under the impetus of its own horror, the creature's belly had been slashed open and its innards, red and purple and blue, hung out obscenely onto the air.

Jack said the words aloud, though quietly, to the wood: "Oh no, oh Christ, oh Jesus Christ, no, no, no, oh the poor poor creature."

And he knew at once, at once, without doubt or pause or understanding: "Cornelius! Cornelius! you bastard!"

Jack turned and ran back out into the sunshine of the garden. Mary Alice had disappeared; the world was turning again, the silence had been slaughtered and was now a crimson scream around Jack's head. He picked up the spade and hurried back into the wood.

As soon as he had buried the cat at the far end of the wood he put on his shirt, left the spade back into the shed, washed his hands at the tap in the yard, and headed out the back gate towards Flannery's General Store. His whole body seemed chilled, although the day was hot. As he passed the kitchen window he saw Mary Alice bent over the sink. She did not look up. He gritted his teeth; his fists clenched and unclenched, he spat short curses into the face of the afternoon.

Cornelius was coming out of the store at the end of the yard, a sack of flour on his back. He was stooped under it, an island Atlas, both hands raised to steady and balance the weight. He stopped; Jack stood directly in his path. Cornelius looked up from under his burden. Jack put his index finger to his mouth, spat on it, and rubbed the spittle along Cornelius's cheek.

"Only an absolute coward will attack an innocent animal," Jack said. "You're lower than the lowest cockroach, Cornelius Griffin, and I hate and despise you with all my soul."

Cornelius smiled up at him in anticipation.

"You just wait now, until I'm finished in the store," he said. "Then I'll lay you straight on the ground."

"I'll not wait, you heap of dog-shit," Jack hissed at him. "You leave down that sack and come out to the side of the lake. That way you won't be fighting on Flannery's ground."

"One minute so, RIC man's whelp, and I'll give you a little somethin' you won't too easy forget. I have to leave this sack above in the shop. I'll follow you down to the water."

Jack knew that his only hope against the much bigger and more powerful man was to try and move fast and often, to stay out of reach, to be a bird, diving and clawing,

95

darting with beak and flying away. He left Flannery's yard and found a fair-sized patch of open, grassy ground at the shore of the lake. If Cornelius could be taunted into foolishness and anger it might help. Jack would use all his wisdom, his speed, his lightness. A small flock of mallard lifted from the reeds on the far side of the lake and flew low and fast over the surface towards him, veering away suddenly and splashing onto the lake far down to his right. He sighed, deeply; how the human soul, he thought, in its most innocent efforts to rise from the drag of earth, is thwarted at every turn.

Cornelius came through the gap in the fence from Flannery's yard. As he strode forward he began to take off his shirt. Underneath he wore braces over a vest that was soiled from sweat and too-long use. He flung his shirt onto the grass. Then he stopped, put his hands inside his braces, stretched them and let them snap back against his chest. He was a powerfully-built man, even more daunting now that his upper torso was visible.

"Right!" he scoffed. "You little squirt. Keep away from Flannery's yard when I'm about. I'm master in that yard and we don't want any of your British-arse-lickin' sort comin' near us."

"I know what's your problem," Jack retorted, "and you haven't got a hope in Hell of getting her even to look at you. All you're good for is killing cats. You're pathetic . . ."

Cornelius made a sudden rush at him, his knotted fists swinging. Jack stepped aside easily and jabbed his right fist at the big man's head, catching him a slight blow on the back of the neck. Cornelius grunted and stopped; he turned and swung his fist but Jack had moved well out of range. Cornelius opened his mouth in an ugly leer and barged forward. Jack skipped away quickly again and flung his fist at Cornelius's ear, hitting him instead on the shoulder, his arm almost numbed; it was like hitting a wall, or a tree. Jack leaned away. He was a butterfly now, skipping and darting out of reach of the big man's net. Jack jabbed again and Cornelius ducked; Jack brought up his left hand sharply into the big man's face; his wrist was stung but Cornelius's head snapped backwards, more in surprise than pain. He raised the back of his right hand and rubbed it across his mouth; there was no blood.

"You can't dance forever," he mocked, "like a woman. You're a yellow bastard, Jack Golden, but I'll quickly blacken you into shite."

Jack laughed, taunting him. He skipped quickly to the right, then to the left, Cornelius stood still, watching him. Jack feigned another jab and Cornelius swung his fist, Jack was gone again, to the side, and swung as fiercely as he could into Cornelius's kidneys. He felt his fist crashing into the flesh and there was great satisfaction in the blow. Cornelius yelped and swung both fists again. Once more his quarry was gone, delivering another blow into the ribs on his other side. Cornelius grunted again. Jack felt elated, then, he felt light, alive, an eagle, in control. Cornelius was wearing heavy hob-nailed boots that kept him slow, sinking in the soft ground.

"You're a thick bull, Cornelius, a shifty, ugly bull. And it's you are the coward. You can fight a cat pretty well, and a boat. But a man . . . ?"

Cornelius rushed again, his fists raised. Jack backed away. Cornelius lunged and a great blow thudded into Jack's chest, knocking him off his feet. He fell on his back, the top of his chest feeling as if it had burst.

"Now, you shite you," Cornelius laughed, "did you like that? Get up now till I knock you down again."

Jack scrambled to his feet and dodged back as the big man lunged again. Jack hit him sharply on the right ear. His chest hurt greatly and he took deep breaths to recover. Cornelius felt his right ear gingerly, his black eyes narrowed in hatred.

"You're slow, Cornelius Griffin, you're too fat, too heavy, too ugly, too stupid, you're a slug, Cornelius Griffin, a slug, a slug, a slug . . ."

Cornelius let out a roar of rage and rushed forward again; Jack had hoped for this and he stepped aside nimbly at the last moment, swinging his arm as hard as he could, striking his enemy on the back of the neck. Cornelius stumbled forward, his arms flailing for balance, and he fell into one of the furze-bushes near the shore of the lake. He yelled in pain as the thorns stung his arms, his chest, his face. Jack felt good, things were going better than he had anticipated. He hopped from foot to foot, he jabbed at the air, he could beat this man, he could win. Cornelius was groaning, turning from the bush, still on his knees; he was holding his left arm and moaning: "Jesus! I've broken me arm; I'm sure 'tis broken. Help me, help me, Jesus Jack will you help me!"

He was on his knees; Jack, surprised, moved towards him, dropping his guard. Cornelius lunged at him from the ground, he was an explosion, rushing at him, catching him about the waist. He stood then, lifting Jack in a powerful bear-hug, his arms clasped around behind his back, pressing the breath from his body. Jack bent backwards, trying to get air into his lungs. The big man held him off the ground, squeezing, squeezing. Jack freed his right arm and drove his elbow down into Cornelius's face, again, again. Cornelius released him, flung him from him, and Jack fell on the ground, hauling breath in out of the air. Without a pause Cornelius kicked him where he lay, a fierce kick with his right boot that sent shocks of pain through Jack's body. Then the big man leapt on top of him, his hard knees pressing into his stomach like iron bars holding him down, grinding into him, and Cornelius's fists pounded down on him. Jack put his arm before his face to shield himself from the blows then swung them up into the other man's face with all the energy he had left. Cornelius yelled and jerked himself upright. Jack scrambled with difficulty to his feet and backed away from him though his whole body was a fire of pain and he felt as if his legs were tied to the ground.

Cornelius took his hand from his face; there was blood coming from his nose and mouth; he looked, astounded, at the blood on his hand. Then he roared, a roar of rage, resentment, horror, loneliness, a roar from the void. He lowered his head and rushed towards Jack, still screaming. Jack moved aside and swung his arm out at the back of his attacker's head; Cornelius, the impetus being so great and Jack's blow adding to it, stumbled uncontrollably and fell forward over the low bank of the lake into the water. The lake was not deep at that spot but Cornelius floundered on his hands and knees, his feet with their great boots thwarting him, and his knees striking against small rocks in the lake-bed, struggling in the soft and muddy bottom. Jack jumped into the water beside him and tried to hold that brute, ugly head under the water. He knew a terrible anger now and a wild elation. Cornelius spluttered and choked, his hands unable to find purchase in the mud. Bubbles of his life rose to the surface. Jack jerked the head up out of the water and the big man gasped to get his breath. Jack pushed the head down again under the surface of the water. The world was one great flame of noise, anger, elation, it was a scarlet world and Jack was in charge of it, conqueror, king, high priest.

It was Gráinne's hands pulling at his arms and her voice screaming his name, screaming at him, "Jack! Jack! You'll drown him!" that brought him back to earth. She was standing in the lake, too, urging him, pleading. Jack let go Cornelius's hair and the man spluttered and gasped upright, on his knees still in the mud. Gráinne was drawing Jack out onto the bank, he followed, dazed. Then he was standing with her at the lake's edge. Together they watched as Cornelius, cowed, wet, gasping, staggered up out of the water. He clambered onto the bank and stood, drenched and filthy, blood on his face. He was sobbing, looking at his enemy as if all life and light had gone from his eyes. He shivered. Jack and Gráinne stood, watching him. She took Jack's hand and held it. Jack, also, was shivering; there was blood on his face, too, but there was a haughty certainty in his bearing. Cornelius moved away from them, emptied, needing to start again from the very ground of defeat and find some way back into the bright air of living.

Jack stood, swollen with the food of battle, bloated with it, his face red with effort and with victory, his mind convincing him of power. His hand held Gráinne's hand and he knew that now he could forever hold his head high before her, he felt he could find the authority to take her to him, to make her, too, yield to the great fury of his passions.

Gráinne brought Jack in the back door of the Flannery house, into the kitchen. There she sat him on a chair near the window, flowed a basin of water from the tap and added warm water from the great black kettle that hissed quietly on the range. She took off his shoes and stockings and rolled up the ends of his trousers. She bathed his feet in the warm water, kneeling before him, saying little, her hands gentle, careful yet firm. Quickly his shivering eased and a glow of warmth and happiness flowed through him. She dried his feet and gave him slippers to wear. She hung his stockings on a bar in front of the range to dry. She poured more water from the kettle and bathed his face with a small sponge, cleaning away the traces of blood. There were cuts under his eye, his nose still bled a little, and his lower lip was swollen and purple looking. Ugly. But her hands tingled at the touch of his flesh, she longed with all her body to fold herself into his life, to know the strength and firmness, the warmth and the taste of the flesh of the man she was coming to love with a deep, pounding love. A great need surged through her that he would desire her, clasp her even violently to him. But she knew she must not force him, he would not understand her needs, her longing, he would draw away from her . . . She turned from him, quickly, her life's weight instantly conscious of the strictures of her God.

"It was the cat, Gráinne," he said. "I couldn't take it when he did that to the cat. He had no call to do that. It was a rotten thing to do."

"I'm sure he'll leave us alone now, Jack, we'll hear no more from him. Poor old Cornelius," she added, almost under her breath.

He sat in her kitchen, his trouser legs folded up, his feet in large slippers, his face looking swollen and sorry. She looked at him, he was hers, and she relished his presence in the intimacy of her home.

Suddenly she knew. It was time to share her secret, to draw him further in along the corridors of her life.

"You must come upstairs, Jack, to my room. There's something special I want you to see, something my uncle Jim has been sending me over the years. It's our secret, Jim's and mine, and not even my parents have seen it. I have never told you about it, either, it was my special secret. But it's time to show it to you, now."

He followed her slowly up the stairs from the hallway. They went along the landing and he saw the almost vertical stairway to an attic room. She looked back at him, smiling. In the white ceiling there was a white trapdoor, smudged and grey from years and fingers.

"I'll have to go up first, Jack, to open the trapdoor, and you'll give me a minute to clear the place up a bit."

He nodded and watched as she climbed. As she rose he could see the flesh of her calves, the hocks of her knees, and then, gradually, the lovely, white flesh of her thighs, under her dress. He coughed into his hand, quietly, and turned his eyes away. Once more he remembered the day she had leaped and fallen from the pier gate, at his insistence, and he remembered Mary Alice's buttocks on his hands, her breasts against him. Once again there was an uneasy stirring of his penis as the closeness of the fully developed body of Gráinne Flannery touched him. But, he thought, she would not be able, she would not understand such urges, he must keep himself aloof from her body. He heard her heaving against the trapdoor. He looked back as she stepped from the stairs onto the floor above and saw her again, the cool white lace of her underwear, the startlingly beautiful and disturbing flesh of her thighs. Then she was gone, and he could hear her moving about in the room above.

"You can come up now," she said then, gazing down at him and smiling. He climbed quickly and stepped into the narrow room she had created. He had to keep his head low as he walked, the ceiling sloping quickly in the middle. Her bed was neat against one wall and through the large skylight he could see the sky, and clouds, their slow-waltz movement. It was quiet up here, a quiet of peace and solitude and books.

She stood against one wall, smiling at him, happy at the wonder that showed in his face as he moved about the room. Then she stood aside from the wall and he saw them, the moths, the butterflies, all pinned in their death against the cabbage-green wall. He stood for a moment, growing aware of what she had offered to display to him. He was angry at once, he felt hurt. He came close to them and reached his hand towards them.

"Don't touch them, Jack," she darted her hand out to restrain him, "they're very delicate. Like dust. Like coloured dust. Jim sends them to me, Uncle Jim, from all over the world."

He gazed at them. His face was white. They were

beautiful, a tapestry of colours and perfect shapes against the wall, wondrous patterns on wings and bodies, stretched and held for awe.

"That's awful, Gráinne, that's awful. All those beautiful, lovely creatures, killed, pinned down, kept because they're so beautiful. And they're so innocent, such wonderful flyers, and now they are pinned to a wall. Can you imagine that? The lovely creatures, in free and wonderful flight, suddenly caught in a net and handled, then killed! Just for someone's silly pleasure. How can you look at them? Doesn't it hurt you to think of them, flying in their own spaces, enjoying their freedom, their flight, their short, brilliant lives, and then someone comes and kills them, sticks a pin into them and holds them forever and ever in their death? Destroying their flight, their freedom, their hopes. I think it's disgusting. I hate them! I think your Uncle Jim must be sick! It's horrible."

Now she was upset, deeply upset. She looked at the lovely creatures again, at her secret that she had offered to share only to have it torn to shreds before her eyes.

"It's Uncle Jim's passion," she said. "He says he dreams of them, bright airy creatures, when he's locked away in the hot, dark engine-room of his ships. He sends them to me, like wishes, like dreams, like – kisses. I think they're really beautiful."

She looked at Jack, his height, his strength, and she could see his future, a certain thing, like sunlight, open spaces, adventure, and she could see her own future, in a chicken-run, in a small attic room, in the deep dank darkness of the bar. That darkness, like the engine-room of a dirty old ship. And what was her dream to be? If not with him, where were her hopes to be? He had turned away from her and from the butterflies and was watching up through the skylight. She saw him as self-centred, then, his eyes turned towards his own sky, his own sky and no one else's. She felt alone, suddenly, desperately, hopelessly alone. Only her God to be with her. Only her God . . . And she remembered the pier, and her fall from his high branch.

"I think it's you who're horrible," she accused. "I bring you up here to show you these and all you can say is mean things. I'm truly sorry I brought you up here. You've destroyed my room. You've dirtied it by being here. It'll never be the same again. Get out now, go down, get your things and go home!"

He saw the tears on her cheeks then, and he moved quickly to gather her into his arms.

"I'm sorry, Gráinne, I'm sorry, I didn't mean to say all that. I know they're very beautiful, but you must remember that I've just seen our poor old cat caught and killed and tied to a tree. And it hurt me very much. And I hate to see you cry, Gráinne, please don't cry."

She had buried her face in his shoulder and allowed herself to lean in against him. He was astonished at how much joy it gave him to hold her like that, to feel her body against his, depending on him, to have her hair against his cheek, her head buried in his shoulder. He hushed her, hushed her, and her sobbing died. They stood like that for some time and he knew the slow rise and fall of her breathing against him, his hands moved gently, stroking her back, petting her, until she shifted slightly and lay against him, her face now in under his chin, resting on his chest, and the lovely breath of her hair rising to him. That lovely river-in-spate of golden hair. She knew the strange man-scent of his body moist from the fight, she felt a great joy in his manliness, in his comforting body against hers. She put her arms about his waist and held him and he knew he had never, ever been so happy in his life.

"I think I love you, Gráinne," he whispered, and the whisper was part of the lovely, rich silence of that high room, part of the clouds and sky through the high window, part of the permanence of the beautiful creatures pinned against the wall. Hidden against his chest she smiled, her eyes closed, her happiness, at that moment, too great for words.

He was beginning to sway slightly against her now, his hands were moving on her back more freely and suddenly he held her more tightly to him and, his hands around her waist, lifted her bodily off the ground. She lay against him as he bent backwards, and she was like an angel in flight, her face looking down at his, her body lying against his bent body, his broken face looking up at her, a great fire in his eyes, a flush of desire on his cheeks, his mouth open. She longed to stoop and kiss that face, kiss it passionately all over, but she was afraid of what that might unleash, she was afraid of that strange fire that had come alight in him, the same fire she felt blazing in her own body. And then he was holding her to him with his left hand only, his right had gone down and drawn up the hem of her dress and his hand was on her flesh, hot and powerful, moving up along her thighs, gripping her buttocks, moving over her flesh, touching her, feeling her, and she cried out with the pleasure of it, the suddenness, his hunger, her hunger, his frightening need, and hers. She could see it, too, in his eyes, in the way the saliva was on his lips, in the way his whole body heaved under her, and she knew she knew that if she yielded to him now she could not stop herself, or him, she knew that it was not right, it could not be this way, it was a sin, it was – evil.

"Stop it, Jack, you must stop it!" she said down at him.

But his hand continued to caress her flesh, to move in under the cotton of her underclothes and she felt his fist holding her, fingering the naked flesh of her buttocks, kneading her flesh, savouring it. She felt his fingers parting her buttocks, one finger searching out the secrecy of her anus, that dark sphincter. She shouted at him.

"Put me down, Jack, now!"

But he would not and she grew terrified as an animal foolishness seemed to take over his features and his hand moved more violently on her buttocks, his eyes wide and demanding, his body shivering. For a long moment she closed her eyes and leant back, giving herself to the awful power of her own longing. For a moment. A short delightful forgetting moment. But her strength was great, and the flushed leering face of Father Wall rose before her.

She reached out then and slapped him across the cheek, quickly and sharply. He dropped her at once, looking at her as if she were a stranger, as if he had stepped off a boat and landed on a strange shore.

"Get out now, Jack, go!" she said, loudly, angrily, pointing at the trapdoor.

As if he were still in a dream he turned and stepped onto the staircase under the trapdoor. Almost as his head disappeared below the level of the floor he looked back for a moment where she stood, her hand to her mouth, the other on her breasts.

"I'm sorry, Gráinne," he panted. "I'm sorry. I'm really, really sorry."

Then he was gone and she sat down heavily on the bed, buried her face in her hands and wept. She did not know if she wept for him, for his heaviness, or for herself, for her strength. Her body shook in the great spasms of her sobbing and when it settled, after a time, into some form of stillness, she knew an isolation and a loneliness that frightened her. On the wall before her the great moths and butterflies hung in their own hopeless stillness.

In the early months of 1938, while whispers of terrible import, whispers of wars and battles to come reached their snakesounds even onto the fields of the island, the famous Burlington Brothers Flying Circus arrived, with a fanfare of lorry shouts and a bunting of car horns, on the island sandybanks. They set up their festive world right in the eyes of the islanders, turning their grey-bleak world of whistling wind and hissing rain into a scarlet-and-gold symphony. There were two young men, wearing strange and cumbersome flying suits, leather caps fastened to their skulls, big awkward-looking goggles covering their eyes. There were lorry drivers and tent-erectors, sideshows and stalls and shops. People everywhere putting themselves through invisible hoops of delight. It was a festival of forgetfulness, a great sacrament of hope.

At the loosely erected entrance to the site there was a woman, dressed in scarlet and gold, with sequins glittering all over her dazzling costume; her face was dark and her eyes, big brown eyes, were wet with the visions of foreign places. Her long lovely legs were bare right up to her buttocks; she wore a sequined jacket that was split down the back revealing more than should be revealed of a tanned and sumptuous flesh; she smiled into the eyes of the stricken young islandmen while she took their money.

Jack was among the first to arrive, breathless, his best

clothes on, his handsome face scrubbed, wearing now a delicate moustache and having his hair brushed stylishly to one side, a long fringe over his forehead held in place with oils. He arrived open-mouthed, silenced, awed at once by the foreign beauty of the woman at the gate. She looked straight into Jack Golden's grey eyes and saw Mary Alice MacNamara's heavy body hovering in there, she saw Gráinne's withholding strength and frustrated longing, she saw desire and loneliness and a lingering haltingness. He was a handsome young man, she saw, bright, too, with a wondrous future if only he could leave the sodden acres of this remote island and take his place among the demanding kingdoms of the world. Her hand brushed against his fingers as she gave him his change.

Jack's eyes were a light breeze on the dark opening between her breasts and then he was gone, his hands in his trouser pockets, his being heavy with his isolation, his head high to receive the grace of the fair. And there, ungainly, blank, dispirited, a monoplane stood on the sandy swards of the island, its heavy head pointed skyward, its propeller still, its tail dragging on the ground behind it. Worn out. A dromedary without a desert. A heavy cumbered thing, like an islandman in his waders, windcheaters, caps, bound by the force of gravity.

Jack noticed, however, the stakes hammered deep into the ground, the strong ropes that held this elephantine monster to the ground. He could hear the wind whistling through its wires and laths, he could sense its cluttered soul urgent for the skies.

Jack stood for a while and watched from a distance the other island people who came cautiously past the exotic woman at the gate. He watched the bangles on her arms and the tiny, golden hairs about her neck. He watched how the wind took her hair and set free a myriad of tiny hummingbirds of all the colours of paradise from its folds. He saw the flesh of her thighs, not white like Gráinne's, but honey-gold, and once – as she felt the heat of his gaze upon her skin – she lifted her eyes and looked into his and he could see the great blue oceans of the Caribbean, the white sands, the schooner birds swooping low over the waves, he could see the dense, wet-green undergrowth of jungle and tropical forest and his body grew warm and peaceful and he smiled. She sank deep into his soul and became forever associated in his mind with flight, with the great thrust of a plane into the sky, with speed, danger, excitement, the high clear skies, and with death.

He turned away then and walked slowly round the great machine, saw its struts and canvases, its many bolts and wires and timbers. He stretched out his hand to touch it and was quickly and roughly warned away, as if it would turn its heavy head and bite him.

He passed among the stalls and sideshows but there was nothing there that interested him. He saw Cornelius Griffin pick up a rifle and aim at some object in a stall; he heard the little crack and saw Cornelius straighten up with delight. Jack moved on, hands in his trousers, brooding.

He saw Gráinne, too, and she saw him. They had not spoken for such a long time now, weeks, perhaps months. She nodded to him, gravely, and that was not enough, Jack turned from her quickly, roughly. She was with her father and together they were standing, dulled and insignificant, against the corner of a high, green-white striped tent.

Mary Alice MacNamara was there, too, and she smiled at him and winked. But she had betrayed him, she had betrayed them all, for Father Wall had called to the house one day recently and begged Jack's mother to allow Mary Alice to come to him, to be his housekeeper. Mrs Golden was surprised, at first, for wasn't she old and didn't she only have a son with her to run the little farm? Father Wall promised he would let Mary Alice come twice a week to do down the house, to sweep and wash and iron, and wouldn't Mrs Golden be saving money that way for Father Wall would pay Mary Alice a weekly wage that would include her days with Mrs Golden. Jack watched her now, her prettiness somewhat dimmed before the orchid beauty at the gate. She stood, down the distance between two stalls, and watched him. He made up his mind he would push the issue between them, one day soon, when she was at the Golden house. He would pluck up his strength, like gathering up a nettle and urge her to complete with him what she had several times tentatively begun. For after Gráinne he had known only sorrow and loneliness and a great regret. And if you wish to fly you must push yourself to a great speed first so that the air can take you and lift you up into its ecstasies where you will be allowed to ride it, ride it wildly and powerfully as you will ride a horse. And as he smiled at her where she stood, her handbag swinging low across her crotch, a man stepped out from a stall to her right, took her arm proprietorially; she flashed Jack a bright smile, then they vanished from his sight.

The world, along the sandybanks, was now filled with colours, noise, movement, music over loudspeakers, laughter. And then from somewhere came a great wailing sound, a siren calling the spectators to the great flying machine waiting on the sward. It was like the turn of a tide, everyone moving excitedly towards the roped-off area that held the plane. Jack got up against the ropes to watch every movement of the display.

They had removed the thick cords that had held the plane, like a hunting bird, a falcon, to the earth. One of the brothers was announced, the metallic voice over the loudspeaker crackling and grinding as it was caught by the island breeze and whisked away to sea. The man, dressed in his flying suit, his goggles, his leather helmet, his boots that looked like riding boots, bowed to the people, accepted the bouquets of their cheers and climbed aboard. Jack watched as the other brother hung on the propeller, swung it fiercely, he heard and saw the engine catch, there was smoke, shuddering, noise and then the creature moved heavily along the grass, lumbering, gangly like an autumn harvester, gained speed, its tail coming up alarmingly and then it lifted, came back down, and then was in the air, circling away from them out over the sea, back to dip and soar above their heads, the pilot visible, waving his hand to them, a long white scarf flying out along the air behind him.

He flew low over the heads of the astonished people, he rose again, banking steeply out over the sea, that sea that they strove so hard, with so many sacrifices, to master, that sea to whom they had offered so many of their own island lives, and there he was, treating it with contempt, dipping so low the little wheels almost touched the wave-caps, then up again, making for the cliffs, head on, then up up up with breathtaking power and back down again to land, in an elegant, slow bouncing dance, before them. Jack stood, shocked with delight; his eyes never for a moment left the aircraft; he imagined himself aboard, mastering the element of air, oh how he would wheel away from the earth, from the sea, up into the sky . . .

For an hour the Brothers flew, changing places, one of them now tied to the fuselage, walking out on one of the wings, and once, the hearts of the islanders frozen like lumps of potatoes in their chests, the plane flew upside down and the man became the wheels and the wheels rode along the ceiling of the air.

Jack was one of the last to leave the sandybanks. As he trailed slowly out through the entrance-way he saw the dark, lovely woman striding with long emu strides towards the Brothers. He watched her, she went up to one of them where they were examining the structure of their plane, and she took him by the shoulders to lead him away. That was all. She had not turned again to weigh his life down even further with the impossibility of her existence. But in that moment Jack was aware of all the possibilities that life had still to offer him, far from here, away among the vast magnificences of the world closed off to him because he was an island, living an island life, circumscribed by tradition, faith, and gravity.

My dear Gráinne,

I am enclosing another butterfly, a special one, and I don't care what your Jack Golden says about them. This fellow is called the kallima butterfly and I bought him in a shop in the Pacific. You'll see the strange, pinkish colouring on this chap. You must remember these innocent, harmless creatures have so many enemies, birds, and bats, flies and wasps, farmers, gardeners, cats, everything wants the butterfly. About three or four of every hundred caterpillars live to become butterflies and then only one or two out of those four live the full length allotted to them. This fellow, the kallima, is an expert in disguise. When his wings are folded up he looks like a leaf, and when he's feeding on a plant the birds don't notice him. So he survives.

Life is about surviving, Gráinne, there are so many things out to get us in life.

That's why I think that every chance we get in life to be any way happy we must take a shot at it. What you told me about your Jack is normal. He sounds like he has grown into a lively lad, young still, and don't forget you're living on an island, none of you have seen the things I've seen, have been where I've been. Look at your walls and see the great variety of moths and butterflies, wondrous, wondrous things. Among them there's the cabbage butterfly, white, veined, delicate. That's you, Gráinne, that's you, there on

115

your island, no less beautiful, but missing the exotic colours and the great size of the others. There's many ways of living, Gráinne, many ways of looking at the world. You've got one of them only, on your island. And it's a good way to live. But it's only one way, only one way. Remember that. Out where I live – for I have got myself a little house on stilts, like a man you'd see in the circus, and Gráinne, ssshhh! Don't tell Fintan nor Nora, I've got myself a dark native wife here in Papua New Guinea – anyway, where I live a lot of the women go round naked and nobody pays a blind bit of heed. That's their way. That's not your way. Where you are the body is a curse, it's a sin, it's to be hidden away. Your God is a heavy old God, weighing down on you from His big black clouds. Might be something to do with the cold and the rain but really it's to do with sin.

Gráinne, don't I remember it all so well. Where I am now there is a vast sky, limitless; to the west of me there is ocean, the Indian Ocean, and at the far side of that ocean is Africa. To the east is the sweeping forest and some great mountains of the Owen Stanley Range. Go north and you'll hit the Philippines. I've been there, too. Go south and it's Australia and then New Zealand. There's the Pacific Ocean and beyond that there's South America and then the Atlantic Ocean and then the other side of Africa. And everything is different, other, sometimes wondrous, often worse than at home. But if it's God you're thinking of then He's limitless, He's as many as there are people, that's what I think, and if you have an island God then you have an island soul. If that's so you have an island life, a small-island life and that's like being blind and stubborn and locking yourself out of the sun to spite your own eyes. Gráinne, what I'm saying is this, if you like your young lad, then you must be able to understand his wonder and his curiosity and his anguish before the power of a woman's body; a woman's body is something breathtaking and demanding for a man, believe me, and to be scared of it, or ignorant of it, doesn't mean he doesn't care for you, for the real you. I'm certain he does. And I'm sure he has his own ideas about the moths and that's alright, too. Anyway he doesn't seem to have been too bad with you, not at all. And haven't we all got our problems, don't we all have to carry everywhere with us our own weight of flesh with its urges and longings. We're caterpillars, Gráinne, crawling through the mud, scared of birds, hauling an ugly weight around with us. But when we're free of it, how beautiful we may become!

Gráinne, it's my advice now, go to Jack and say hello to him again, and smile on him, and be great again. Don't be stubborn, Gráinne, nothing is ever served by being stubborn. I'm certain you have taught him a lesson, an island lesson, and he's just unable to come and say that he's different. Don't be lonesome in life, above all, don't be lonesome. Go to him, Gráinne, please, go to him.

I'm wandering the world still, like an albatross. Leaving my own dark darling at home for long times. I watched a man fall overboard the other day under the sudden strike of a wave, a freak wave in an innocent sea and it was only then, from the water slipping already behind us, that he screamed to us that he couldn't swim, though he's been at sea for thirty years. He was gone by the time we got a small boat out. Just gone. You cling on to things, Gráinne, you cling on, for though we're heavy flesh and bones and our heads are dense with weight, the slightest thing can whip us from our holding-place and we're gone.

Gather rosebuds, Gráinne, gather rosebuds. Look at your moths and butterflies and think of possibilities, think of love, Gráinne, think of open spaces and freedom and love.

Gráinne, bless you, little friend. Give my love to Fintan and Nora. And don't tell them at all about this letter. And write to me soon. Your letter might have to follow me over the seas but never mind, it'll come.

Jack stabled the old donkey and left him to his feed and to the slowly gathering dusk. Then he passed down along the out-houses and hoisted the small turf-cart bodily, holding it by the shafts, and pushing it backwards into the shed. The big wheels chuckled on the soft, turf-mould-covered floor. Hours he spent now, sometimes, high in his trees, hugging their bark in his loneliness. He went to the corner of the shed and he washed his hands in the water from the outdoor tap. It was a sultry evening, it would be filled with a grey light for some hours yet. The swift and swallow were chasing and cavorting high in the dim sky. The grove was still, as if it were tired from movement. His mother would be heading down to Cafferky's soon, to spend the evening with Mrs Cafferky and her friends. Talking out of her own loneliness and emptiness for she had greatly loved that tyrant, Ted, Jack knew it now, she had loved him. In spite of all . . . Jack shook his hands to dry them. Then he went into the shed and took off his overalls to hang them on the hook.

When he turned back Mary Alice MacNamara was in the doorway, standing between him and the light. He had almost forgotten, today was her day in the Golden home. She was as lovely as ever in his sight, her breasts full, her hips large and shapely. She stood watching him for a moment, her hands lightly resting on her hips.

"How is my little saddle-boy?" she said softly to him, her voice coming to him through the dusk like the distant sound of a thrush at evening, and at once that dull pain hit him in the stomach and a trembling began somewhere in his chest. "Almost a man now, I'd say, able to carry me away." She was wearing a bright cotton dress, lemon-yellow with tiny pink roses all over it, short sleeves, and it was open at her neck. He picked some little courage out of the dim light of the shed.

"I wish I was your saddle-boy," he said. "I miss that. I just loved it when your weight was on me. I mean, when, the bike . . ."

She advanced into the shed towards him. She was laughing lightly, she was a small breeze stirring the tips of the trees that had been still for a long time.

"A man!" she said, reaching her right arm towards him and touching him on the shoulder. Even in the dimness of the shed he could see the soft hairs on her flesh, he could see the full shapes of her breasts. "Fit to take all of my weight, fit to be my saddle, my throne, my donkey. Down on your hands and knees then, on the floor, and you can be my little pony and I'll ride on you, I'll ride on your back and we'll go to the market. My little pony will take me off to market."

He looked at her, but her strength and certainty as well as her beauty had him at her command. Her smile was gentle though mocking, and even in the gloom of the shed her eyes were warm and filled with laughter. Her body was full and beautiful to him and at that moment he would have died for her. He went down on his hands and knees on the soft turf-mould. She chuckled, then, lifting her dress high above her knees she straddled his back. Slowly. She stood over him for a moment, and he could see the shine of her black shoes on either side of his body, and the tiny dark hairs on her bare legs. He wondered again if she were wearing anything under that lemon-yellow dress. She waited for a while, teasing him, rubbing the insides of her legs against his sides, and he did not dare look back up at her. She laughed, brightly, her laughter shaking him in the echoing gloom of the shed, then, lowering herself slowly, she sat on his back, she sat heavily on him, settling herself, lifting her feet from the ground so that her whole weight was on his back and he found it difficult to stay as he was, bearing her weight, knowing again the delight of the pressure of her buttocks against him.

"To market, little pony, little pony, little pony . . ."

She was laughing, shifting her weight on him, and he loved the wonderful fullness of her buttocks, the way they moved on him, and the fierce and agonising longing of his own body.

"Hup, there, pony," she said and began to move on his back, slowly at first and then more rapidly, up and down, forward and back, making little clicking sounds with her tongue. He was breathing hard, trying to maintain his position, but her weight was too great for him and he collapsed on his face in the mould. She laughed loudly, now, and sat there on him for a while before she hoisted herself onto her knees.

"You're not strong enough," she said. "You're only a young pony yet, you're not able for me. You better turn over now."

He turned under her and lay on his back, looking up at her. His hands hurt where they had pressed into the mould under her weight. He looked at the palm of his right hand, it was covered with tiny pieces of black mould and here and there were the white marks of the pressure. She was kneeling over his chest now, holding her dress above her knees, and the shape of her breasts loomed above him.

"So," she said, down at him. "My little Jack is as innocent as ever." She sat down on him again then, squatting on his stomach, the dress drawn well up on her thighs. He felt her weight on his stomach and on the lower part of his chest. He could see the gleam of her lovely flesh as she sat there, heavily, how high she had her dress, how close . . .

"I just love your weight on me, Mary Alice," he panted up at her. "I'd love to be pressed down forever into the earth under you."

She chuckled again. Then she hoisted herself from her straddling position and sat down fully, squatting higher up on his chest. Her knees were raised now over his face and he could glimpse into the wonderful cave of her darkness. He was in ecstasy under the great burden of her weight. She chuckled again, rocking herself slowly on him. She moved a little further up along his chest, until the lemon-yellow dress was covering his face and the backs of her lovely thighs pressed against his cheeks. A little further and she would cover his face. She sat quietly for a while. He would have stayed forever.

"Spread out your hands, now, like a cross," she commanded.

She stood upright again, moved back a little, then lay forward on top of him, her whole body pressing him down, her breasts against his chest, and she stretched her arms out on top of his spread arms, lifted her knees and feet until they rested on his. Now her whole weight was on him, and she put her face down to his and kissed him on the lips, a long, lingering kiss.

That was the moment when Jack heard a sharp cry from the door of the shed. He lifted his head quickly. Gráinne Flannery was standing in the doorway, looking down at him.

"Gráinne!" he said, and his whole life crumbled into mould.

Gráinne cried out again, an inarticulate cry, then she put her hands to her mouth, turned and ran from the shed.

Mary Alice lifted herself carefully off him.

"We always seem to be interrupted," she laughed. But he rose, too, hurt and bewildered. He looked at Mary Alice and only anger and resentment flooded through him.

"You've ruined it," he said to her. "You've ruined it."

"Oh have it your own way," she retorted at once. "What do I care? You're only a little squirt, anyway. Haven't I got my Father Wall? And as many men on the island as I want to? Why do I bother with a little squirt like you?"

Jack turned from her then and stumbled, blinded by frustration and despair, back into his deserted house.

Two

The old man put his hand on the doorknob, paused a moment, and opened the door. It sighed softly as it yielded to him. There was a faint light from the window falling like sleep across the room. He held the door and looked cautiously around it. She was lying on the bed, sleeping. For a long moment he watched her, watched her peaceful stillness on the bed, and he could hear the slight rhythmic sighing of her breathing. She was propped up on the pillow, her hands folded on the counterpane, she wore a pink nightdress and he could see she was wearing a soft pink dressing-gown, too. Her hair was a small summer cloud about her head, ready to vanish at the slightest breeze. Her eyes were closed.

He looked quickly about the room. There was a wardrobe, a dressing-table and beyond the dressing-table a view down over dim countryside, the corner of a graveyard just visible behind bushes, headstones and crosses leaning and bending like a crowd of old gossipers, then the trees that belonged to the ruined abbey. He knew that, just beyond the old abbey and the trees, there was the sea, the ever-patient, ever-grumbling, sea. The walls of the room were coloured a light blue, there was a dark blue carpet on the floor. One picture of a long, golden beach with multicoloured crowds leaping forever at the edge of the waves. Blue sky. Silver light.

He gazed at her again. He was still half in, half out of her room. His heart thudded heavily inside him. He rapped softly on the door once more. She did not respond. He glanced quickly out into the corridor. It was deserted. He went into her room and closed the door after him.

He went over to the bed, the weight of his own body settling quickly on him again after the climb up the stairs. His right leg was paining him, sharp, quick pains flowing from his thigh right down to his foot. He sat down quickly on the small armchair beside her bed. Still she did not stir. She seemed at peace.

He sat a long while watching her. Outside the room there was silence. He seemed to be with her in a world beyond a world, the earth itself a grey and shapeless mass somewhere out of reach. He leaned forward and touched the back of her hand. She did not respond.

"Darling, darling, darling," he whispered, softly. The words were as gentle as breathing. She did not respond. He sat back in the armchair again. He would be content to stay for as long as they would allow him. Or until she told him he must go. He felt at peace, with her, at last. He breathed easily.

Once, while he sat, perfectly still, watching her, something like the shadow a small cloud makes over a summer meadow passed across her face; it passed quickly, but he noticed it, and it hurt him. As if somewhere she was in pain, or as if a black thought had suddenly covered the sun shining in her mind. Then it was gone, and her face was as peaceful as before. Her breathing continued, soft, regular. He watched her.

And once he heard footsteps coming along the corridor. The door opened and a nurse came into the room. His heart hurt him now with fear; would she tell him to leave? before he had been able to speak with her? But the nurse, young and harried, merely nodded to him, then placed her small white hand on the woman's forehead and gazed down into her face a while.

"No change," she said, "the poor creature."

He looked up at the nurse and wondered. But he smiled and nodded an agreement to her words.

"I'll come back soon," she said. "If there's a change, just you ring the bell. OK?"

"Yes, I'll do that."

She smiled brightly at him and then she was gone.

In the ensuing silence he gazed more closely into the old, still lovely face. And then he knew, he knew it suddenly and overwhelmingly, he knew such stillness was not natural, such absence, such a regular rhythm of breathing, no movement other than the slightest lift of the chest under the light blanket, not even the smallest riffling of the perfect sheet. He suffered then, he suffered as much in that moment of intense realisation as he had suffered for years and years before. Quickly now he reached his hand and touched her forehead; it was cold, too cold. He called her name, loudly, several times. There was no reaction. Not the slightest movement. He stood up then as if flung out of the armchair onto his feet, his hands raised to his face in sorrow and terror. His right leg caved in under the suddenness of the movement and he fell heavily onto the side of the bed, his arms falling on her shape under the clothes, and he stayed there, on his knees beside her bed, as if he were praying, praying, praying . . .

She did not stir. He knew now it was finished. He suffered the whole weight and heaviness of all his years, as if he had been keeping them for so long high above his body and now they sank, all at once, on top of him. He buried his face in his hands and laid his head down on the counterpane beside her form.

"I'm sorry, I'm so sorry, so sorry, so sorry." He whispered the words into his hands. He could feel his spittle touch his flesh. He did not care. He looked up at her face again.

"I love you, I love you," the words were spoken loudly to her now. He reached his hands and held both of hers where they lay, fingers wrapped together, on the bed. "I have always loved you, always, and never for a moment did I cease to love you. I was born loving you, and I love you now. I will love you forever, no matter where you are or where I am, I will love you. Forever." He laid his head down on her joined hands and stayed there, growing still himself beside her silent shape. And the tears would not come.

He was scarcely able to rise again and get himself back into the armchair. Now his whole body had seemed to collapse inside itself, imploding, as if all the pressure from within that had kept him going for so long had collapsed, yielded at last, and with relief. He sighed hugely. His eyes were dry. His whole life seemed to be urging itself to one great word. One word that would explode out of him with tremendous import, holding all of his life in it, all of his hopes and failures and despair, all of his sorrows and efforts. He breathed in, deeply, slowly. He raised his eyes towards the white ceiling of the room and his body shook. He would curse, now, he would let all his anger rage against life, against the barriers, invisible and visible, that make living such a difficult thing. He would scream. He opened his mouth. And he could not utter a sound. His hands were fists again, his body was a tightened coil. His mouth was the barrel of a gun. And no words came. He sank back again into his chair, closed his eyes and let his head fall heavily on his chest.

He had embraced death before and had survived, shaking it off. It had scared him, like a great river of flame he had to swim through before coming to the other side. He had laughed, later, though he bore the scars of that embrace. To face the death he had faced was almost an easy thing, he had gone towards it with his head high, his fists raised, his soul challenging. He had faced it, then, as an equal, as soldier to soldier, fighter to fighter, hero to hero, naked and unarmed before it, and he had survived. But this was different. He knew it now, he would be drained utterly of all life, the way a fox could suck an egg dry, leaving the shell intact. His being would be an empty space, hope and faith and all of self would be drained away. He would sag before it. Utterly. He would be vacuum.

Slowly he watched around the room, looking for some escape from his position. There was the window. His eyes rested on it for a long time. The curtains were not drawn. The room, its light blue walls, the white jamb of the doorway, were faintly reflected in its glass. He could not see, from where he sat, out into the growing darkness beyond. An overwhelming lethargy had settled on him. A heaviness that seemed to be a pressure from within, passing outwards. He had sunk down into the armchair. She had not stirred. Not moved. He tried to stand. It was almost too difficult. As if all the energy he owned had been drawn out of him. All physical energy. All the energy of grace. He tore himself suddenly from the chair with a low growl, the effort tumbling him forward once more against the side of her bed.

He was standing now, his heavy coat still about him. The room was warm. He had only a vague sensation of the blues and pinks of the room blurring together about him. He moved the few steps needed to take him to the window. It would be easy. Easy. He was high up. The third floor. The earth would take him, mercifully, filling his emptiness with its hard, forgiving mass. He could not see beyond. For him already it was dark night. There could be no reward, either this side of his own, pitiful reflection in the window, nor on the other side. He could still wonder, still admire, how deeply pathetic is all the ministration of the world, and all the foibles, fears and antics of the human soul. How empty is the entire world, how hollow its mass, how great the void. And how it yearns for God. And how God has failed it. Truth, he thought now, truth is on the side of death. On the other side of suffering. Beyond the darkness.

The window was low. He could rush and fling himself bodily into that darkness. It would be easy. Just to find the energy. Now. Without further thought. He gathered himself, summoning all the energy that absolute despair could give him. He turned his shoulders. He clenched his fists. He turned to look at her for the last time.

Her eyes were open, watching him. A thrill of unbearable terror went through him, as if he had been stricken through by lightning. Her eyes were open, fixed on him. And focused. He cried out, a short, strangled cry, and all his despair turned at once into a violent, bursting flame of gratitude. He turned back towards her, away from the image of himself in the window, back to her where she still lived, waiting. It was an instant only, an instant when the world had halted, an instant in which he had gone beyond that dark mirror and found himself still alive, because of her, because of the gift of her grace. Her eyes had closed again, and for a moment he was uncertain whether she had looked on him at all or whether his awful need of her had made his eyes see what his soul screamed for. He fell on his knees by the bed, calling her, touching her hands, caressing them, those old, long fingers. She did not respond. She had come from death a moment to touch him with her eyes. She had saved him. And had gone.

In the awful silence that settled back about him he began to tremble. He sat back in the armchair, frightened, shivering with the cold proximity of death. He shivered with the memory of it, with the memory of that impossible emptiness that death had held out before him as its calling card. He felt chilled where he sat, and suddenly tears came, rich, warming tears, a release, tears for himself and for her, and for all humankind.

Suddenly he remembered. He reached to the bell that lay close to her hand and he pressed it, several times, trying to convey his urgency through the wire. The old woman looked exactly as she did before, still, unmoving, gone, but he knew, he knew . . .

Jack Golden got on the train at Victoria Station. London. England. When he arrived he could hear the noise of voices and trolleys and steam, as if the world were normal again; there was human animation as if the world were on holiday, buckets and spades at the ready, picnics packed. The engine breathed quietly, little impatient foot-tappings of steam from its sides, its wheels; the carriage doors stood open, a long line of them, open and inviting as if here you could find your own private pew from which to worship. Camaraderie under the high-arched ceiling of the station, back-slapping and mustachioed bravado.

Jack (Jackie) Golden slipped through the many soldiers and their wives and girl-friends, slipped through them unnoticed. Wasn't he one of them? Indistinguishable now, with his fine and fair moustache, his uniform, his youth. Laid on the altar. Offered to that dreaded god of war. For what do the young know of war and death and brutality? They stride firmly towards the future, knowing little of the lessons of the past, casting their bodies in vigorous denial against the world, as a challenge to earlier generations, as a defiance of all they had been bred to believe.

He stopped suddenly; ahead of him three soldiers had huddled to light their cigarettes from one match; for a moment, a second perhaps, no more, the three intent young faces peered onto flame and their skins were lit from the match; he saw them, all three, taken in a pit of flames and burning swiftly in intolerable pain; he cried out and leaped towards them, his right hand reaching. They did not notice; there was so much noise, so much shouting, so much raucous bravado. They drew back from the flame, contented; there is such camaraderie, such willing unknowing in the wearing of a uniform; one of them shook the match in his right hand and flicked it against the great flanged wheels of the train. Jack stumbled on, embarrassed, shaken, and surprised. It was the dreams, he excused himself, the dreams and nightmares he had been having at the base. It was a time for nightmare, human ranged against human, heavily armoured for the strife. The soldiers drew deeply on their cigarettes and moved up along the platform.

Foolish visionary; coward; madman. He mocked himself. From somewhere and for the first time in these months of war, fear had fallen on him now. Fear; because the great iron gate that he had been longing to open was now beginning to creak and he feared what he would find beyond. What would find him . . .

He looked up. Up above the noise, the clamour, the movement, a city pigeon was flying among the high blackened beams of the ceiling. High, high up above the soldiers, the airmen, the women. Under the smoke-blackened glass dome. Flying slowly, in freedom from any memory or anticipation. Free, in its own, dumb nature. Enviable so, and enviable in its power of flight. The bird vanished among the beams and darknesses. Beyond that the heavens, betrayed, he knew, by man's instinct for slaughter, heavens now so often filled with man's expertise to kill, to bomb; the heavens, another world inhabited by the murdering, destroying villains of creation.

He shook himself out of his reverie. He felt alone, hopelessly, utterly alone. Around him carriage doors were slamming shut. He stood, entranced by fear. He could run away. Now. No one would ever find him. Back. Back home. Back home to Gráinne, to the island, to . . . He could explain, it was nothing to do with anything, only the brute and mindless urgings of the flesh. She would . . . Someone took him suddenly by the shoulder. It was a soldier.

"Canterbury? The Canterbury train?"

Jack nodded, helpless.

"This is it, then. Better be getting aboard." The soldier grinned at him, another young face bearing the first proud growth of hair above his lip, his eyes already visionary beyond death. There was talk, fervid and barely voiced talk, about a great push against Hitler, about a fierce and overwhelming gathering of the forces of life against those of death, one, great, effort . . .

Jack moved, like a ghost, collecting his bags, climbing into a carriage, sitting down among the others, hoping the train would never start. Such a sweat and frisson of cowardice that shamed him, here among the raucousness of his companions, these strangers with whom he shared a small space for a time.

The train shuddered, jerked, and moved forward. It stopped, shuddered again, as if unwilling to start. Then it was moving slowly, the engine puffing loudly, and the train moved out into the light from the cave of the station. He was astonished then; for a while he had thought it was night time when he had been standing in the station, waiting. Now the early afternoon sun lit the carriage and they moved out over the streets of London, rattling, hissing, puffing. And his sense of dread lifted as if he had taken off a heavy, sodden overcoat.

He was the only airman among a troop of soldiers. RAF uniform. His wings. He was glad of that; it held him apart from them. He did not want to speak. What did he know of this war? What did he care? He had his own, lonely war to fight, he had his wings, he would fly. He settled back; they would ignore him. They had gathered to play poker. There were five of them, young, innocent-looking, eager, ignorant, unknowing. They laughed as if they were on a day's outing instead of heading for their part in a deadly war. Perhaps for them, too, it was an escape, a way out of some emptiness that threatened them. One of them dealt the cards. They took out coins, ha'pennies, farthings, pennies. One of them glanced at Jack and caught his eye. "Join us, sir?"

That "sir" bothered him momentarily though he knew it had been offered with innocent deference. Jack shook his head. "Thanks."

He was running away, he knew that, running away from Gráinne and from Mary Alice, running away from the emptiness that had settled on him after that day in the turf-shed. Running away from the island. Society, when the heart hurts, is the darkest of caves in which to dwell; it is full of condemnation, of memory, of association; the way out of it is isolation, and Jack had left, left to be alone, lured, too, by the call to the great world that was in turmoil, lured by the possibility of real flying, of aircraft, of the sky, the clouds. That vision of the heavy tail of the plane dragging along the earth and then lifting, miraculously, into the air. Freedom.

He had gone to her and she had shut him out of the

yard. Cornelius sloped about, like a quietened dog. Jack envied him his obtuseness. His big-bodied, awkward, committed relationship to weight and slowness. Jack waited. The day grew dark. She did not appear. He hefted his jacket higher on his body and merged with the shadows in the doorway of the store. If he could explain to Gráinne the longings of flesh . . . but she would not know them, she would not understand. It rained. He waited, the rain taking him, bit by bit, wetting him, the doorway being narrow and the rain slanting softly in across the yard. Cornelius switched on a light in the fuel shed and beckoned to him to come. Jack hesitated. He was beginning to shiver and still she had not appeared. He raced across the yard and in the door of the shed. Cornelius watched him, wordlessly. There was a great hill of coal in one corner of the shed. Cornelius's face was splotched with the dust.

"She's away to her room. This hours past. She's distracted. Best go to her or go on home with yourself."

Jack looked at him, surprised. There was a rough kindliness in the face he had not seen before. Cornelius fustered with some bags of turf.

"Cornelius," Jack began. "Thank you. I never – I mean, it was never a thing between me and you. As if you – and me – I mean, it was over Gráinne. That's all."

Cornelius looked at him and grinned.

"That's all right, Jack," he mumbled, embarrassed, too. "You bate the shite out of me and I hold you in respect for it. That's it now! And herself, Gráinne, sure I know she has her mind on yourself and whatever 'tis has her bothered 'tis you can overcome it."

He nodded his big head, slowly, and Jack took comfort from him.

"Thanks," he said again. He reached his hand and Cornelius took it, swaying his big head in delighted embarrassment. Jack left the shed and went to the back door of the Flannery house. He knocked. There was no answer. Again. No answer. He pushed open the door. Gráinne was sitting in a corner of the kitchen, bent over a book, a letter, something. She did not look up.

"Gráinne." He said it loud but it was a whisper, hoarse and hesitant. She did not look up.

"Gráinne," he tried again, his back against the door, his body wet and cold. "You've it wrong. There's nothing, nothing . . ."

She closed what she was bent over with a slap and stood up, without looking towards him. She moved slowly towards the door to the hallway on the other side of the kitchen. She was pale, he noticed, trembling too. He could have run to her and held her to him, he should have run and cried out against the world that they two, together, they two of all people, should have any pain, any misunderstanding between them . . .

She had turned, half, towards him.

"You have no right being here," she said to him. "No right. You and I have nothing to say to one another. Nothing. I forbid you to come here. There is no word, no deed, no . . ."

She sobbed, loudly; her hand went to her throat. Then she looked at him, quickly, and there was such despair in her eyes, and such a flame of anger and dismissal that he crumpled up on the floor as if his knees had melted into water. Then she was gone, and she had closed the door behind her. Leaving him, sodden, on the floor of her anger, kneeling, as if in prayer . . .

Someone laughed, and Jack was back in the carriage with the soldiers. One of them was standing over him, holding out a flask of something, offering him some, welcoming him, speaking. And Jack had not heard any of it. Nothing.

He shook his head, slowly, and tried to smile. But he knew that the sadness was in his eyes, too, and he did not try to speak. An islandman, facing all the ruck and roister of company, takes on himself an even thicker, heavier weight of armour. Surfacing from an island life and being flung, like a landed fish, on the dry and burning shore of the great world. The soldier shrugged his shoulders and turned away.

The train continued slowly, stopping at small stations for no obvious reason, sometimes stopping between stations. The fields seemed normal, there were men working, there were cattle, horses, sheep, there were orchards, too, with their blossoms. Normal. As if the world had not exploded into curses and spittle and blood.

Once they halted inside a tunnel; they were in a blackness within utter blackness. "It's a raid," someone whispered, as if the words might be heard from the sky above to draw down the wrath of death upon them. They waited, helplessly, the train hissing softly at times within the impenetrable darkness of war. They were silent, each man forced deep within himself, forced to search again whatever emptiness within that he tried to fill. Until the train stirred again, there was the dim light of dusk, and their words came as if a door had opened onto a familiar room filled with familiar guests.

It was quite dark when the train pulled into Canterbury station. Gradually the men had fallen silent. Some of them slept. In their sleep they stirred and moaned as if a small swarm of nightmares had buzzed about them. Others sat and smoked, staring out at the darkness outside. The train, too, was dark, for fear of attack out of the sky above them, it was a long, black worm making its way fearfully across a dark and threatening field. Jack's mind was restless, he was unable to sleep. Soon, he knew, soon he would be with others, up there in those skies, a bird, an eagle, a hawk. But now, and always, there was the burden of himself. It is a question of being delivered from the self, he thought, a question of flight, a question of war, a question of love (and he had lost?), a question, perhaps, of death.

When the train stopped nobody stirred. Here and there in the darkened station, someone moved with a torch, or a lantern, the lights small and hesitant, the silence overwhelming as the great steam-engine died. They would sit there waiting, until dawn. Then they would go their different ways, some to the front, some to the coast, some to the airfields, some to the ports . . . Jack tried to sleep.

He dozed and for a moment Pearse Plunkett Keane was walking with him again. Pearse was the only other Irishman at the RAF College at Cranwell. Together they had climbed into the sky for the first time, Pearse in the front cockpit of the "Maggie", the rickety trainer plane, the *Miles Magister*, made of wood, capable of wild acrobatics in the air. The plane had lurched and yawed. Pearse had screamed with delight as the wheels ticked off some leaves on the top of an elm at Cranwell. Then they were climbing, Jack's stomach pressing down inside him, fear brushing his hair, his face. He could see the world below shrink rapidly. He looked back to the controls in the cockpit. Then the clouds were above them and Pearse had plunged into the strange wispy dreaminess of their grey half-being. Soon they had come out on a new world, a world of azure and silver-blue, of bright sunlight with an endless vista of rolling clouds. Jack took control. At the sense of the power at his fingertips all fear left him and all that remained was the exhilaration, the joy, the sense of escape. He held "Maggie" in a steady flight, then turned, dropped and skimmed the top of the clouds the way a skua skims the surface of the waves. Pearse had turned to him, a great grin on his face, his two thumbs raised.

What can they know of war, the young? It is an ocean in turmoil about them and they are the sprat, swirling and

leaping in their millions before the slaughtering shoals of
mackerel, or they are the mackerel, gaudy in their speed
and strength, the impulse to hunt and feed driving them
on.

When they touched soil again the excitement in both of
them was too great to contain. Their first flight without
instructors had been perfect. They undid their flying
clothes, their whole bodies tense still with the wonder and
sensation of the flight. They were trembling, the words
they had were inadequate. They left the base and wandered
into the little town. Pearse was young, too, clean-shaven,
intent, bright and candid; he was a big man, and Jack was
glad to have him as a friend. They drank a little in The
Crow and Lark. But it was still too much for them; they
watched each other, grinning, unable to express, or to
contain, their excitement.

Two young women had come into the Inn, one of them
dapper, good-looking, young, the other large and
somewhat plain. Pearse and Jack drank a little more; the
women drank a little; from their places they watched each
other; the men were exhilarated and young; Pearse was
confident about the world and soon they were walking the
quiet streets of Cramston, and Pearse walked with the
pretty one, Jack beside the plain. How he remembered it all
now, all of it, in detail, second by second, floating slowly
through his half-dozing mind. How awkwardly he had
doffed the hero's armour to lie naked, fragile, alien, along
her bed.

She was called Louise and she had already lost her
boyfriend to the war, somewhere in the north of France,
somewhere fighting those awful bastards, and oh how she
wished Jack luck, to go out there and rid the skies of that

terrible enemy. Revenge, she wanted, he should drop down death on them from the skies . . . She stood, naked too, for a long while at the window; the curtains were drawn back, there was no light in the room and the streets outside were unlit. Jack saw her big body gleam like alabaster in the failed light of day; she was not beautiful, but Jack's terror was still great. She stood, watching away from him into her own war, and the silence of their separateness settled on them, like a chill air. Jack thought fleetingly of Gráinne, and of Mary Alice, and how he longed for Gráinne now, Gráinne, to be with him, here, at this moment. He thought, too, of the spaces and confines of his island, and sorrow surged for a moment through his life. Quickly he put the images from him, concentrating on the large buttocks of this unknown woman. He whispered then into the dimness: "Louise!" She turned from the window, sighing heavily. Then she came towards him.

It was an awkward, fumbling and unhappy event. Always remembering Gráinne, her eyes, her gentle shape leaning towards and away from him, Jack had wanted to be tender, gentle, even loving. But Louise had needed more than that, much more, she needed to be taken with an urgency and a violent passion that would sweep her out of her sadness, out of the river of misery that was her war, into some oblivion, however short. She had pulled at him, urging him, and he had grown conscious of his ignorance, the unreal expectations of flesh, how much of an island he still was.

They lay together, then, side by side, unsatisfied, ill at ease, like spars thrown up on a beach. And then the sirens blared, they heard the bombers coming from a long way away, they heard the thuds of the falling bombs, the screams of the planes, they saw flashes of light and the ugly glow of fires and she had rolled suddenly over on top of him, holding him, pinning him down under her weight, holding him, needing the security and companionship that another body can give. He had loved it, learning again his own pleasure at feeling the weight of a woman's body press him down, knowing her breasts against his chest, her limbs stretching down over his, and enjoying the heaviness of her body as she pinned him down. She was sobbing with the helplessness of it all, he could feel the moisture on her face, her cheeks, and then he was holding her, kissing her, loving her, his breathing difficult under her, his arms around her now, pulling her even more heavily onto him, his hands fondling her, along her back, her buttocks, the backs of her legs and then his need for her became so great that he hoisted her off him and entered her, working frantically into her cries of pleasure and for the first time in his life he knew the full abandon and glory of giving, of offering his own body as a gift. He knew the exuberance of flight, the weightless, unforgettable hovering at the edge of a profound abyss of pleasure. The bombs dropped not far from them, buildings crumbled and collapsed, fires raged and explosions flashed their quick lights on the two naked bodies. Until they stilled, and the world stilled, and Jack breathed deeply and peacefully once again.

He had won his wings.

He stood, conscious of the dapper and haughty statement of his uniform. Now the jacket fitted him, the cap did not come down over his face, his hands did not stick out from the sleeves. He lifted one sleeve and fingered the crown embossed on the buttons; the brass was cool and he breathed on it; then he watched the dulled brass gradually brighten again as his breath faded from it. Alone but not lonely, he raised his right hand and saluted, smartly, his absent father Ted.

Jack Golden, he told them, Jack Edward, he signed it, Jack E Golden. It was Pearse who christened him then, seeing him proud and tall in his uniform: Jack E Golden. Jackie. Jackie, mustachioed, uniformed, flying hero.

He had been shown the Browning mechanisms in the Spitfires; he could strip the guns, and reassemble them, he could identify and clear any stoppage along the machine. He had practised high-speed, low-level bombing and forward-firing gunnery in the Miles Master 2. He had grown his moustache and become Pilot Officer in the RAF. He became a man. But in the game of flight and war he knew he was yet too raw. The young men were queuing up to pass through the doors of courage into the halls of glory and he was one of them, caught up and rushed and harried into war.

The night chilled. He got out of the carriage and walked on the platform, up and down, up and down. At times other trains passed through, their sound coming out of the darkness, with only a small red light high in front. They loomed, huge, heavy, ponderous, dark, shunted slowly past and vanished into the darkness on the other side of the station. War, the violent passage through darkness into . . . ? Then there was silence again, a few soldiers restless about the station, the tiny red glow of a lit cigarette, and the great world beyond as if it did not exist. *I am that which is, thou art that which is not.* Once a train stopped and the soldiers that had been with Jack trooped wearily aboard. He stood, watching them, their bodies stooped under the burden of their destination, their fear, the way their thoughts turned inward in the darkness of the night, when words fall away and loneliness, big and dry-bodied and heaving, shoved hard against them. *I am that which is, thou art that which is not.*

Before dawn, a one-carriage train drew into Canterbury station. Jack dozed in the carriage of the London train. He was roused. With a dozen others he boarded the new train. They were all silent, too lost at that unreal hour to speak, even to think. Slowly the train moved out, heading now towards the dream and the nightmare. Almost at once Jack slept, rousing himself for a moment when the train stopped again, at Ashford, to take on another ten or twelve airmen. The light was still faint in the sky, as if they were surfacing from very far under water.

He had seen a Spitfire once come in on fire, when the recruits were taken to Kenley to see the plane and to begin an acquaintance with it. He had watched while twelve Spitfires had taken off from the base to escort Blenheim bombers on a mission somewhere. He had loved the perfect lines of the craft, the economy of shape, line and power, its perky head raised towards the sky, its bullet nose, the way it rested on its wings with a self-conscious nonchalance.

He loved the magnificent dance they made across the airfield as they rose, one after the other, into the air, how they gathered quickly in formation, how soon they had vanished, leaving silence, the wind shushing through the grasses where he stood. But within half an hour, he was watching the fire tenders race out over the same field, he had seen the Spitfire, alone, emerge out of clouds, trailing black smoke, the sound of its engine now a broken, stammering appeal. It staggered, and stalled, and caught again. But it approached steadily, dipping sickeningly all too soon, losing altitude, and Jack moved forward as if to sing out a warning when suddenly it was down, crashing straight into the earth and exploding with an unreal, faraway sound, almost gentle, as of a drum smitten once, and then a cymbal allowed to tremble into silence. There was a hillock of flames, yellow, scarlet, orange, and then only a pillar of dense black smoke rising silently towards the clouds.

In the train Jack jerked again out of nightmare. A morning sun was shining brightly on a station platform. They had stopped again. In the carriage the young airmen stirred. Jack stood and opened a window and leaned out. Along the platform a small group of children came chattering, holding one another by the hand, a teacher in front of them, another teacher behind. They called and laughed loudly; they stood then, waiting; they carried buckets, spades, picnic packages, balls. They bobbed and fluttered without rest, an endless excited movement, like small birds scurrying and scooting along the edge of the sea. As if the world were normal, as if the sand would suffer their digging and building, as if the waves would be gentle about their small bodies, as if this were home, and the past, and other. Jack saw the station name written on a small wooden placard along the wall: Maidstone. It was a place of contradiction for him, a world outside a world, real and unreal. Childhood found and lost as soon as found. He sat down heavily again, remembering the gate where he had climbed to find flight, where he had hoisted Gráinne, urging her into the same chapter of childhood as himself. They would have flown, together, they would have flown . . .

The train moved again. On the rack above his head was his new suitcase, and beside it the kit he had collected at the receiving centre in London. Before that he had stripped naked in a room in Cannon Street, doctors had examined him thoroughly, his strong island body resistant to their probing, their fingers, their instruments. To distract himself he had dreamed they would discover wings budding from his shoulder-blades, they would see strange, powerful muscles coming to glory high on his arms, his face would have begun to grow into a bird-face, proud and sharp and cruel . . . His fear was that they would find him lacking, that they would send him away, back to his island where he felt useless, unwanted, out of place.

He had bought the suitcase in Flannery's General Store. Fintan Flannery stood at the counter, a dull-brown shop-coat hanging open over his white shirt, his braces, his black trousers.

"I'm for England, Mr Flannery," he said, his voice flat, and dulled. "I'm for the RAF. They take volunteers, you know. I'll learn how to fly. Maybe even the Spitfires."

Fintan Flannery had looked at him.

"There's a war on out there, Jack," he said, "people getting killed. It's a terrible war. Not our business. You know that. We're neutral, here, not taking sides. A kind of benevolent neutrality, Jack, that's what it is, that's what Dev wants, benevolent towards one side, while not wanting to antagonise the other side. The RAF, Jack, airplanes, the Battle of Britain was a desperate thing, so many young men killed, shot down out of the sky! It's unthinkable, Jack, so young, so many of them, and horribly mutilated. No young man in his senses . . . "

"I have to go, Mr Flannery. I have to. I'd never live with myself if I didn't go. It's in my blood, I suppose, from my father . . . And I want to learn to fly. I've always wanted to fly. Do you remember that plane over on the strand? The Burlington Brothers? This is a great opportunity for someone like me, out here on the very brim of the world, it's a chance, I've got to take it, and maybe after the war I'll get a job as a pilot somewhere, flying . . ."

The older man was silent. He looked into Jack's eyes for a while and Jack looked away.

"A suitcase, Mr Flannery."

"Yes, Jack. Just a moment now. I've some fine new ones came in just the other day. I'll be back in a minute."

He left the shop and disappeared through the door into the house. The shop was empty. Jack was alone, gazing over the shelves, somewhat depleted now since the war had taken hold of so many lives and turned the concerns of the world towards arms, destruction, defence, warfare. The silence in the shop was great, filled with dust-motes, a sad, echoing silence for Jack, an ending.

And suddenly Gráinne was there, beautiful in a light-blue dress, a dress suggesting the hopes of spring and new growth in the burgeoning of flowers and blossoms. Her face was animated and her colour high. She came up close to Jack who held himself stiff and wary before her coming. When she was near she raised her face to him and he could see a sadness in her eyes that shook him deeply so that he longed, urgently, to gather her to him and to press her body against his, for comfort for them both, and for love. But he had been so far unable to handle the urges of his body, and if he were again to be repulsed . . . He made a small, involuntary movement towards her, then, afraid of her reaction, afraid of himself, he drew back again, cursing his fears, cursing the barriers that had risen, invisibly, between them.

She stopped. Her fingers fidgeted with a button on the front of her dress.

"You're for England, then, Jack?"

"Yes. The RAF." His voice was unsteady, his body trembled. He leaned his elbows back against the counter.

"You're going to join the war. To fight."

"Yes, Gráinne. I have to."

She looked up into his eyes and held them.

"Jack, you don't have to."

He felt that now, if he could, he might break through a wall and be close to her again. But he had brooded long on the demands of the flesh, on how the pull of a woman's body seemed impossible to resist, how merely physical had all his longings been for Mary Alice, how Gráinne had surrounded him with a gauze of guilt and a strong resentment rose now against her, and now, holding back a sob of self-pity, he turned from her to look along the high shelves of the store. What right had she, she above all people, to judge him and condemn him because of the strength of his urges, because of something he had no control over . . . How could it be she did not understand the urge of the flesh . . . ?

"I'm looking for a suitcase. I asked your father . . ."

Gently she laid her right hand on his arm. The touch was soft, but it felt as if he could fall under it, fall easily and melt away into the ground at her feet.

"Don't go, Jack, please don't go."

It was even more difficult then, but his resentment, his churlishness, took strength from her pleading, and for the moment he was relishing the small power he had over her, her pleading, her gentle, almost loving, touch.

"I have to go, Gráinne. I have to get away from this island. There's nothing here for me any more. I've lost it. There's no future. And I feel hemmed in, tied down, earthed if you like. There's nothing at all . . ."

She withdrew her hand and looked down towards the ground. Again her fingers toyed with the buttons on her dress. He looked at her, at the magnificent golden sheen in her hair, at the full and lovely form of her body and his heart throbbed wildly, flung about between longing and despair.

They stayed still and silent for a long moment and all their childhood years flowed away from them and vanished down some dark gulley. They waited, and he could not move towards her.

"I'll miss you, Jack," she said, but she was already turning from him.

"I'll miss you, too, Gráinne."

She turned back for a moment, smiling at him, though sadly. Then she moved to the door and as she opened it, she spoke to him again.

"May God keep you safe, Jack. May He keep you safe and warm in the hollow of His hand."

Then she was gone. Gone.

The train stopped, at last. It was in the tiny station of West Malling. Kent. England. Still without speaking the four young men gathered themselves, their kits, their baggage, out of the carriage onto the platform. It was mid-morning. The sun shone on the small station buildings, gleamed silver on the sheen of the tracks that curved away into the future and away into the past. The shadows of the leaves moved gently over the platform. There were blackbirds, thrushes, wrens, robins, finches, singing the joy of living. In the near distance Jack could see the spires of a church in the village of West Malling. All about him the trees were rich, the fields heavy with life. The morning was warm. Peaceful. The world seemed so innocent, so much at peace. He was no longer an islandman, he was no longer an insular person, his was no longer an island life.

The airfield at King's Hill, some three miles outside the little village of West Malling, was a great field breezy with emptiness, reminding Jack at once of the sandy banks of his island. The sky stretched immense and welcoming, and the grass rolled gently to the horizon distant in every direction. It was a place for skylarks. A space for the windhover, a world where the human soul could expand outwards from the straitening confines of the body. Two enormous hangars stood at one side of the base, great doors on oiled wheels had been rolled back to reveal a black emptiness within. They were huge, dim caves, echoing only with an occasional shout, the clang of a dropped spanner. All the planes were scattered about the base, making their targeting by marauding bombers a thing of greater difficulty. Jack stood a long time at the edge of the airfield; he could breathe deeply here; the world, filled with sunshine, open to every gentle breeze, seemed here flat as the ocean, limitless in scope, inviting him to reach out, out and upwards, upwards and beyond.

It was only five days before Jack went into action for the first time. It was shortly after dawn. He woke, cold and still heavy with sleep. There were three other pilots in the hut, all of them already veterans. Jack went out into the brisk, demanding dawn. There were bushes away in the distance to his left; the two giant hangars were barely visible through a dawn mist, far away across the field, to his right. Close by – the four magnificent Spitfires. There was a terrible shortage of pilots now and a terrible shortage of fresh young men willing and able to take on these planes. But he had proved himself, he would have to prove himself again. The small and sacred cell of the plane seemed the place of worship for his soul. He walked towards it, appraising it as a child would appraise a new, gleaming bike. He slapped his arms together for warmth. How cocky the plane looked, standing there, waiting, head high as if disdaining the earth, the propeller blades still, their curved surfaces breathtakingly honed, the hoods closed over, the tiny tail wheel at an angle. He had flown a few trial hours in the air, under the watchful eye, the guiding voice, of the base Controller. The plane had been called *Irene*; Jack did not dare inquire about the last pilot. He renamed her *Polka Dot*, remembering the beauty of the creature he had seen pinned to the cabbage-green wall in Gráinne's attic room. They were, as yet, an untested team, *Polka Dot* and Jackie Golden, but he felt already they were friends, knowing one another's moods, one another's capabilities. They had found an instant understanding as if she, in the perfection of her form and design, had taken to her heart this young, eager, lithe body that knew already how to handle her, gently but firmly, above all with love.

Jack had seen, once, a huge formation of British planes, bombers and escorts, fly low over their airfield, heading towards France. They circled the village of West Malling until they were joined by another squadron from that base. Then, with a power and surge that made the air tremble, that shattered all the precious glass in the ancient Church of St Leonard close by, they wheeled away for the sky.

They had been very high, then, so high they seemed like a swarm of black beetles, but he had heard the great drone of their engines, even from that wondrous height, he could imagine the whole sky and earth below them tremble with the shuddering of their passage, and the sound had filled him with a sense of urgency, to be part of that awesome movement, that power.

When he went back into the hut the others were having breakfast. There was a small coal stove in the centre of the hut and he tried to warm himself against it. Someone poured him a cup of tea and he cupped it gratefully in his hands. He lifted it to his lips and took a sip. And then, as if that had been a signal, the call came at the other side of the room. The Leader answered the phone and sang out the word to them: "Scramble!" The cup fell out of Jack's hand and shattered on the wooden floor.

"I hope you handle your Spitfire more carefully than that, young Jackie Golden," the Leader laughed at him.

Before he was fully aware of what was happening, Jack was climbing into the cockpit, the engines were roaring, there was smoke, like the snorting of a huge race-horse, and he could feel the Spitfire throb and stamp under him, eager to be off. The calm, certain voice of the Leader, Captain James Mellor, in his ears almost drowned by the thudding drum-beats of his heart and the tense brass noises in his brain, Jack taxied out with the others and soon was in the air, drawing the hood of the Spitfire closed above his head, breaking away steeply over the hangars and climbing, swiftly, up towards the cold source of the sky. At twenty thousand feet they levelled off and flew steadily, easily, south towards the coast.

He was a knight on a fast courser, riding out, armed for

battle. Breastplate, cuisse, gauntlet, knee-cap, helmet, visor, fauld. His trusty steed was heavily caparisoned, too, steel shield, hauberk, and sabaton. He was a chevalier, his game was war, and his war a game. Like chess. Like moving the pieces. Plotting. Manoeuvring. Bluffing. Like shifting the pieces about the board of the sky. A tournament. Chivalry. War.

They flew higher. They were joined by other squadrons of Spitfires. They were flying now at twenty-five thousand feet and Jack could see a plane to his left, another to his right, several in formation ahead. He was part of a great force. The whole sky trembled with their sound, their power. He whooped with the tremendous, shaking thrill of it. Soon he could hear the voice of the Sector Controller passing on instructions. They were to intercept and destroy a force of German Dornier bombers heading north along the coast of France. Jack's stomach began to churn. The bombers would be accompanied by a small force of Messerschmitt BF 109s. They were to stay high, and come down on the formation from above. "Good luck!" The cool, distant, calming voice.

Jack flew mechanically now, fear clutching him. He knew the great power and versatility of his aircraft; it responded almost to his thinking. He knew, too, that he had never yet fired any of the guns of the craft. His thumbs touched the buttons of the guns. He gazed forward through the target-sighter; the tail of a Spitfire was held in its delicate, cobweb network. Jack shivered. His neck felt stiff, as if he could not turn his head. He thought he might be ill. He wanted to draw back the wheel and lift his Spitfire above all of this, out of the tourney, above the chess board, high into the pure, uncluttered sky. The Spitfire squadrons droned on. The heroes, riding out, heavily armed, into war.

And then – suddenly – it had begun. As if it had always been like this. As if he had been living these moments all his life. He could see below him three long lines of German planes, like great threads pulled taut, Messerschmitts in line-astern formation, innocent-looking against the vague field-work map of the earth below. Far, far below. Jack realised he must be well in over France. A calm but urgent voice stayed in Jack's ear, giving instructions, coolly, as if this were a school outing and all the exercises and all the tests were understood and it was simply a matter of going through them, one by one. The Spitfires wheeled together and were diving down out of the sun on the German planes and Jack already knew the shuddering anger of his aircraft, the dreadful fear eating his stomach from within, and he held the wheel tight, and uttered a prayer to his unknown God.

Jack saw several of the German planes burst into flame almost at once and he was still rushing down towards them. As yet he had not even put his thumb on the firing-button, he was gripping the wheel too hard, holding on in fear. And then the German planes had banked steeply away, and Jack had passed through their formation and was still diving at killing speed towards the patches and shapes of the fields of France. Small grey clouds waltzed slowly beneath him. He pulled the plane back level and in his ears now were the urgent voices of his comrades, urging one another, warning one another, cheering, claiming victories. For a long moment Jack could not see another plane. He pulled back the wheel and rose steeply again. And at once he saw a German plane coming down towards him. Out of nowhere.

Coming at him. Diving. Jack held tight for a time, fear numbing him, as the sleek machine hurtled towards him. There was a sudden thud against his plane and Jack knew that the German was firing. He pulled sharply to port and was in the clear again. The moment had caused him panic but he had escaped it. In his ears, now, were the long screams of the planes as they dived and manoeuvred, flinging themselves in pursuit or attack, side-stepping, dipping, lifting. Jack again rose higher, unsure where to turn.

As he rose another German plane appeared from nowhere and came at him from the starboard side; Jack was certain he could see the track of the bullets as they passed just above his hood and he dipped again, violently, and dived. At once a Messerschmitt floated into the net of his sights and Jack found himself directly astern, in command. He put his thumbs on the buttons and waited. He could not push. The sounds from his brain were too loud, too much threaded with fear and horror and he let the opportunity pass. The Spitfire was going faster than the German plane and Jack found he had to lift the stick violently or go straight into the tail of the Messerschmitt. The German plane veered away to starboard as Jack flew just above it.

Fear held him still. He was a novice on a football field, running frantically, but running away from the ball. He was a chess-player, interested only in defence, unable to attack. He was a pawn, small and vulnerable and expendable. He veered and rose and dived, avoiding often by good luck, the attacks of the German planes. Sky and cloud and wonderful open spaces alternated in his line of vision with the fields of France, with aircraft intent on their murderous missions, and sometimes with planes in smoke, or on fire.

And then Jack saw a Spitfire below him, being pursued by two Messerschmitts; he saw the Spitfire stall, its nose dip sickeningly, and then there was a gentle line of smoke, clean, light-blue smoke, and suddenly the plane was a ball of fire below him. He watched in horror as the hood was slid back, he saw the pilot scramble out into the air and fall, he saw the parachute open and then Jack had passed too far out of the view of the pilot. He turned in a long, perfect arc, his stomach one tight mass of terror, his teeth clenched, his mind a mess of fear and shame and hesitation. Again he could see the pilot dropping away far, far below, the parachute bellying beautifully against the day.

Without thinking any more he flung his Spitfire in pursuit of the Messerschmitt. He came down at an acute angle and was almost at once on the tail of the German plane. There was spittle on his lips and his thumbs pressed eagerly at once on both firing buttons and he felt the fierce outreach of his plane, like the screeching, hissing, sudden clawing and spitting of a ferocious cat, as the bullets flew into the flesh of the Messerschmitt before him. The German plane seemed to lurch, there was the same small cough of smoke, then the plane rolled onto its back, slowed, and dropped swiftly under Jack's fuselage. Jack banked at once and came round again. He watched as the plane fell, trailing grey-black smoke, and he saw it hit the ground far below in a great lurch of flames and smoke.

As they returned to base, Jack could hear the voice of the Captain cool and gentle in his ears. They were answering to their names, one after the other; there were several gaps, there were too many silences. Jack answered to his name and the quiet voice murmured to him: "Well done, lad, that was a fine shoot-down. First blood to you!"

But there were tears in Jack's eyes, and his body trembled as a child's. Automatically he flew and the coast of England offered him little cheer. Then they were landing, sweeping in one by one out of the sky, back onto the grass field of King's Hill. Jack saw the small houses of the village, the fields parcelled and plotted and worked, the trees in rows, the apple orchards, all the ordinary signs of human grace, but none of it offered him any comfort or peace.

His plane slowed to a halt. He unstrapped himself, pushed back the hood and clambered down, almost falling off the wing of the plane. Then he fell on his knees on the earth and was sick, violently sick.

After the first killing, there will be many more. If the chessboard were to be covered with real blood, with the torn limbs and broken bodies of the pawns, it is not certain that the game would die.

Jack's Spitfire Squadron often flew, Jackie Golden becoming expert in the ways of flight, and in the ways of battle. At times they were thick as a flock of giant starlings at evening, darkening the sky. The Germans sent up flak against them and long, reaching fingers of light. Jack knew they must be terrified down there, he could almost sense their terror from up in the sky, that awful, slaughtering power hanging over them, shadowing them, waiting to wipe them out. It was almost too easy, the Spitfires patrolling the skies while the bombers dropped such loads of bursting stars on the city that the night became like a scarlet day and the moon that had hung white and virginal at the far end of the sky became a moon of delicate pink against the strange, beautiful killing pink of the sky. Jack could imagine he heard the cries rising to him from the ground, he thought he could hear children's voices, like the soft, strangulated cries of kittens. He shuddered, knowing that what he could really hear were the voices of the pilots and the squadron leaders calmly talking them through the night. The flight back to King's Hill, back to base, was a silent one, the night darkening once again, the moon standing out calm and white, as if nothing out of the normal running of the universe had taken place. The Spitfires flew on the pure, straight road laid out for them across the sky by an island moon.

On other days Jack was a bird, riding clouds and air-currents, updraughts and thermals. He was a falcon, a peregrine, an albatross. He was Daedalus. Once when he looked out the window he was startled to see a big, fat figure of a man go strolling purposefully by on the top of the clouds. Smoking a pipe. Gobbing into the clear air. He was a fine-looking man, tall, handsome and bearded, wearing a long, flowing robe that looked like the alb a priest wears during Mass. He glanced over towards the plane and raised one thumb in salute. And then Jack knew him for who he was, that thumb, that cocky salute, that proud bearing: it was his father, Edward (Ted) Golden, RIC man, constable, offering his ghost frame in the complicity of the war. For a moment Jack waved and then, suddenly terrified that he was losing some control over his own mind, he wheeled the Spitfire round and the figure disappeared.

Jack, Birdman, was wearying. Wearying from the blood-soaked fields of the sky.

Look! I'm a bird, I am a bird, I am an angel, I can fly! But the skies were filled with slaughter, with engines, steel, fire, smoke; with sudden mutilation and death. A slow mist of blood tracking across Europe. From East to West and from West back to East. Every time he went into flight, Jack had to urge new reserves of will-power to overcome his dread, his sense of sickness, his fear. It was as if the world had been turned upside down; he thought of the word 'base': bad, corrupt, sordid, vile, lowly, menial, mean, the basis, the core, the essence, the heart: the airfield, earth. And he thought of the sky where he had hoped to find release from the weight of earth. Now, up there, suffering the endless intensity of the murderous game of chess across the sky, pitching his courage and despair together into a febrile activity that passed almost beyond what he could endure, it seemed that the sky was filled with baseness and that release and freedom could be found only back on earth, back on his island, back at his own, true, base.

He was always weary, now. The bullets, the flak, the bombs, crossing and recrossing the spaces of the sky, made of it a vast bird-cage of slaughter. Heavy bombers trundled along the sky like haywains loaded with the heavy dead. He had lost his *Polka Dot* and acquired another he called *Falcon*. That, too, had been shot from about his body. He was given another. *Peregrine*. He had twice fallen from some twenty thousand feet, the parachute opening with a great slap above him, the jerking of his body out of free-fall, the terror of his escape, the smell of cordite in his nostrils, the fear of the burning oil, the jarring of the Spitfire as it shuddered in its death throes about him – and he was dropping through a strange silence, his hands raised, gripping the cords of the parachute, cold breezes round him, the villages and hedgerows, the meadows and rivers and ploughed lands dancing their slow-motion dance far below, his body heavy with its weight of sorrows, memories, weariness, and he hated the thudding, always-too-sudden and humiliating slump back onto the earth, as if his God had picked him up between his vast, red fingers, had led him breathlessly about a sky that had been blue and beautiful but that was grey now, streaked with red, had grown tired of him and had dropped him back into God's own indifference.

Yet how the heart lifts, when it can, over the labyrinth! Once only he fled that dreadful game, once when he had strafed to pieces a Heinkel bomber, had watched it burst into flames as if its heart had exploded, had seen it spin crazily out of the sky and fall into the sea below, had known that not one of the crew had been able to escape, suddenly he had fled, lifting his Spitfire off the terrible battlefield, and flying higher, higher, away from the killing, into the world he had hoped to find. He took off his helmet and the Squadron leader's voice died from his ears.

It is a question of being delivered from the weight of self. He came out high above the clouds on a perfect skyscape. Far below were the surfaces of the clouds, great rolling plains like those the first explorers over an Antarctic wilderness must have seen, undefiled, white, going on forever. And all about him the purest sky imaginable, an azure sky that shaded to light blue and into white on the far horizons. He was flying through an ice-cold purity, his body gripped by the medium, as if he had died and had become immortal, alone in a new, untarnished Eden, pure, silent, measureless. He rose as high as his craft would take him, until his breathing became difficult and the Spitfire shuddered about him. And then he killed the engine.

For a while he was afloat on perfection. He pushed back the hood and was stricken by the fierce knives of cold that darted in upon him. There was a silence that was beyond silence, only the sound of the fuselage of the plane through the thin air, sounds that wings would make if they had sprouted on his shoulder-blades. He shivered with the cold, he trembled, inebriated by the magic of his isolation. Now it was as if there were no such thing as time, he was here, in this purity and at this height, and it was this moment, and that was all there would ever be. There was no future. There was no past. And he was innocent, up here, isolated from all the burdens of the flesh and the struggling soul. He tried to cry out into the virginity of the moment, he tried to beg pardon, pardon, pardon on behalf of mankind, but his breath would not come in that awful purity. He tried to rise from his seat in the tiny cell of the cockpit, to reach out further into that purity, but the pressure on his body was too great. He drew the hood closed again above him. He breathed more easily. He knew now that there were only two moments of perfect nakedness in life: the moment of birth and the moment of death. And he knew that death, when it did come, would be like this, it would not be life, it would be immortality, a purity the flesh could not cope with, that immortality would not be a prolongation of life, it would be other, demanding, exhilarating, pure. He closed his eyes and would willingly have taken on, there and then, the nakedness of death.

He was falling. The plane had stalled and it was beginning to spin uncontrollably. Soon he would touch the clouds again and fall out of the clouds to a certain death. He touched the motor and it caught at once. And soon he had left that moment and had fallen back into time, back into the demands of the flesh, of the Spitfire, of the war.

One day, early in spring, 1945, Jack's Spitfire squadron took off from King's Hill on a mission to strafe an enemy airfield. The day was fair. On the base the daffodils along the far hedgerow had already begun to fade back into themselves. Jack had strolled beside them in the morning, and the bluebells that had appeared in clusters under a small copse of elms. Bluebells, a blue like the late blue of a bright afternoon, high above the clouds that covered the earth. Jack had called his Spitfire *Gráinne*, and he spoke gently to her now, while the squadron leader's voice gave precise instructions into his ear.

The mission was an easy one. Jack flew low over the enemy airfield several times, so low he could see the terrified faces of the Germans peering from a shed door at the perimeter of the field. Jack watched as several bombers exploded into fire on the airfield ground. They were waiting there, helpless, like cattle waiting for the slaughter. The war was almost over. Soon, Jack dreamed, soon he would be starting for home.

The squadron lifted gratefully into the sky and turned for England. They eased out together at sixteen thousand feet. They talked quietly and calmly to one another across their easy spaces of sky. And then a small formation of Messerschmitts was on them, coming from nowhere, emerging violently from the fist of God, from above and below them, and from port and starboard. They flew past like a thought and Jack's evasive action was not fast enough. He could see the bullets coming through the air like sprung wires and at once there was a great flash of heat through his right leg. He flung the Spitfire up and about to starboard and dived for the cover of a cloud. His right leg burned with a long, agonizing pain. He glanced down but could see little from his cramped space in the cockpit. Then he was out of the cloud again and there was a Messerschmitt directly below him, he could see the dark helmet on the pilot's head through the hood. He slewed his plane and fell in directly behind the German. His thumbs moved to the firing buttons. The German plane moved into his line of fire but instantly jerked away. Jack's plane had been spotted. The Messerschmitt dived rapidly and Jack dived after it. The German veered and twisted, Jack following as if glued to the great swastika on the German's tail. Once he pushed the button only to see the traces of his bullets go harmlessly into the sky past the German's wings. The Messerschmitt suddenly stalled and Jack, zooming past, almost clipped the tip of the tail and suddenly the German was behind him and Jack was veering and diving in a frantic effort to escape.

Almost at once there was a great ripping noise as a swarm of bullets tore through the fuselage of the Spitfire and shattered the glass of Jack's hood. Tiny fragments of the perspex glass dropped onto his lap and glittered there, innocently beautiful. The rush of wind into the cockpit stunned him for a moment but his instinct had taken him down into a near spin out of the German's clutches. The aircraft shuddered under the pressure, the noise of its screaming engines and of the wind rushing past his head almost deafened him. Then he was levelling off again, the coast of France just visible below him. He tried to look around though the wind made it difficult. The German was still on his tail and Jack could imagine the man's laughter, his sense of victory, his exhilaration. Jack rose suddenly and flipped his Spitfire over on its back, looping perfectly to come down almost on a collision-course against the Messerschmitt. Jack's whole body seemed to be pounding with the excitement of the fight; his hands were tense but there was no fear. His whole being was intent on surviving and on destroying this pilot who had challenged him. Jack levelled out and again he was behind the German who zigzagged wonderfully before him. He had time to admire the German pilot's skill before his two thumbs pressed the buttons and he saw the tail of the plane shatter into fragments. It lurched drunkenly and then fell sideways out of the sky, sliding through the air the way a leaf will slide, helplessly, shifting from left to right, and then it plummeted towards the earth. Jack glimpsed a figure falling from the plane and he hoped the parachute worked.

But suddenly, as he was again examining his leg to see what damage had been caused, another German plane appeared directly in front of him and Jack could see the bullets coming at him, like a fist aimed directly into his face. It was now as if in a dream he saw the Messerschmitt dive in under him as his own plane was torn to shreds by the hail of bullets. There was an overwhelming smell of cordite in the tiny cell of the cockpit, there were frightening hisses from the pneumatics and the instruments on the panels before him seemed to disintegrate together. The plane lurched as if it had hit an invisible wall and flames burst instantly from the fuselage in front of him.

The engine died. The silence was a silence of wind and fire and there was a great sensation of heat all about him.

He fumbled at his harness to release himself from the cockpit. The plane was vibrating violently as if it would collapse into tiny pieces about him. Fragments of perspex were everywhere and the whole plane seemed to be a mass of flames. Jack managed to haul himself out of the fuselage. His hands grasped the red-hot metal and for a moment he caught the stench of burning flesh. He was in the slipstream of the spinning plane for a moment then he was free, out in the sky and falling. He pulled the ripcord of the parachute and heard, gratefully, its loud slap as it opened above him. His body was jerked upright and he began to float gently towards the world.

After the intensity of the noise of the battle and the flames, the sudden silence about him brought Jack back into the real world of his own suffering. He could see that his right leg was bathed in blood, from the thigh downwards. His leg was numb now and there was no pain. He could see, too, that his flying suit was on fire, there were black stains of oil everywhere and the fire moved silently and swiftly, fanned by the wind of his falling, up along his body. Jack swung his body frantically to try and quench the flames. He looked up. Several strings of the chute were on fire, too, and tiny tongues of flame were moving towards the stuff of the chute itself. Again he caught the dreadful stench of burning flesh.

He could see his plane, a great ball of fire, vanish into the sea below him. The sea was black, small strokes of white showed here and there and disappeared. Jack dreamily admired the beauty of the sea. He felt little pain. Soon, he knew, soon, he would strike the surface of the ocean. There was no sign of land anywhere. The flames snapped through several threads of his parachute. He was falling faster. The troughs in the sea were growing bigger. Only the whispering of the flames about him could be heard. He saw the flesh on the palms of his hands; his skin had turned black and here and there he knew he could see the naked purple flesh beneath. He began to pray, quietly. He knew no fear. No regret. He thought, fleetingly, of Gráinne Flannery, of her quiet, of that soft summer dress, the light blue with its patterns of small meadow flowers. He smiled with a strange weary happiness. He closed his eyes then, and braced himself to strike the ocean.

Three

The old man leaned in over the bed and looked more closely at the woman's face. There were lines and ridges in the flesh, he could see the faint rust colour of the lips, there were bulges of old flesh under the eyes. The hair, that hair that had been a golden harvest, so beautiful and abundant, was now like the gleanings left after a haystack had been taken away. And her body lay small and still under the blanket, as if a wind could rise and lift her from the face of the earth. But she breathed still, he could see that, and he had seen her eyes, those clear, intelligent eyes had watched him, even for a moment. So . . .

The door opened quickly and the same young nurse came back in. The old man sat back and pointed, his hand shaking, pointed foolishly at the form in the bed.

"Her eyes opened. She's alive. She's alive. I'm sure she needs help."

"Well, Mr . . . Ah, Mrrrrrr . . . ? Yes. You know she's quite likely to make an occasional movement. But it's just, like, instinct, like the ongoing natural functions of the body. But it's just the body, like, you know? The mind's totally gone. That stroke was enormous. Finished her. There's nothing there. Not really. You know. We told you that. We phoned. Someone phoned. And you said not to call you, and the doctor agreed, until and unless the change began, the final change, I mean, like. So you mustn't be

175

surprised if she jerks, or the legs move, or even if she opens her mouth, or her eyes. Or anything like that. You know?"

The old man gazed at the nurse without comprehension.

"But she looked at me. I saw her. She was watching me."

"Now, now, I told you. She'll do things like that would make you think she's still really in it. But she's not. The brain is gone like. She's not there, actually. Just the body. And she could last like that right through the night. Nobody knows. What I'm saying is, she's, in actual fact, dead. There now. Don't let yourself be distressed over it. It was quick. And very easy. I'm sure. I'll look in at her again later on. Soon. If you'd like to stay with her that's all right but I don't think there's any point. You mustn't upset yourself."

And again she beamed him that lovely, youthful smile and then she was gone again, a flash of white, a toss of hair, and the door had closed gently behind her. He turned again to the shape on the bed.

"Oh darling, darling, darling!"

His voice was only a whisper, but it sounded loud and startling in the small room.

"Darling, I'm so deeply, deeply sorry! But I'll stay with you, if you'll let me. I'll stay with you now for whatever length of time is left. I'll stay with you. If that's all right?"

He leaned over her and put his left ear down closer to her mouth, hoping for an answer, any answer. A sign.

But there was nothing. He watched her lips. They remained closed. He watched her eyes. They were closed, too. She seemed to be in repose. Resting, merely. Perfectly at peace.

The old man put his right hand on top of her joined hands.

"Do you remember the story of the prince?" he spoke quietly to her. "He saw this wonderfully beautiful princess lying in a glass coffin. She was dead, at least that's what everyone believed. But he had her taken out and he kissed her. He kissed her, she was so beautiful he couldn't stop himself. And she sat up and smiled at him. And they got married, and lived happily ever after."

He chuckled quietly to himself. She did not stir. He got up and leant over her. His lips touched her forehead so very gently. Her eyes were closed and there was not the least flicker in response. He watched her. Then he stooped again and kissed her on the lips, gently still, so very gently. He kept his lips on hers for a while, closing his eyes. There was still no sign. He sighed heavily, and sat back on the chair.

He sat on for a while, gazing at her. Then he shook his head.

"That was a stolen kiss," he said to her. "I'm sorry. I shouldn't have done that. Please forgive me. That can't count. A kiss stolen is a soft fruit spoilt. But maybe . . . well, it was a kiss from me to you, that's all, a gift. Nothing asked for in return. That's all it was. A gift, from me to you. With love . . ."

There was a long silence while he sat there almost as still as she was. He watched her face for the slightest sign. He watched the slow rise and fall of the light coverings over her breast. He watched her fingers. There was nothing.

"I believe you're still there," he said softly, leaning towards her. "Somehow I believe you're still there. And you can hear me. And you saved my life already, opening your lovely eyes. So let me say it again. I love you. I have always loved you. I never stopped loving you and I have never loved anybody else. Never anybody else. Only you. Always. It was always only you."

The darkness was settling about the grounds outside, rubbing its black fur softly against the walls of the home.

"Don't die yet, my love," he said. "Don't die without some word to me. Something. We could have been so wonderful together. Magnificent. It's a wide world, wide and broad and deep. But it all comes down to a small island in the end of all. Our own small island. Where we set out from. The tiny islands of our sad little selves where we try and survive, where we try to make sense out of things. I was the one who wanted to rise high above the world. You were the one who were all grace. I'm begging you not to die without a word. Without forgiving me. Just one word of forgiveness. That's all. Just one sign. Any little sign. One tiny word, even. A word. Of grace."

Gráinne was in the tiny room in a corner of the store, the small office that was the only post-office on the island, when the telegram came through. She wrote it down quickly and then stood a long, long time, watching the contours in the grain of the wood on the counter top. At last she took out one of the dark green envelopes from its niche, slipped the telegram inside, and walked slowly out of the store. She left the till unlocked. She left the door of the shop wide open. She left the phone off its holder.

She had been toiling, long now, between store, yard and office. She spent the late afternoon and early evening in the licensed premises in the darker backroom of the store, suffering almost more than she could bear. Out of the sunlight. Among dark-wood panels and dark, low beams, where dead men sat on old forms and drank, slowly drowning themselves into a stupor that was their only escape from an even dimmer living.

"Gráinne!"

"Yes, Patsy?"

"A pint a' stout there, an' a whiskey, like a good girl."

Her hand to the lever. Behind her, the whiskey bottles, the gins, the brandies, the quicker, neon ways out of the sodden fields and the rough, unproductive seas, out of the boglands, away from the emigration bus.

"Terrible slaughter agin beyant in France, Gráinne."

"It's heartbreaking, Patsy, heartbreaking."

"Hard to imagine it, though, bombs falling out of the sky like rain, like big black hailstones, wha'? An' that bollocks Hitler spoutin' an' rantin' out a' himself 'till you'd think he was God almighty above in Heaven decidin' the rules an' regulations a' the world. Wha'?"

"True for you, Patsy. Like the end of the world it is out there, I'd say. Thousands and thousands of innocent young men, getting killed. And for what, I ask you, for what?"

"Thousands, Gráinne, it'll be millions, I'd say, before 'tis over. Killed. An' mutilated beyond all humanity. An' driven stark, stone crazy by the horrors they see around them. On land, Gráinne, on sea, in the sky, till that oul' bollocks Hitler has destroyed with his filth the entire world we live and move and breathe in. Wha'?"

The brown door opening again. Another, a younger, refugee. Willie, the twin, Butler. Twenty-eight years old. Or less. But weary and worked out as any old tree in the western gales.

"Patsy!"

"Ah! Willie!"

"Ay. Gráinne. How's things?"

"Fine, Willie, thanks, fine. Grand day, thank God, grand day."

"'Tis, begad. Sunshine an' all. Give it a week an' we'll have the turf saved. A large Paddy there, Gráinne, please, when you're ready. An' a wee drop a' water."

A large one. But only the first one. Of many. His open-necked shirt showing the dirt and the whiteness of an unwashed baby, the strength of a young horse, the despair of a ghost. Willie. Took his place in the darkness along with the others. The weighted ones. Boulders in their lives crushing them into the earth.

"Any word of young Golden, Gráinne?"

"No, Willie, nothing, as far as I know. He drops an odd line to his mother, I believe. But nothing now this long while. This long, long while. She's fretting something, above."

"Always a class of wildness in him, though, wasn't there, Gráinne? No steadiness in him. No sense. Like his father, old Edward himself, God rest him, made himself a class of an outsider."

"He was always wanting to fly, Willie. To leave the earth and take to the sky. Nothing to do with politics."

"Couldn't keep his feet on solid ground, Gráinne, not like the rest of us. Wha'? On solid ground. Hah!"

And he lifted his drink solemnly towards his mouth. He would bump and barge his way homewards in the dead darkness of the night.

Now Gráinne walked, slowly, towards the Golden home, the green envelope held out from her body. It was near dusk, the air was fresh and pure over the island. She held the telegram slightly away from her, as if its touch could soil her. High among the branches of a tree there was a thrush singing, invisibly, filling the evening with a sweet nostalgia. The world, otherwise, seemed still, and at peace. But she knew how fragile such peace could be, as if the evening were a great sheet of glass and someone, carelessly throwing a stone, could shatter it, utterly. She knew, too, on an evening such as this, still, and grey, and heavy, how old the earth, how strained and weary under the fierce, demanding selfishness of humankind. She was lonely, lonely, lonely.

She had told her Uncle Jim about Jack Golden. She had nobody else she could speak to, no one to consult, no one to whom she could unburden herself. How hurt she had been, she told him, how deeply shaken by Jack's untruth. Jim was so far away she felt it was safe to tell him all, it was like whispering these things to God when she was in her attic and only the stars watched in upon her. Jim had laughed; Gráinne knew that the letter from him was mocking her, she could almost feel it shaking under the impulse of its laughter. He said the word in that letter, too, the word "love". And when she saw it, written down in his beautifully legible hand, she knew at once how true it was and what the great, hard lump that lived and shifted about inside her, distressing her, always with her, really meant. But Mary Alice . . . ? And the weight of her body down on Jack's, and her lips on his lips, her breasts on his . . . ? And again Jim's note was flushed with mockery. Flesh, Gráinne, flesh, it said, the natural urge and need of two people, one male, the other female, a demand, a necessity, a curiosity. Nothing more.

And don't you, Gráinne, don't you ever feel such urges? Such a need? Such curiosity? Of course she did, she answered him, but she quelled all of that instantly, for it was sinful and there was God . . . and, in any case, was she not surrounded now only by great rocks of young men, or by shivering old snipes, all of them grovelling in the darkness of the Flannery pub, many of them slobbering and maudlin when they turned their attentions towards her young, full body?

"God, Gráinne, do you know what? but you're a bosomy young woman now, after all."

Little drops of sweat mingling about the lip with the porter froth.

"'Tis your hair, Gráinne, 'tis so long and lovely and

gold, do you know, a man'd think he'd love to leap off a high cliff and drown in its deep pool. Be like fallin', I'd say, into a jar a' honey."

A long, scarred wrist reaching from a dirty jacket sleeve, fingers calloused and chapped and hard as hurley sticks, thick black nails at the end, reaching for her.

"You're getting gorgeouser by the minute, love. Come on, Gráinne, come into the bushes and crush us."

Repulsive they were, all of them, repulsive. Their flesh repulsive to her, their minds and spirits held to the damp, black stuff of the earth, unable to shift upwards even the breadth of a feather from its clasp. And more often than before she would stand in front of the cabbage-green wall of her attic and roam through the wondercolours of the moths and butterflies, their stillness, their completion, their delicate colouring, their patterning, their urge towards flight.

There was, of course, Cornelius. Big Cornelius Griffin. Atlas. Who heaved and hauled the sacks and barrels as easily as she could shift the cups and saucers. Who seemed able to bear the deadly weight of Jack Golden's victory over him and to support her own, unyielding scorn, and still carry on quietly, patiently, among the dark props of his living. He was present still about the yard and store, never venturing into the pub. He was calmer now, a quiet presence, and Gráinne sensed some contentment about his life. As if he had learned more than she had about life and its burdens.

Once she watched him through the storeroom window; he was kneeling on the cement floor of the yard, working under a warm sun with tools and timber. His great, naked back towards her. And his trousers, as he bent, fallen low about his hips. And as she watched the healthful glow of his flesh the terrible lonesomeness of her life struck her a blow so hard she almost ran to him, she almost ran to plead with him that he offer her the comfort of his great, strong flesh, his arms, his chest, his whole body, his sex. She gasped with the urgency of her impulse and when she ran to her attic room and lay sobbing on her bed she let her hand move urgently over her body, imagining the great naked body of Cornelius Griffin pinning her down, taking her, raping her, and she cried out with the pain and pleasure of her slow release. When she quietened, her whole flesh revolted again under the sad, demanding, hurt gaze of her God.

Sometimes, too, she had asked Cornelius to take the van and drive her places, to the mainland, to the quay, to make special deliveries. And he had always done so, graciously, without the slightest impropriety, so that she began to trust him, quietly, and even rely on his strong presence outside the pub. And when she delivered the eggs to the presbytery she always asked Cornelius to drive her there and she would stand at the presbytery door, the front door, and Father Wall would come out and stand there, too, looking towards the van, fumbling for the money to pay her with.

Mrs Golden kept the old back gate of her driveway locked. She rarely left the house now and was always grateful for a visit from Gráinne. Mary Alice came, too, still once a week, touching the house, the outhouses, keeping everything in order, clean, tidy, sure. There was little to do, God knows, little to do with only old Mrs. Golden there, and no one else. And Cornelius came, perhaps once a month, and tidied up the gardens, the hedges, the small flower bed.

Gráinne touched the iron handle of the small front gate.

She paused, looking at the dim windows of the house. For some reason she thought of Mary, the Virgin of Nazareth, how she must have been going idly about her ordinary nothings in the house when the angel grew into her presence with his overwhelming news. Good news. Good, difficult, even dangerous news. How Mary must have been left stunned amongst the familiar things of the house, how those nothings must have taken on a totally different look when the angel had emptied himself away again. How Mrs Golden was probably knitting by the fire now, her mind half-conscious of the sounds from the wireless, a cockroach, perhaps, daring to venture out from under the skirting-board onto the kitchen floor, the clock ticking away on the mantelpiece. And how could she, Gráinne, interrupt that quietness with what she had in her hands, how could she ever, ever survive the news she had to bring?

Almost instinctively now Gráinne pushed open the little gate. It gave out a low, iron moan. As if it knew. Perhaps, inside the house, Mrs Golden heard that moan, and knew, too. Slowly, to allow more time, Gráinne turned to close the gate behind her. She wished she were coming out that gate again, the message delivered, the annunciation made. She paused, looking out over the island, over the small, dull fields, unproductive, heavy with rushes and couch grass, furze bushes along the hedgerows, the near hills small and useless, the long, slow slope down to the seashore, the seaweed down there lolling and rolling and the mud of the foreshore breathing and bubbling uglily.

Gráinne decided then and there that she would have to move tonight. Tonight. There was still time to get Cornelius to drive her. And he would. Without question. She would leave a long, long letter for Fintan and Nora, explaining, and they would understand. They would have to understand. And Father Wall would come and talk to them. Calm them down. Explain. If he could explain.

Twice she had gone to him, gathering up all her disgust and her horror before him and putting it away somewhere in the back of her soul. She had knocked on the kitchen door and Mary Alice had opened it for her. With that awful, Mary Alice grin. That conspiratorial, all-knowledgeable smile of a priest's housekeeper. Mary Alice. Ministering to Father Wall as his housekeeper. And again Gráinne forced all other thoughts out of her soul and allowed herself to be led, in a hot silence, through the kitchen and hallway and into Father Wall's room.

Mary Alice knocked loudly, almost contemptuously, on the door, her left hand already holding the knob. There was a mumble from inside. Mary Alice turned and winked at Gráinne. She opened the door.

"It's Gráinne Flannery, Father, can you see her?"

There was another mumble from the cave beyond. Mary Alice reached out and half-tugged and half-pushed Gráinne into the presence. Gráinne heard the door close behind her. She heard Mary Alice's footsteps in the hallway outside. Father rose out of some lair of darkness in the corner of the room.

"Ah, Gráinne," his syrup voice intoned. "Glad to see you, girl. You haven't been to see me this long, long while. On your own, I mean. Without your escort! Why not, I wonder?"

He was coming across the dark and darkly furnished room towards her, and she found herself pushing back against the door. He wore a grey-white shirt, sleeves rolled up, under his open, black waistcoat. He did not have his

Roman collar on. For some reason Gráinne's eyes fastened on the one white button she could see on the front of the shirt, hanging half-alive from a piece of thread. His face was round and red-looking as he emerged from the darkness by the fireplace. His hands were big, the forearms fat and hairy, and Gráinne dreaded those hands.

"I want to become a nun, Father." She had blurted it out, too quickly.

He stopped, as if stricken. His hands dropped to his sides and rubbed fretfully against his trouser legs. He took his right wrist in his left hand and began massaging it gently. His mouth stayed half-open. His eyes watched her.

"That's quite a shock, Gráinne, quite a shock." His voice was unsteady. He was adjusting to her. To himself.

"I've been thinking about it for a long while, Father."

He stayed, now, at a real distance from her and she sat beyond him, her nervousness gone, her mind certain. He questioned her, gently, but deeply. Probing. Testing. He counselled her. He advised. He questioned again. She insisted. He gave her names. Contacts. Places. He would write. She would write. He would drive her to see Reverend Mother. No, no thanks, she would have Cornelius drive her, not to waste Father's time.

"And your parents, Gráinne, how do they view this move?"

"They're against it, Father, dead set against it . . . They have no one, in the store, I mean, the house . . . Cornelius . . ."

He promised he would speak to them. He was kind. Positive. Helpful. He would pray for her. She should pray a great deal. She might pray for him, too?

"Arise," he quoted, and the words came from his lips like a slow fall of grace along the edges of his darkness,

187

*"arise, my love, my fair one and come away. The flowers have
appeared in our land, the time of pruning is come and the voice
of the turtle is heard."* He giggled. "You know, Gráinne, I
used to wonder, as a student, about that – the turtle, I used
to wonder what a turtle sounded like. It's the dove of
course, the turtle dove. It's the voice of peace, Gráinne,
that peace we all long for, in our world, in our minds, our
souls and our poor, shivering bodies. Peace. Peace. Peace.
We are lonesome creatures, Gráinne, lonesome loons,
solitary herons, wrapped in our own silences and our
terrible desires, and how can we ever reach out and enfold,
and be enfolded by, another such as ourselves?"

The fire in the hearth in that dark priest's parlour
began to collapse, the evening came darkly through the
big, bay window. Gráinne shivered, but she had been
happy then, happy to have his approval, his assistance, in
spite of all . . .

She sighed now and turned, with extreme reluctance,
towards her task. Walked slowly up the short, shingled path
to the front door. She paused, her hand moving towards
the old, brass face that was the knocker. But before she
could touch it the door opened and Mrs Golden stood
there, waiting for her, small, pale, dressed all in black, her
hair white, her eyes moist.

Mrs Golden said nothing. She held the door open and
Gráinne passed by her, down the small hallway and into the
kitchen. She waited. Mrs Golden stood at her front door a
while, watching the evening light. She closed the door and
turned back towards the kitchen.

"Don't read it yet, dear," she said as she closed the door
of the kitchen behind her. "Sit with me a while first, before
we let this bit of news bring in a heavier darkness."

She sat in her small armchair by the fire. The kitchen was lit only by the small glow from the turf.

"I saw you on the road, coming slowly, reluctantly, and I knew, Gráinne, I knew already."

Gráinne sat without words, the green envelope lying in her lap.

The older woman picked up her knitting and was quickly busy. Her hands moving expertly, almost instinctively, creating a net of threads against the future. And against the past.

"Last night Jack was here." She spoke very quietly into the gloom. "Here with me. I was bending over the fire, throwing in a few sods, poking it into life and I heard this noise in the room behind me. He was there, taking off his jacket, the way he used to when he'd come in from the workshop or from the meadows. He'd hang the jacket up there, on that hook behind the pantry door. 'It's hot in here, Mammy,' he said. 'It's roasting. Stuffy as an oven', he said. He began to peel the shirt off himself, too. Stood in his vest only, waiting. 'I'll fry up a few rashers for you,' I said to him, 'and an egg or two.' He only nodded. I went into the back kitchen and fried up a fry and left it in for him on the kitchen table. Just there. Behind you. With soda bread and a pot of tea and he sat down to it. He was humming away. I went back to the fire and sat down here, just like this, and I was wild contented in myself. He wolfed into the food as if he hadn't eaten for days. God help him. I turned back then, to poke at the fire some more. And when I looked round again he wasn't there any more. I didn't expect him to be. I saw the grease congealing on the rashers and the eggs. They weren't touched. I saw the steam dying slowly from the lip of the teapot. Like a ghost into the air. So I was waiting for you, dear Gráinne, I was expecting you."

Gráinne was sobbing, soundlessly. They were both silent for a while. The turf shifting lazily in the grate. A thrush or a blackbird in the distance keeping away the night. As if there were no such thing as time. Mrs Golden sighed heavily. Gráinne opened the envelope and unfolded the telegram.

"It's from the War Ministry," she said. Mrs Golden nodded. Kept on knitting. "It's dated today. It reads: *Deepest regrets. John Edward Golden reported missing in action. Presumed killed. Valiant pilot skilled in flight. Letter to follow.* And it's signed, Flight-Commander William J Trigg."

Mrs Golden had stopped knitting. She sat perfectly still. There was silence.

"It's getting very dark now, Gráinne," she said then. "I think I'll try and sleep. Thank you for that. Thank you. It wasn't easy for you . . ."

"I'm so dreadfully, dreadfully sorry, Mrs Golden . . ."

The old woman smiled sadly. She said nothing. Gráinne got up and left the telegram on the table. "If I can do anything, anything at all . . ."

"No thank you, dear, no thank you. I'll go to bed now. I'll be alright. You go on home now. You've been very good. And sure you were a little bit fond of him yourself, I know that."

Gráinne stood looking at her for a moment. Mrs Golden rocked ever so slightly where she sat. She looked old, suddenly, much, much older. But she had already gone into the world of her own thoughts and memories and any other words would be intrusion. Gráinne left her still sitting by the fireplace, the darkness closing in about her, the fire dying. She left her to begin her rooting among her memories for consolation. Gráinne knew she could not root among her own memories for such consolation. She moved quietly from the kitchen. She closed the door softly behind her. She went out into the evening.

Show me, you whom my soul loves, show me where you spend your day, where you lie down at noon, so that I may no longer wander after the footprints of others.

It was a dark, dark night. Gráinne lit the lamp in her attic room. She undressed completely. Carefully she folded and put away her clothes. She took out a small, red-leather suitcase from the wardrobe and put in some underclothes, some stockings, some night-things. She could hear the island winds ranging round the corners of the store, sliding down the attic roof. She stood still, a long time, naked, her shadow thrown large across the cabbage-green wall with its kaleidoscope of butterflies and moths. She gazed at herself in the mirror. She was beautiful, she knew that, in the full grace and loveliness of her waiting virginity. Her hair was long and golden, flowing down below her shoulder-blades. Her face was pale, her lips a dark red against the pallor. Gently she touched her lips with the tips of her fingers. *He shall kiss me with the kisses of his mouth.* She shuddered.

It was cold. A fistful of rain-pebbles clattered over the roof, onto her attic skylight. Her breasts were full and firm. Waiting. She touched the nipples, softly. Forever, she thought, forever now only he will live there, there between my breasts. She brought the tips of her fingers together and drew them slowly down the cleft between her breasts, down over her stomach. She touched her navel, her fingers

191

moving down, touching the small cotton-soft blossoming of her pubic hair. She shivered violently, her whole body trembling. *I am the flower of the meadow, I am the lily of the valley.*

Rapidly, then, she dressed in older, rougher clothes. Hiding away that lovely body. She reached under the bed and drew out a small, wooden tobacco box. She took out the bank-notes – five-pound notes, pound-notes, ten-shilling notes. She put them into an envelope, all but one five-pound note which she put into a pocket of her rough skirt. She put the envelope into the suitcase. Her dowry. She sighed heavily and gazed fondly around her attic room. The moths and butterflies were beautiful as ever. As she looked at them she remembered the day Jack had climbed into her secret room and had hurt her, deeply. She almost imagined him with her in the room again, critical, angry, annoyed too about the step she was going to take. Out of her loneliness. Out of her body. She glanced anxiously about the attic. He would be a ghost, forever stern and critical, in this high space where she had found some happiness. Another fistful of rain was flung against her attic window and she could hear the rush of the wind across the sky. *I opened the bolt of my door to my beloved, but he had turned away so quickly from me, and was gone.*

She shifted a chair out on the floor, as softly as she could, and stood up on it, opening out the attic window. She shivered again as the edge of the island wind touched her. Quickly now she moved to the cabbage-green wall. She unpinned the small moth at the top, the striped morning sphinx, and laid it on the palm of her hand. It was so light she could sense nothing against her skin. She brought it to the window. Slowly she stretched her hand out into the wild, dark freedom of the night. She opened her hand. At once the morning sphinx was swept away into the universe. For an instant she could glimpse a flash of scarlet from its wings as it was blown away, colouring the darkness, on its last flight. On her palm remained the faintest sensation, like the memory of a kiss.

Next she took the golden dog-face butterfly from its place and held it in her hand. For the last time she admired the symmetry of its colours, the two little sprigs of pink on the yellow, lightly-veined wings. Then she let it, too, free into the winds of the night. It flew for a moment, as if it lived again, gratefully and then it disappeared, taken too by the awful forces of the world. She took the orchard swallowtail, the morpho cypris, the brimstone, the butterflies and moths, one by one, from their places, and let them gently fly away into the night. She imagined their feckless careering flight as they left the comfort of the attic for the great expanse outside. She stared after them into the darkness.

She kept on working, saving till last the large butterfly she loved most of all, the tailed birdwing of paradise. She laid it on her palm. She felt she could know the trembling of that tiny body as the light green wings prepared for flight. She blew gently on the wings. Fly, little creature, fly, she whispered. It does not rain in paradise. You will not be alone any more. You will be free, with your kind, in flight. She let it go, reluctantly, into the darkness. *Many waters cannot quench love, neither can floods drown it.*

"For you, Jack," she whispered after it into the night.

She shut the window, as soundlessly as possible. She put on her plainest, oldest coat. It was almost one o'clock in the morning. She picked up her suitcase and looked again about the room. The cabbage-green wall was forlorn, nude, the names of moth and butterfly remaining, in her own handwriting, like ghosts. She turned down the wick of the lamp. All the light went out. She began down the steep stairway, cautiously.

On a dark, dark night. Gráinne was deeply anxious not to disturb the house. And yet her anxiety was mingled with a new excitement as she began on a fresh, great venture. She crept down the attic stair, slowly, every creak of the timber sounding too loud to her ears. She stood then on the carpeted landing and breathed more easily. Everybody in the house was sleeping. She had left a note on the pillow of her bed. Her whole heart seemed on fire in the darkness. As if that fire within her was lighting her way she went more quickly down the main staircase. She was glad of the darkness that hid from her the familiar things of her home, the small objects that were warm with memories and love and that might hold her heart from her desire. Tonight, she thought, lover and loved one would be joined forever. She stepped out onto the road and at once the rain and wind seized her. She welcomed them, their snatching at her was a caress. She raised her face to the wind and rains and closed her eyes; she, too, was a butterfly released on the great pathways of the world.

She closed the door quietly behind her. On the other side of the road the van was waiting. She ran over to it, eagerly. As she climbed in she felt she could be climbing into the cockpit of an aeroplane, like Jack must have done. It was small and cramped. Cornelius sat on the driver's side. At once she handed him the five-pound note.

"Thanks, Cornelius," she whispered. "Fly!"

Gráinne Flannery was admitted as a postulant in the convent of the Little Sisters of Perpetual Adoration. She arrived with the dawn, when the Sisters were already singing lauds. She waited outside the grille in an ante-room to their chapel. She heard the high, sweet voices as they sang. Like a flock of goldcrests in the high branches of summer pines. She could not see them, the grille was closed over; they were a choir of angels high in the sky; they were gentle thoughts in the attic of a troubled mind. *The beauty of the King's Daughter is within.* In the dark room Gráinne prayed fervently, her face buried in her hands, her whole being aflame with hope and love and longing. *As the apple tree among the trees of the wood, so is my beloved among the sons.*

The hero clothes himself about with armour, but the saint goes naked through the world. Gráinne was clothed in the habit of humility, a rough brown smock, a plain black belt, the dark brown postulant's cap and veil, flat shoes like clogs. With two others she received instruction, studying the Rules and Vows, reading the *Office of the Blessed Virgin Mary*, the *Imitation of Christ*, the *Book of Wisdom*, the *Song of Solomon*. She worked in the kitchen, washing dishes, peeling potatoes, scrubbing the stone floor; she worked along the outer corridors of the convent, polishing, dusting, sweeping, cleaning windows; she worked in the convent grounds, weeding, gathering leaves, cutting grass edges; she worked in the laundry-room, suffering the depredations of steam and sweat, her hands growing red and swollen, tiny purple veins beginning to stand out on her cheeks. She did all the menial jobs with joy and enthusiasm, her eyes turned down, her mind turned to things beyond the sky. The noise of her devotions covered over the clamour of her young, demanding life. The whisperings of the angels occluded her loneliness.

The postulants were allowed only into the back pews of the chapel, to attend Mass and meditation and to listen to the Sisters sing the hours. Gráinne spent two hours every dawn, between four o'clock and six o'clock, kneeling in adoration at the back of the chapel, while two sisters knelt on the prie-dieus before the sacrament exposed, like a tiny white and distant sail on the great green ocean of the altar. Quickly, the last remaining strips of worldly clothing were falling away from about her and she was admitted, on a sacred day, to her first profession of vows.

Set me up with flowers, compass me about with apples, because I languish, I grow weak, with love.

During those two hours before dawn, Gráinne was in a fever of agitation in the pew at the back of the Church. The sanctuary was brightly lit, candles throwing their still, white light on an array of flowers about the great gold monstrance. She raised her head and watched the host and imagined that it stirred, like a white cloud, calling to her. The high windows of the chapel were dark but she knew that light would soon come pouring through. She longed to pronounce her vows. It would be the first loud knocking she would make on the door that opened through the blue wall of the sky. This would be her day. That light would be her light. She would feed forever on that light.

After the frugal breakfast she took for the last time with the other postulants, Gráinne was brought by two sisters into the same ante-room she had first entered. They sat her down on a low stool. She folded her hands over the rough smock on her lap. One of the sisters removed the cap and postulant's veil. Gráinne's lovely hair flowed down over their hands, as if it breathed again with the relief of its release. It was a river of gold. It was a gift, a grace, a mirror in which God's creating eye had loved to gaze. The other sister caught the hair roughly in her left hand. Gráinne heard the sharp cutting of the great scissors from the kitchen. She could feel the small tugs against her head. She could feel the parcels of her hair fall soundlessly down her back. Soon, about the legs of the stool, her hair lay strewn in thick, hopeless mounds. Like a shipwreck. Like flotsam and jetsam from a world of wonder. Not a word was spoken, but Gráinne almost swooned with joy.

By mid-morning she was led up through the centre aisle of the chapel. All the sisters were standing in choir. There was silence. Only the soft shush of her stockinged feet as she moved behind the same two sisters. They left her standing at the altar rails, alone before the wondrous brilliance of the altar and the white demanding presence of the host. She wore her old brown smock, her cap, the postulant's veil.

To her left the grille was slipped open. Gráinne prostrated herself on the marble foreshore of the altar. Then she rose and approached the grille. From the dark otherside of the grille came the voice of the Bishop, questioning her, insisting, questioning, questioning if indeed she were prepared for the total dedication of her life that Christ, her Spouse, was demanding of her. She answered in a firm voice. She stood erect and kept her head lowered, but her answers were heard by the community gathered behind her in the chapel and by the other community, her reluctant parents and some of the privileged of the little town, in the darkness of the ante-room beyond. The Bishop pronounced her ready. She could take her vows. She would be able to stand forever in the great company of the sisters, no longer a solitary soul but one of a great sisterhood of love.

Gráinne was led once more to the sanctuary steps. Once more she prostrated herself on the marble shore. She remained there during the long Mass celebrated by the Bishop himself. She trembled with joy and gladness. Her name was mentioned among the low pleadings offered before the throne by the Bishop. She was named among the angels.

When the Mass was ended the Bishop seated himself to the side of the altar on a marble bench. The sisters led Gráinne from the chapel. In a room apart she stripped herself of the rough brown smock, the black belt, leaving on the cap and postulant's veil. She was clothed, then, with the flowing blue habit of the Sisters, a white cord about her waist. She was given two flat, brown shoes. One of the sisters placed in her hands a bouquet of flowers, white passion flowers, lilies of the valley, snowdrops, camellias and roses. She walked again up the centre of the chapel, a sister on either hand. She knelt before the Bishop who slowly removed from her shorn head the cap and veil of the postulant. In the ante-room her mother, peering through the grille, wept at the sight of that small, shorn, vulnerable skull.

The Bishop placed on her head the special, flowing blue

veil of the Little Sisters of Perpetual Adoration. He placed about her waist the great, brown rosary of the Order and solemnly requested her to pronounce, before the world, her name.

"From henceforth, to eternity," she enunciated, in a voice that trembled with joy, "I am to be known as Sister Mary of St John of the Cross."

She then spoke aloud the solemn vows of her first profession, offering herself to God as his lowly servant maid forever, promising to observe the sacred poverty of the Order, holy chastity, perfect obedience, and dedication to adoration of the Blessed Sacrament.

As the sisters behind her began to sing the great *Te Deum*, Mother Abbess came and placed a crown of thorns on the new Sister's head. She was reborn. She was betrothed. She was delirious with happiness.

Sister Mary knocked, timidly, on the door. The new clothes, the habit, cincture, beads, the long veil, all felt strange about her but she relished their embrace. She was a soft hushing breeze along the short corridor. When she stepped into the small parlour Nora moved forward awkwardly to greet her, not knowing whether to reach for her hands, or to offer to kiss her. She stood, then, distraught, her mouth open. Fintan Flannery, island merchant, was standing at the small window, looking out. Beyond him was a patch of green; beyond that a high, cement wall.

"You're like a prisoner in here, Gráinne," he said, without turning round. "It's dark and grey and ugly. And those high walls!"

"I'm very, very happy in here," she said, quietly.

Fintan turned then, abruptly. Humphing with impatience. He was wearing his best, grey suit, a black tie that bulged in a hard lump, and his brown hat was in his hands.

"You can come straight home with us now, Gráinne," he urged, "and not one more word need be said about all this. Come on home with us now."

Nora looked anxiously between her husband and her daughter.

"I can't do that, father," Sister Mary said, still quietly,

her eyes lowered. "This is where I am meant to be. I will find God here. I will miss you all. But I'll be very happy. *Winter is over now, the rains are over and gone and the new flowers have appeared in our land.*"

"What are you talking about?" Fintan retorted. "It's July. And it's still raining. And they gave us a miserly cup of tea. A few sandwiches. Something like cress in them. Grass sandwiches! I ask you! And buns you wouldn't give to a cat!"

"We eat simply in here. The sheer weight of the human body drags us down, Mother Abbess says, but the gravity of the spirit is all upwards, into the light of heaven."

"Gravity, indeed. You won't put on much weight in here. You don't eat at all, as far as I can see," he went on, accusingly, "you're thin, and pale . . ."

"And your hair, Gráinne!" Nora rushed in. "Look what they have done to your lovely hair!"

"It's a vanity, mother, a girl's hair, and it has no place among the sisters."

The parents fell silent. She was standing before them, motionless, her head lowered, her eyes bright and alert. Submissive, but steady in her posture, not easily to be moved. Like when she was a little child and came in to be scolded, Fintan thought, and his heart lurched with sadness. He was turning and turning and turning the old brown hat between his hands. Nora looked frail and uncertain. There was silence.

"You ran away," Fintan accused her. "You ran away like a hare before hounds. And we didn't think to look for a note for a long while. You ran away and left all the burden on us."

"Burden?"

"Yes, the burden! The store, the pub, the house, all of it.

It was all meant for you. And, we had hoped, for young Golden if he hadn't been such a fool and got himself killed. And there's Mrs Golden, too, she's a burden on us, now."

"We want to try and look after her . . ." Nora began, and faltered.

"How is poor Mrs Golden?"

"She's failed, Gráinne," Nora said. "She doesn't hardly come and go any more. We have to deliver everything to her. She just sits. Or wanders about like a ghost in her own house. Mary Alice brings us in her order. And I go and sit with her betimes."

"I came after you, you know," Fintan continued. "When I found out. I asked Cornelius. He was reluctant, but he told me. And I took out the car and came after you."

"I know that . . ."

"They wouldn't even let me see you . . ."

He stopped. But he was careeing through his emotions. He went on again, hopelessly.

"I came to fetch you back, bring you home."

"I'm sorry, father," the voice was a whisper. "But I know my place is here."

"We'll be all right, child," Nora was anxious. "We'll miss you, greatly, but we'll be all right."

"It's worse than if you died, Gráinne," he went on. "Let me say it. It's worse than if you died. Because you're still alive, but we've lost you."

She looked up at him. There were tears in her eyes.

"You know that's not true, father. You haven't lost me. I'll be closer to you than ever I was before. I love you both, very, very much. And here I can think of you and pray with you always. I'll be as close to you as God is close."

Gráinne stood, tears on her cheeks, watching him.

"Well, anyway," Fintan muttered, his hat crushed between his hands. "For the last time, Gráinne, please, I'm begging you, give up this foolishness and come home. Now. With us."

Gráinne held her two hands firmly together. She was squeezing them, for strength.

"Please don't ask me that, please," she said. "I know my life must be here. I have given myself to God. Like a bride. I cannot . . ."

"A bride!" Fintan almost spat the word onto the polished wooden floor. "Come on, Nora, I can't listen to any more of this. We've lost her. She's lost to us, lost!"

He brushed past his daughter, quickly, opened the door and went out into the corridor. Nora held Gráinne tightly for a moment, her arms about her, then kissed her quickly on the mouth.

"God bless you, Gráinne," she whispered. "Sister Mary . . ." she said the name cautiously, with a little wonder and a certain fear that the name might hurt her tongue. "Pray for us . . ." and she, too, left the room. Sister Mary stood, watching the open door. She heard the footsteps move away down the corridor. She heard a door open, and close noisily. The echo moved quickly back along the corridor. Then there was silence, a deep, resonant silence.

"Heal me, Christ, heal me," she whispered to the air. "Send no further messengers to me from the world. Let me die here, with love for you. Come, end my sufferings because it is only You I long for. Let my eyes see you, the true light, let me rise from the darkness of this earth into your wondrous light. Raise me, raise me high into the sky of your love. Kill me with your beauty, your love. Only your presence, Lord, can bring me peace."

Sister Mary was given a cell on the second floor of the Convent building. It was a small room, one window looking out onto the small front garden and the enclosure wall that reached as high as the window. In the cell there was a washhand-basin and a jug. She filled the jug with cold water and washed herself in the basin. There was a thin, small wardrobe with one drawer at the bottom where she kept everything she had at her disposal. There was an iron bed with a thin mattress, sheets, two blankets. On the pillow there lay, always, a small brass crucifix. At the side of the bed, on the rough timbers of the floor, was a thin mat to kneel on. And that was all. This was her life.

That evening she knelt and prayed. The summer night was settling in, a gentle sky beyond the wall still reflected a little brightness into her cell. There was no lamp in the room. Jesus was her light. She would feed on that light, on the light of her faith. Her love. She could hear the birds sing in the distance. The rest was silence.

"You, Lord, are my love. You are the heights of the mountains, you are the valleys with the lonesome trees, you are my strange and distant island, my running streams, you are my loving, wandering winds. This is my night, as beautiful to me as the dawn, here is all my music, all my food. Here is our marriage bed, safe and secure from harm, here is our dwelling-place, our house of peace. You are all the path I long for, you are my sacred wine. Deep in the cavern of my soul I will find you, drunk from your love I will stagger through the world until I am with you. From this day on, I will not be found among the haunts of men. Let them know I have gone mad with love for you, let them know that I am lost and dead, but here have been found and come alive again."

As the room grew dark about her and only her own words sounded within an even deeper silence, she knew a joy and ecstasy that she had never felt before. Even the words within her then fell silent. She closed her eyes against the solidity of the walls about her. She reached deeper into her own darkness. Her knees hurt against the hard floor. And she joyed the more in her discomfort. She remembered her father and his anger and her heart lifted the more strongly towards her lover. Tears came again but they were tears of love and fervour, offering herself, body and soul, into the arms of her Lord. She was a flame of love, a fire that took both body and soul and burned from within; and her great Lover came and ripped the soft covering that kept her still from him. She felt a searing pain, a tender wound, as if a loving hand had searched inside her body and held her, killing her almost, while offering her a greater life. She moved in a realm of light, a white-hot light that held her utterly and nowhere in her was there left the slightest taint of darkness. She imagined she rose softly from the earth, gently rising, her eyes still closed, voyante, the universe spread out beneath her as if she were an eagle, a falcon, an angel, flying high above a world that was all light and warmth. She heaved deep sighs, she was in love, she was at peace.

A gentle tap came on her door a few minutes before

four o'clock in the morning. She woke at once to find herself lying on the mat at the side of the bed. She was stiff and cold but she was at once deeply happy again. She heard the whispered words outside: *Laudetur Jesus Christus*, and she responded at once, *In Aeternum. Amen.* She bathed her face in the cold water of the basin. She raised the crucifix from the pillow and she kissed it. Then she went down to the Chapel to take her place in adoration before the host.

She was a novice now. Admitted, named and clothed. In three years' time she would make her final profession. She knelt on one of the small prie-dieus inside the white marble altar-rails, below the first marble step leading to the paradise of the altar. At four o'clock the nun on her right-hand-side, at another prie-dieu, rose quietly, prostrated herself before the altar. And left. She was replaced immediately by another nun. Sister Elizabeth of Saint Francis. Now again they were two, two sisters in adoration before the wonder of the world, praying for themselves, for one another, praying for the end of wars, praying to God to sustain poor heavy humanity in its slow but certain fall into the wet soil of the earth.

There were candles, and flowers. There were lights. Behind her Sister Mary sensed the dark, breathing cavern of the chapel. Its small benches. Empty now. Still trembling with the echo of prayer and psalm. She knew the books that were lying there. The Little Office. The prayer-books. The personal prayers and devotions of the Sisters. The hope-filled lives. Dedicated.

To love.

Brides. Of Christ.

Silence surrounded the two nuns. They were islands washed about by the most wondrous of oceans. Sister Mary could hear the gentle breathing of the other. Sister Elizabeth was older, experienced in the ways of God, exalted by her contact with the Lord. Sister Mary closed her eyes. Already her knees hurt, her elbows, too, against the hard wood of the prie-dieu. She shivered a little. It was cold, here, in the pre-dawn hours. For a moment, the image of Jack Golden as he leaped off the top of the pier shone before her mind. She opened her eyes, quickly, and fixed them on the white purity of the host. It was still, a steady brightness, while all around it the tiny flames of the candles flickered gently in their own, devoted, dying.

Arise, make haste, my love, my dove, my beautiful one, and come. The winter is now over, the rains are over and gone. The flowers have appeared in our land. Let my beloved come into his garden, let him eat the fruit of his apple trees.

And then I entered in, but where it was I do not know. And I stayed there, still unknowing. Transcending every knowing. Wherever I was, as soon as I was there, I understood great things at once. I cannot say what it was I understood, all I can say is I stayed there, still unknowing, transcending every knowing. My wondrous understanding came from peace and love, from deep solitude after a path directly taken; it was all done in total secrecy and there, stammering still, I stayed, transcending every knowing. I was so drunk with knowing, so much absorbed, carried away, that all my senses were simply deprived of feeling; my whole soul was gifted with an understanding that yet did not understand, transcending every knowing. Anyone who has truly reached that place must shed her self completely; whatever was known before seems foolish now; her knowing grows so gently that she remains still unknowing, transcending every knowing. I rose and rose towards the heights; the more I rose the less I understood that cloud so tenebrous that lit up that night; so that anyone who has known it stays always still unknowing, transcending every knowing. This knowing and unknowing is of such a high power that all the learning of the wise men can never comprehend it; that their knowing will never understand without understanding, transcending every knowing. That wondrous summit of knowing is of such surpassing height there is no faculty or knowing that may ever comprehend it; he who ever overcomes it, by understanding beyond understanding, will forever transcend all knowing. Oh you who might wish to hear, this high and wondrous knowing is a sudden sense of the one Divine Essence; it is the labour of His clemency, to allow you to remain without understanding, transcending every knowing.

On feast days of saints and virgin martyrs the novices were permitted to leave the strict indoor enclosure and spend an hour about the enclosure grounds. Here they could walk the gravel footpaths among the flowerbeds, the roses, dahlias, lilies, reciting the hours of prime, terce, sext and none. To the right rose the high enclosure wall, covered here by trellises of clematis and climbing roses. Here she walked, the *Little Office* in the great sack of a pocket in her habit, her hands tucked into the sleeves over her breasts, her eyes caressing the flowers. *My love is a garden enclosed, a fountain sealed.* At one end of the garden, under the high elms, was the convent cemetery. Sister Mary walked among the simple plots topped by a small iron cross that bore the name of the sister and the year of her death. No more. She admired and envied the achieved anonymity of these great Brides of Christ. Flowers bloomed in the sunlight. It was a corner of peace and rest, of gently shifting shadows, and embedded in the high wall there stood a Calvary, the figure of the Christ hanging in a Grecian repose, his body coloured like sand, the wounds in his hands and feet and side delicately stylized and painted red. Beneath the Cross, her hands folded in prayer, the Mother of Dolours, her mantle painted a soft-cream blue. The Magdalene was there, too, on the other side, her mantle brown, her eyes cast demurely towards the ground.

For a long time Sister Mary stood, beyond the graves, gazing at the figure on the Cross. A delicate scent from the flowers wafted over her. Like a warm summer breeze blowing across the island. There were bees working everywhere and high in the branches of the trees the tiny whispering calls of the goldcrest. She stood, still as one of the painted statues. From beyond the wall the echoes of the turning world were muted. Once, as if suddenly dropping out of a startling, empty sky, she saw an aeroplane, falling in total silence, falling in flames, and Jack's eyes watched out at her, staring helplessly from behind the glass. She started, and moved slowly back towards the enclosure door. How she longed to die, to be laid, among the softly murmuring voices of her sisters, in the quiet patch of sunlight among the flowers, there to rest for ever in perfect peace, disturbed only by the prayers of the sisters of those endless generations yet to come. *Put me as a seal upon thy heart, as a seal upon thy arm, for love is as strong as death.*

A letter from Mary O'Boyle to Mother Abbess.
Little Sisters of Perpetual Adoration.

Dear Mother,

You asked me to write. To explain why I left, so hurriedly. What can I do but tell you of Sister Mary. It is she . . . no, Mother, it is I . . . let me tell you how it was. She stepped into our days, like many more, tall and kempt and full of history. Her eyes were unfocused, giddy as sanderlings before the waves. She had enough of the world but, like us all, she brought the whiff and rumour of the world with her when she came. Miss Gráinne Flannery. That sunshine of golden hair! That pale and querulous beauty!

Mother Abbess, she brought me such disturbance in my soul, such whisperings, echoes, tremors . . .

One of the most difficult duties of our lives, as you know, is to accept and tame the wild spirits that break in on us from the world. Those reaching memories of ours. Trailing clouds of passions as they come! We live to ignore the created, the inferior; our lives are burning only for the Creator. And every step we take is on another road, turning and turning, inwards, always inwards. Only. Seeking the Lover. Only. Offering love to the creator of love. To Love Itself. This you know. This you taught us, often. I knew it, too, its truth, its undoubted truth. But I also knew the human heart, Mother, and mine was a heart, is a heart, all too human.

Our world, outwardly, must be at peace. Inwardly, a battle field. My soul was a minefield. We wanted no drama other than the dropping of a spoon on the refectory floor, or a sudden sneeze during adoration, a voice out of tune at Office.

Ours was a death, the peace of death. But a living death. But then, death is a lovely thing, the filling up of the void with love. It is the creation of the void that is the difficulty. That making space within an unruly life that will allow for the glorious entry of the Lord. The filling of that void with love is the consummation of our marriage. Sunlight at last, and love.

Forgive me.

Very quickly and admirably she shed her history. Our Community was fervent, filled with generous chosen souls. I was one of them, too, you knew that. You encouraged me. Often. Soon, settling amongst us like a white dove among white doves, it was clear that Sister Mary wished indeed to cast off the chains of the world for the freedom of the Cloister. Almost at once her hair was shorn and whatever was left was hidden away under our plain, novice's cap. Those deep eyes, roving and filled with a hot, profane wisdom, had been lowered and stilled, deep waters, cool and watching inwards. And that rose flesh paled, at first, then gradually turned red again, the healthy red of our life locked from powders and unguents and offered to the Lord of the fields. Quickly and well had Gráinne Flannery, Miss, shed the false clothing of the world and taken on the habit of perfection, the habit of our order, and taken a name, a special name, a difficult name.

I admit now, and I relished then, surprise that she had not taken the name of the glorious Francis we all venerated so much. She reminded me of Clare, Clara, that wondrous hair, that simple, immediate devotion, that single-minded attention! My name was Francis, Sister Teresa Elizabeth of Saint Francis. What a name! What a burden I had imposed on myself. Fool that I am. Proud fool. I exulted in him. In my father, my protector, my mentor. May God forgive me!

That day, in the Chapel of Our Lady of the Angels, she and I adoring together, side by side, small souls, sand-grains on a magnificent shore, I allowed my eyes to become moths, to land on our Altar of Cararra Marble, to touch the alabaster throne of the Monstrance, to rest on the great light of the Monstrance itself wherein is the Blessed Bread by which we live. I allowed myself some moments of selfish joy in the treasures of our adoration. And then my eyes touched again on the young novice, on Sister Mary of St John of the Cross. And this is my witness and it is true. She was kneeling, humbly, adoring, alight with grace, some several feet above the prie-dieu! Her knees supported on the air. The way the angels kneel. On nothing. On nothing more than her holiness.

I tell truth here and that you may be sure I tell the truth, I admit that a great red worm of envy crawled in through my eyes and slithered down my throat into my heart. I was worn and exhausted by the trials attendant upon our life of adoration, enclosure, and penance. I had often stood to listen to the bustling sounds of the little town outside our high enclosure walls. I used to hear the train, pulling slowly away out of the station, I heard it gather speed, momentum, rhythm and slowly, slowly, slowly, steam away into the wonders of the world. And my heart sagged, my soul drooped, and tears of loss wet my face. And still, for all that beauty I would not throw away my precious soul. The taste of all that mortal joy would ruin the palate and destroy the appetite for immortal bliss. The generous heart will never falter on its way, will never weary, will remember always that pleasure is a stone to drag the spirit down out of the highest reaches of the sky, that stone heaped on stone heaped on stone will keep the soul buried on earth for ever. I raised, so often, my weary head to the One above, the One of greatest charm, and offered Him once again my whole being. And never, never once, down all those years, was I offered the smallest savour of such grace as lifted Sister Mary off the earth! Oh it is hard, hard, hard to be a lover! I am a holy person, without pride I say it now, I am a holy person still, all for God.

One night she and I shared the night-time watch, she and I together, kneeling in adoration before the Lord. I remember it well, rising long after midnight, rising out of black, because my life was so tired all the moments I could sleep I sank into a total blackness. I came into the Chapel, trailing sleep behind me, and another Sister bowed her body to the ground and left. I knelt in my place, knelt straight up so as I could hold myself awake. Devoted before the Throne. And prayed. I spoke to the Lord and the candle hissed at me and the golden nails from the Monstrance tore my hair.

I heard a Sister enter and kneel on the prie-dieu at my left. I did not lift my head. My eyes were on my absent Lord. I prayed and I dozed, because the sleep within me murmured and honeyed me like a summer afternoon.

And then my elbows must have greased off the elbow-rest because I was suddenly wide awake. I was sweating.

Now, the habit and all the harnessing that I wore were hot in every sense, smothersome-hot betimes. But this was more. There was a furnace. I looked to my left, away from my Lord. And there was Sister Mary, on her prie-dieu, no, no, no, above her prie-dieu, kneeling, unsupported, on the air. The ecstasy of levitation. And more. She seemed to be on fire, burning. In fact, I was almost certain that I saw two of her there, one kneeling on the prie-dieu, head lowered over joined hands, another kneeling above her, kneeling on the air, head bowed over joined hands. And the one lifted above the other was on fire. It looked like flames, rising from her breast and joined hands and from her head, bowed in prayer. Since I knew Love, I knew He could perform wondrous works. There was His lover, body heavy and struggling, no doubt, like mine against the forces of gravity, and soul burning with a flame so fine and fragrant I expected her to be wholly burned away.

Silence, though, perfect silence. I knew what those flames were. I knew. And the flames had never been for me. Not ever even the merest candle-swish. My heart failed within me, for sorrow and emptiness and dryness. And jealousy. Of course, jealousy. I was a sow, fat and heavy and sweating, slavering about in my sty of prayers. Muttering a few Paters, a few Aves. And filled only with the weight of stone. Earthed. Earthy. Hopeless. I gave up and simply watched Sister Mary for a time, the silent Chapel alight with her fire, the walls and floor and ceiling, the furnishings, bathed in a soft, orange glow. For me it all became a kind of entertainment. I laughed to myself. I got off my knees and sat on a bench. And watched. Bemused. But deeply angry.

The heat of the occasion forced me to loosen the veil

about my head. I did so, softly, not to interrupt the pair of lovers. The veil fell off my head onto the floor with a soft, whispering reproach. And the relief was quite simply more than I could bear. I stood up at once and left the Chapel, walked along the corridors to my room, took off my habit and all my trappings and lay down on my bed, luxuriating in it. I slept, a blessed sleep, long and sound and dreamless. And the next afternoon I was on that train as it went puffing its way out of the town into the little fields, the lovely little fields on which my eyes feasted.

After the midday meal the Little Sisters worked for an hour at various tasks about the convent grounds, or in the corridors. In the kitchen. About the altar. Answering correspondence with the world beyond, letters of petition for prayers to be offered before the Sacrament exposed. The postal orders and small notes included in these requests were carefully acknowledged and handed over to the Bursar. Others worked in the kitchen garden, their sleeves folded to the elbow, raking, hoeing, planting. Several sisters selected flowers for the altar, replaced candles. Only the Mother Abbess, and sometimes the Procuratrix, were allowed to treat with the public – that dangerously polluted flood sometimes fetching up against their walls – at the front parlour grille. Here the visitor could hear the Mother's voice but could not see her face. Blessed rosaries, holy pictures, were delivered by means of a small rotating plate fixed underneath the grille. Otherwise, throughout enclosure, silence was the rule.

Silence was the rule, except for half an hour between two-thirty and three o'clock, the second half of their labour hour, when they could speak. They were allowed to knit, to make rosary beads, to crochet. They were allowed to speak, on holy topics, in lowered voices.

Sister Mary sat in the small yard off the kitchen. To her right Sister Bernardine, a sister whose hair was white, on whose chin and cheeks grew tiny tufts of white hair, whose face was lined and wrinkled like the grease that dribbles down a candle's flanks. Her habit seemed much too large for her as if she had diminished within it. Then there was Sister Catherine, baby-faced, the chin and nose small and perfectly shaped, the eyes light-blue and clear, the skin as smooth and pink as a baby girl's. She smiled a great deal as if the world were benevolence itself. Her hands were perfect, the fingers long and aristocratic, the finger-nails short but perfectly rounded, fingers fit to caress the very body of the Lord. The fourth stool remained, for the moment, unoccupied.

Before them, on the rough cement of the yard, was a large enamel bucket filled with potatoes. Another bucket waited. Tomorrow's potatoes were peeled today and kept overnight in water in the cool-house behind the kitchen. Sister Mary found the water in the bucket very cold, the white flesh of the potatoes chilling on her fingers. She relished the chill. She kept her hand longer in the water than she needed to. Sister Bernardine sneezed suddenly.

"Bless you, Sister!"

The kitchen door was opened noisily. It was, of course, Sister Adrian. Sister Adrian was a country girl, big, red-faced, physical, all elbow shoulder and knee in spite of the all-enfolding habit.

"Sorry, Sisters," she offered, her voice solid as turnips. "I'm late. Sister Athanasius has not been feeling all that well. I brought her over to the infirmary."

She hefted her habit high up to her knees and squatted on the stool, her heavy body thumping it so that it seemed to wince under her weight. She planted her feet too wide apart, firmly, firmly on the earth. The Sisters noticed she was wearing no stockings. If you looked closely enough you could see the rough cloth of her underwear above the great red hams. The sisters did not look. The Sisters made no remarks. The ankles, too, were red. The legs were covered in a fine, golden hair. Sister Adrian's face was the image of health, speaking of farm mornings, the shifting of churns, great hanks of homemade brown bread, chipped mugfuls of buttermilk. A curl of light-red hair always slipped down somewhere from under her veil and she blew upwards at it, curling her lower lip. A wench. She dipped her hand in for a potato, forgetting to roll up her sleeve.

"Shite!" she muttered.

The others paused, fingers poised over their work, the parer hesitating in the flesh of the potato.

"Pardon me, Sisters!" The voice was alive with laughter. The offence was not treated by that voice as an offence. Sister Mary thought of one of her moths, bright-red and shapely, falling out through the darkness of night.

After a few moments of silence, Sister Adrian spoke again.

"Sisters! Do yiz know what?"

The sisters were still sitting behind a delicate sheet of gauze they had drawn before their faces at her first word.

"What is it, Sister?" Bernardine asked.

"I'd give my left elbow for the pull of a cigarette!"

Sister Bernardine let a long, dark curl fall from her potato into the bucket. She chuckled quietly. Babyface smiled a condescending smile. Holier than thou smile. Beneficent.

"Any o' youze got an oul' butt?" The big body at work, the big hands running expertly over the potatoes. "Sister Mary? or did you shake your habit?" and she laughed more raucously than a sister enclosed ought to laugh.

Sister Mary did not lift her eyes from her task.

"I was lucky enough never to have smoked, Sister," she said, sweetly.

"Ever guzzle a bottle of stout, any o' yiz?"

There was a silence. Busy. A little strained. Sister Bernardine sighed.

"I've always been very dry myself, Sister."

She looked across at Adrian, a bright twinkle in her eye.

"Like the desert, I mean," she went on, looking down again at her work. "I live in a desert, without favour of my God. It's a question of the will only, a question of faith sustained by will. When I try to meditate there's nothing there. I'm like an old shipwreck, tossed up high on the beach. Too high for the waters to touch me. Sleep is the only consolation. And what I miss most is being able to cry. Sometimes I long to weep, to weep and weep and weep. I can't even do that. I'm dry, Sisters, very, very dry."

The only sound for a time was that of the peeling skin and the plop of the water.

"What about you, Sister Mary? Are you enjoying the favours of the Lord?"

"Me? I'm very happy here. Very happy."

An even deeper silence followed this remark. Sister Mary could have told them about the pub, about the drink, the stout, the blackness, the darkness. But she did not. All of that did not exist, for her, any more. Sister Adrian hummed as she worked. She plunged her great hand into the bucket of water.

"Just a small drop of stout would be great for the soul!"

Sister Catherine looked offended.

"Not even the smallest drop of wine ever touched my lips," she offered, "but I once saw the inside of a bar, with my father, it was sad, dark and musty and very, very sad."

Sister Adrian sat back on her stool in an unsisterly manner.

"I'd love to wallow in that darkness for a wee, wee while." She bent forward again, peeling. "Ever been in love, girls?" She threw the words into their little circle where they fell about, noisily, on the ground.

Mary stopped. She kept her head lowered. She said nothing.

"Oh yes," said Sister Bernardine. "I was very much in love. But my parents wouldn't have it. He was too plain for them. Too poor." She paused.

"What happened, Sister Bernardine?"

"Oh he went away, that's all. He just went away. I never knew what happened him. It's a dull story. A dull story."

Sister Adrian noticed how pale Sister Mary had become. And was that a tear? It was quickly brushed away. Or was it just a stray drop of water from the bucket?

"What about you, Sister Mary?" the big nun prodded.

"I am in love with the Lord, Sister Adrian. Human love is an unsafe thing, you cannot rely on it. It is hurtful and cruel. The love of Jesus is a thing of truth and beauty."

Sister Adrian, her two great knees exposed to the winds of the world, eyed the younger sister closely.

"If you ask me, Sister Mary," she began, "I should say that you might just be . . ."

The small bell sounded in the corridors of the Convent. Obedience demanded instant and complete compliance with the signified will of the Lord. They finished their task in silence, each one set apart again inside her individual shell, suffering her individual burden.

Report on Sister Mary of St John of the Cross submitted to Mother Abbess by Sister Bernardine of St Joseph.

"She and me were beside one another in choir. She was a distraction to me. I admit distractions come easily and my life seems to be a battle with them, but still, this was different. I could not avoid being aware of her and she took my prayers and meditations and flung them into the wild winds. With her about I couldn't concentrate. Often I heard her sigh deeply, long, heartfelt sighs. She would have her eyes closed and yet it looked as if she was seeing something. Her lips moved, too, though no words could be heard. The word I would use of her is 'rapt'; she seemed rapt out of herself as if her body had been taken over and she could see what none of the rest of us could see, hear words the rest of us could not hear and sometimes tears flowed down her cheeks and she would not move to wipe them away. And once, when I was in the Enclosure garden, I watched her. It was early afternoon. She was standing below the Calvary, utterly motionless, like a statue herself, her arms outstretched as if it was she who was on the Cross. I moved along the gravel walks, quietly, so as not to disturb her. But when I came past the graves and turned by the end of the walk I could see her face and I got a fright for she was dark and distorted as if she was undergoing great suffering. Her eyes were wide open, fixed on the Christ, but she was rigid as a post, unblinking. I coughed out loud, deliberately, and she did not stir. Nothing. I was anxious for her. Envious, too, in a way. I had no doubt she luxuriated in the sensible favours of God. I remember some of the men I used to know at home, those that had strange gifts from God, cures, the seventh son of a seventh son, that kind of thing, and I envied them, even in those unholy days of my life. Anyway. She was stiff as a stick, yet I felt a small breath of wind would brush her away into the blue sky. And leave me standing, my whole body heavy as a load of wet peat, fixed here on the earth. She had once spoken to us of a flame, a fire of love. The kind of stuff she'd say during recreation. Never speak of things of the world. As if the world wasn't there. I expect maybe she was trying too hard to keep the world on the other side of our wall. She experienced things, then. Nothing I've ever experienced. I believe such favours to be real but I believe, too, they can distract you from God Himself, fill up the place that ought to be empty so that God can take over. God, and not the favours. Goodness knows but I'm empty enough myself and there's no God filling my void. But maybe that's just envy speaking. Forgive me. I do not know. Anyway. I know that Sister Mary hardly ever ate anything, picking like a sparrow at her crumbs of bread. And she did penances, of that I'm sure, far and above what we all take part in. And I'm certain, for instance, she put pebbles in her shoes for I saw a few of them fall out once in choir. Anyway. The Convent bell rang three o'clock and I turned my mind to praying for our benefactors when Sister Mary gave a kind of gasp, a small cry and she staggered a little as if smitten, and fell forward on her hands and knees. I moved to help her but I didn't, for her face was so serene again, so filled with joy and peace I knew I would be only an intrusion. She seemed to feed on pain, and gain sustenance from it. She got up and turned in my direction but I know she did not see me. She went into the Convent and sat down on a window-ledge. I followed her. She was vulnerable, I felt. She seemed exhausted then, worn out, pale. I made signs to her, asking if she needed help, a Sister Infirmarian, but she shook her head, slowly, smiling at me. A foolish kind of a smile. A happy smile, and exhausted. I remember shrugging my shoulders and leaving her. She was not of us. She was floating in a different sky above our world. Somehow I knew she would fall. I expected it. I was jealous, I admit that, and I pray for forgiveness. But I pitied her, too, for such flights are often followed by a fall. That's what I think. That's what my parents always told me. Feet on the ground, they'd say, and hands on the rail. Anyway I worried a bit for her. And I know I pitied her. Though I gloated a little when she fell. And for my jealousy, and for my gloating, I will do penance until the day I die.

Sister Mary loved it best in the evenings. After Vespers. After supper and the reading aloud of the *Imitation of Christ*. The soft blessing of the bell. The beautiful, dignified, slow process into the chapel. Into choir. Into her place. That whispering movement, regulated and soft, like the coming on of night itself. She loved the darkness that settled about them, the way a hen settles herself down onto her eggs. Compline. The sweet voices in harmony. *Now thou dost dismiss thy servant according to thy word, in peace.* She was tired. Tired, even worn out. If it could be like this to die . . . like a psalm fading into its own echoes, among the lights and the flowers, among the radiant, golden arms of the monstrance . . .

She lived, but without living within herself. She had eaten almost nothing for weeks on end so that now her bones were a burden to her, and the habit was a cross. She lived, but she was dying because she had not yet died. Every hour of the day was a dying for her because she had given herself away and God had not yet taken her offering. Her bones were the bones of a bird, a wren, a goldcrest, but she had not yet flown to her God.

It was winter. The convent was warm. She had turned off the radiator in her cell. In the warmth of the chapel she felt caressed, and the music and sweet words were food enough. Her living was all privation. It was a privation to be still alive. She would go on dying until she lived in Christ. Hear me, my God, this is not the living I desire, I am dying because I have not died.

And then the voices rose in the final hymn; *Salve Regina*. Mother Mary. Hail our life, our sweetness, and our hope. The Latin words lifted and sank in a soothing melody, it was like flying on clouds, up, and down, gently. To thee do we send up our sighs, mourning and weeping in this valley of tears.

She stumbled as she left the chapel and had to catch hold of the end of the pew to stop herself from falling. She sat down a moment, breathing heavily. Sister Bernardine touched her on the shoulder but she merely shook her head, gently, patiently, waved her hand, and did not look up. The words of the hymn still sounding about the rafters of the little chapel, singing like angels in the air: *After this our exile show unto us the blessed fruit of thy womb* . . .

She climbed the stairs with great difficulty. She was tired, that was all, tired. And weak, suffering in the service of her Spouse. The more she lived, the more she would have to die. She closed the door of her cell behind her, gratefully, and lay back against it for a while. It was cold. There was darkness beyond her window but a faint glow was visible beyond the high wall, a glow from the lights of the town. She was protected from it. A garden enclosed. He shall abide between my breasts. After supper this evening she had to go to the washrooms, quickly, and she had vomited back the little piece of bread she had forced herself to swallow.

She found it difficult to get as far as the side of the bed. There was an ache in her stomach she put down to her longing. Her longing to be with her lover. She fell to her knees. She leaned forward over the bed. She buried her face in her hands. She shivered with cold. *Let him kiss me with the kisses of his mouth.*

For a time she knelt there, her mind a strange blur of emptiness. The weariness in her limbs had tired her out. She would sleep tonight, she would sleep a while, gratefully, so that she could be fresh and alert again for her morning adoration.

She heard her name called, as if from a great distance.

"Gráinne!"

Her heart soared with joy. *Let my beloved come into his garden and eat the fruit of his apple trees.* She raised her eyes towards the window. She could see nothing but darkness. The faint glow in the sky from the lights of the town. She listened, intently, with her whole being. And she heard it again. Distant. But certain. Her name, called:

"Gráinne!"

Her name, called with love.

"Jesus!" she whispered into the darkness. She struggled to get to her feet. Oh she was weary, weary. She stood up, barely able to hold herself erect; she moved to the window. She leaned her arms against the window frame. She stared out, at the wall of darkness, at the soft glow from the town.

"Jesus!" she whispered the name again, into that darkness.

Almost immediately she heard the answer, faint, beloved, her name, called out loud with love:

"Gráinne!"

She pressed against the windowpane. *Arise, make haste, my love, my dove, my beautiful one, and come.* Her whole body trembled. She fumbled with the window-cords. The top of the window dropped a little. A wave of even colder air touched her. She gasped. Then she heard the voice again, closer now,

"Gráinne!"

The voice, familiar, touched her somewhere old and wounded and vulnerable still; and then again: "It's me! It's Jack! Jack Golden!"

For a moment she stood shocked, perfectly still, staring out into the blackness of the world. She was a butterfly, pinned, and then released and held, ready to be blown away into the darkness of the universe. She shivered, a quick, violent shivering. She put her hands to her face and screamed, a weak, shrill cry of terror. Then she fell, her body crumbling under her, like ash. She fell back onto the wooden floor of her room. A flame gone out. A fire dead. A moth, unpinned from the wall and allowed, at last, to float out into the air of the world.

Four

The old man sat quietly by the bed. He felt as if he had been sitting there for years. Forever. She did not stir. She would not stir. He might have to sit on forever, becoming a stone, becoming a skeleton, becoming a ghost. He dozed once, waking with a start, as if she had said something.

"What?" he called to her. "What did you say?"

But she had not moved. Her lips looked dry, dry as sand on a high beach. He dipped his finger in her jug of water and touched her lips with the water, gently, gently rubbing. Again. And again. There was no response.

Outside it was quite dark now and the light in the room seemed brighter. It was warm, too, comfortable. He could stay in this room forever. If only he could translate his panic into some other emotion. He imagined himself rising, younger and stronger than he was; he imagined her opening her eyes again, the way she had done if only for a moment, earlier on; he imagined the light in her eye that had given her consent. He would have leaned in over the bed and pulled the covers back, have put her dressing-gown about her shoulders and hoisted her into his arms, lifting her bodily from the bed, wrapping the gown about her, then he would have carried her away, out of this cell, down the stairs, out into the night, and away. He imagined all this, his old blood quickening in its pulsing through his body. He closed his eyes and imagined it, trying desperately, in the silence and the absence, to fill up the void.

He stood up, abruptly. He must not yield to despair again, he must not dwell on loss and sorrow. He must not grieve because grief does not change anything. He moved, slowly but restlessly, about the room, glancing at her often, hoping for some trace of movement, some signs of life. His eyes met his own body in a half-length mirror above her dressing-table. He was shocked. He looked, he could see, as pale and absent as she. He peered more closely at himself, at those eyes that had tiny suitcases of flesh hanging under them, at the few traces of hair that still struggled to grow where once he sported a moustache. Above all the neck, what a mess it was now of fallen flesh, hanging in useless strips like an old curtain. Scrawny, lank, lean, gaunt. He chuckled and stuck his tongue out at his own reflection.

"Ugly old bastard," he muttered aloud. "Ugly, foolish old bastard!"

The gaze that looked back at him, he knew, was still a keen gaze, perhaps keener than it had ever been before. He could see himself now, he could see himself as he really was. And what he saw was a man whose feet were planted firmly on the earth, whose flesh had filled out and then fallen back with age, an age that had filled up, like concreting a wall, all the little fissures through which his life had tried to attract light from other worlds. Now all such light was blocked out, forever, forever, by the hardening concrete of his blood. Feet on the ground. Planted. Firm. And so – finished!

He turned quickly, as if he had heard a change in the breathing of the old woman, as if he had sensed something. She seemed the same. He moved back, quickly, to the bed and spoke aloud to her again.

"I still believe you can hear me, I still believe you are

there. My darling. Maybe I'm just an old fool but I know that I'm an old fool. And you must know that you are still loved by this old fool. I have no illusions left, none. I will not carry you away from here, like a hero rescuing you from a burning castle. But wherever I am, wherever you are, I love you. I love you. And I will go on loving you. That is no illusion. It never was. My feet were always on the ground when it came to you."

He sat down again and reached forward eagerly and took her two hands in his own.

"I followed my dreams, darling, and so did you. We each followed our own visions, our own dreams. But we went separate ways. My fault. My fault. I admit it, to my deep heart's grief. We followed our visions but mine was always to become one with you. My other visions now are embarrassments in the old trunk of my life, I was hurrying after lights, after shapes of air, after dreams, but you were always the true light, the real shape, the real dream. And look at what these other visions have left me with, flesh like wet sand, crookedness in my limbs, a tick under my eye, the left side of my face turned up at the corner, and that awful dead weight lying like an ulcer on the floor of my stomach, my loss of you, a perpetual taste in my life like bitter lemon and sour cream. We die often, dearest love, we suffer many, many deaths, we endure them, pains and agonies and deaths, and we come out of them again, by painting them over with our dreams and our hopes and our visions, by filling up the emptiness we should carry about with us, filling up the emptiness with new visions, new dreams, so that we can call each death a victory. Oh yes, how I fooled myself down all those years, death upon death upon death, suffered and gone through – and then I was reborn, moving onwards after new dreams, convincing myself I was growing from victory to victory. It was a nightmare, darling, my dreams were all along a nightmare. Because I lost you.

"And now, dearest love, I plead with you from the deepest, most honest part of my soul, do not let me die in nightmare. I do not want to die in this old, ongoing nightmare. It is only you can save me from the nightmare. Only you. It is a question of being delivered from the self, that's all it is, that's the dream. And I have not been able to do it, not through all these long, heavy years. Not without you. I have been lacking grace. Without you. Without you. Gráinne. Gráinne. Gráinne."

There were tears on his face, now, tears. Real tears for which he was grateful. Softening the rock-hard ground that had been his life these last years. And yet she had not stirred. Her hands lying stone-still in his. He let her hands lie gently on the counterpane and he sat back, took out his handkerchief and wiped his face. He sniffled and blew his nose. But he had released something into the air about her life, something he had wanted to tell her, that he had to tell her. And she was with him still.

He sat another while watching her. All sounds seemed vague and distant. Sounds from the world outside were banished here. They were alone together, in a world between worlds. He knew what else he had to tell her. He leaned forward again, happily, and took her hands once more in his. A little reckless now.

"I'm going to tell you a little story now, an old story, to while away the time we have to wait. And I know you can hear me. I know it. So. Here we go.

"Once upon a time, yes, yes, once upon a time, darling, darling, darling, a long, long time ago . . ."

They had written the name in rocks on the headland that jutted out over the Atlantic Ocean, written it clear and big, in great rocks they had liberally covered with whitewash, EIRE, so that there could be no mistake, so that no plane, American, British, German, could fly in from the sea and, mistaking where they were, drop its load of death. For they were not part of this awful war, they were outside it, they were an island people, here on the Atlantic coast, where only echoes of that war came, faint but real, from a very great distance. As if all of it had been happening on the other side of a high, impenetrable wall. As if Ireland had grown so weary of its own wars down all the centuries that it could never, never contemplate arms again.

And now the war was over! And what had been left? Scars, great, deep scars. And even yet there were long claws reaching out from that great hell of death and suffering. Reaching even here, even this far. As if the human body, torn apart and dead, still jerked and reached out from its spasms. For if the human being does not go to war it seems the war will come to him, as if it were in the very substance of human flesh that it suffer the pains of war before it can be purified.

One evening, as he stood outside the Church after hearing confessions, Father Wall heard the low, deep growl of an aeroplane. Clouds were heavy over the island. At times a thin curtain of mist moved steadily across the fields. As usual. Comforting. Well known. There was little breeze. He watched into the grey and heavy skies. The drone grew louder. He could see nothing. It was a heavy plane, that much he knew, the sky seemed to throb under its force and he feared it. He blessed himself, muttered the name of Christ into the air. And then there was a terrific bang, a sudden, horrific crash that shook the very foundations of the island.

"Bombs!" he said aloud, and his heart almost failed him.

But then there was silence. A deadly, sudden and overwhelming silence. He knew at once that it was not bombs, he knew that the plane had gone straight into the side of the mountain, away up there, in the mists of the high hills. And still the greyness seemed to move about him, almost solid, almost tangible.

Father Wall moved quickly. At Flannery's stores he got Nora to use the telephone, to call up every available man on the island, women, too, those who were young and strong and willing. They were to go at once in the name of Christ to the rescue of whoever it was had broken their lives against the mountainside.

They were like pilgrims, then, the people of the island, climbing the high mountain slopes. All evening, and far into the night, the same men, and others, who had climbed into the RIC barracks many years ago, Patsy Mulqueen, Wheezy (The Wheeler) Wheelan, Mick Mulvanny, Seamus Sweeney, trudged up and down the mountainside, moving like ghosts along the dripping heathers and scutch grass, picking their way among the boulders and rough land, sinking in the soft, peaty earth, getting drenched to the very heart by the persistent mists, circling the black and silent corrie, to where the plane had crashed. They found seven men – young, clean-shaven, innocent. Dead. Their bodies strewn about the mountainside, broken, torn, shredded like the metal strips and heavy iron parts of the fuselage and engines of their plane.

It was a plane that had strayed from its reconnaissance task, strayed so far from the world of struggle into this remote island. An echo, merely, of what the world had suffered. A reminder. A warning.

All evening, and far into the night, Father Wall moved among them, encouraging them, cajoling them into further effort, bearing with them the ripped-open bodies of the young men on makeshift stretchers, laying them out on the benches at the back of his island church, trying to piece them together, to hide the horror of their dying from the children. He was strong and determined, speaking calmly to them, speaking of Christ and his cross, of suffering and its attendant glories.

"The body of a man must be worn to the bone to keep the flesh from dictating the pace," he told them, convincing himself, too.

And with him the same men laboured, older now, weary from their years and the weight they had had laid on them, up and down the mountainside, hardly speaking, stricken by the horror of these deaths. The mountainside smouldered under the mist. In the darkness of the night little fires could be seen. The women came, too, with torches and lanterns, uttering their little cries and working with a strength and austerity the men could only silently admire. Their expert hands, used to the tasks of midwifery and of the laying out of bodies, helped to straighten contorted limbs for the stretchers, their tears flowing silently for these unknown dead as they murmured prayers for the repose of their souls.

Cornelius Griffin was among the men, sweating and silent, his face registering the horror. He heaved and lifted with the others, his big, rough face barely able to contain the pain of what he was witnessing. And Mary Alice MacNamara was there, too, and he watched her, his lonely soul aching, his eyes slyly seeking her out, his silence pleading with the soaked mountainside to take him to itself. Mary Alice MacNamara was no stranger to death, and she, too, was stricken by the pilgrimage on the mountainside. Once she knelt beside Cornelius Griffin and watched as he hefted a broken body from among the rocks, great manly tears coursing down his big cheeks, the sweat of his effort glistening along his forearms, on his forehead, his eyes softened, her eyes stricken. Once, too, they paused and their eyes met, drawing them together, like a hand suddenly taking them and bringing them from mighty distances to touch one another. Softly. As if in promise. And atonement. As if out of the heaviness and misery of violent dying a strange new plant, a wild orchid, could blossom and survive the harshest winds.

And both of them, Cornelius and Mary Alice, were stung to silent admiration by the untiring labours of Father Wall, pastor, servant, priest. He had taken off his jacket, his waistcoat, his collar. His black trousers were soiled and wet with the mountain clay. There was blood mingled with the wet stains on his shirt. He did not seem to tire, returning with each stretcher to the church, coming back up the mountainside again to fetch more bodies. Striving, urging, working.

The young dead were English, they could tell from the uniform, from the small brass buttons with the embossed, brass crown. They could tell from the markings of the plane. Returning from some mission out over the sea, the clearing up of the awful battle ground of the twentieth century, only to end up under the quiet lights of candles in the island church, the wind stilled about them, the pale mists moving in a silence beyond silence, Father Wall speaking words of prayer over them, pleading with an absent and a demanding God that some small whisper of understanding might be afforded to him in this fierce world of agonising human flesh.

Cornelius Griffin worked sometimes, where Gráinne had worked, in the dark womb of the public bar. He was at home there, grinning, strong, in charge. Sometimes, too, he was sent in the car with messages, to the doctor's house, to the hotel, to the ferry, to the priest's house. He was reliable, quiet, strong.

A few days after the terrible crash on the mountain, he knocked on the back door of the presbytery with a box of groceries and Mary Alice MacNamara opened for him. She was beautiful, he had always known that. Tall and black-haired, her face bright and clear with wisdom. Made a little sombre, now, by the tragedy of the mountain, her eyes hurt with the memory of young bodies broken in death. Her body mined with the motion of time.

He stuttered a little before her. She smiled back into his face. He followed her into the kitchen with the box of groceries. She sat him down on the form beside the rough-wood kitchen table and offered to make him a cup of tea. He did not want tea. But he wanted to be near her. To watch her. He assented, nodding his great head.

"Father is out on a call. Won't be back for hours," she smiled at him as she busied herself near the Rayburn.

His big elbow rested on the table. His eyes rested on her body. Her back was to him. She took the hem of her skirt in her right hand and lifted the handle of the kettle

240

with it. The dress rose along her calves and Cornelius saw the white of her flesh, the tiny light hairs that stood on that flesh. She leaned in over the Rayburn. He saw her buttocks strongly outlined against her dress, the dress that rose above her hocks, hurting him, far, far down in his stomach. He realised she had turned her head and was watching him. He felt his face glow with shame. He had not asked a woman since Gráinne . . . She smiled.

"There now," she said, "won't be a minute. Are you in a hurry, Cornelius Griffin?"

"No," he answered, "no hurry. Just a few small deliveries left. Here and there. That's all."

She sat on the form beside him, her left hand resting beside his right hand on the wooden table. She watched into his eyes. She knew that he, like the other island men, was afraid of his own body, of the urges it cast up, of the force of his own desires. She was so bright, he thought, so beautiful, she knows so much, she is so very strong . . . and his own eyes moved away from hers, quickly, searching for something to hide in.

"You were wonderful up on the mountain," she told him. He blushed at once and rubbed the back of his wrist along his forehead.

"I saw tears on your face," she said, quietly. He pursed his lips and looked down at his knees. She moved a little, settling herself, and the flesh of her arm brushed against the flesh of his arm. He drew back, quickly, as if she had struck him.

She sighed.

"So, Cornelius," she pouted. "You don't like me?"

"What?" he gasped. Turning back towards her. Stunned into it. "Of course I like you. You're – you're, ah, beautiful."

When he had got it out he felt released, as if a word could take him and shake him and leave him free of something that had clogged him for years. He smiled at her. Oh God she was lovely!

"You were pretty good yourself, up on that mountain," he added.

She pressed his arm, gratefully.

"What's it like here?" he asked her, to escape. "I mean, in the priest's house." He giggled then. "I'd love to see the priest's house, I mean, is it – is it different?"

She laughed at him and caught him suddenly by the hand.

"Come on, then," she laughed. "I'll show you," and she led him, the way a teacher leads a pupil in school for the first day, down the long hallway. It seemed dark to him, a faint light coming in through the coloured glass diamonds in the front door. She opened the door of the priest's parlour.

"It's dark in here," he said, awed by the big dark-leather furniture, the high bookcases, the heavy curtains on the window.

"He sits by himself in here, reading, drinking, too, sometimes," she commented. Then she giggled again. "And I have to bring him in his bed-time drink – cocoa!"

"He takes a cup of cocoa before going to bed?"

"Yes, and not only that, but he takes liberties, too!"

He looked at her. She was still holding his hand, smiling up into his face. It felt good, holding her hand like that.

"What do you mean, liberties?"

"He touches me, he makes me sit on his knees, he fondles me through my clothes, touches my breasts, my bottom, that kind of thing!"

He was astonished, his face gone wide with wonder.

"The priest? Does that? And do you let him?"

"Oh yes, I don't really mind. He's a man, after all, he has his needs, too, God help him, and he's good to me, I mean he never really does any harm and I can ask him for whatever I want. And he's a good man. I know every man has his needs. Every woman, too. And there's no harm in it for him, he means no harm. He's a good priest, a strong priest, for the people. That's maybe because he knows the urges of the body. And then – " and she chuckled wildly at him, " – don't I fancy a bit of sex myself and never get any? Sure doesn't every girl like to be prodded and touched and loved?"

He did not know what to say, nor where to look. She was holding his hand, firmly. He looked around the room with new wonder, and gazed especially at the big, deep armchair where Father must have sat, this beautiful woman sitting on his knee.

"There?" he asked her, pointing. "Do you sit on him, there?"

"Sure, and I enjoy it, sometimes. I like to have my full weight on top of a man, you know, it gives me a sense of power, I can make him as happy as sin, and why not? It doesn't cost me anything. It feels good to have the whole weight of my body pressing a man down onto the earth. It feels good. Comforting, somehow. And it stirs me. And once I came in and found him stretched out on the couch beyond at the window, he had been having a nap or something, and he beckoned me over and I sat down on him, down on his chest, they way you'd sit down on the form in the kitchen, side-saddle like! And I laughed down at him and chatted to him, and I could see that he was

243

finding it hard to breathe, what with my weight down fully on his chest and he was loving it, every bit of it, poor man. Sure doesn't a lonely girl like myself have longings, too, and nobody around who can lift her out of the sorry emptiness of a priest's parlour?"

He gazed at her. She was radiant. With mischief. With innocence.

"God almighty," he breathed. "I never thought I'd see the day when I'd envy the priest his life!"

She laughed aloud and reached up her face and brushed her lips softly against him.

"You need not envy the priest anything, Cornelius Griffin," she taunted. "It's all there, you know, for the asking."

Then she dropped his hand and moved quickly out of the parlour, back down the hallway into the kitchen. He followed her, stunned, delighted. Shaken.

She poured boiling water from the kettle into a teapot and rinsed it out into the sink. He sat on the form again, watching her. She reached high and took down a tea-caddy from a shelf, spooning three spoons of tea into the pot. She looked over at him. She smiled and the smile warmed him through. She reached the tea-caddy back onto the shelf, her breasts strongly outlined as she stretched. Then she poured the water from the kettle into the pot and left it to the side of the Rayburn. She turned then, skipped a little, and sat down on the form beside him. She looked into his eyes. He was imagining the priest, Father Wall, the man he had so often confessed his most secret thoughts and longings to, stretched out on the leather sofa in the parlour, and this beautiful woman sitting down heavily on his chest. How wonderful that must have been, he was thinking, how wonderful, that lovely body, that weight, that lovely, full arse heavy on his chest.

She moved her hand then and laid it deliberately on his arm, holding him softly but firmly. She moved her hand up along the strong curve of his arm, knowing his strength, the smooth, firm flesh of his body.

"You're a fine cut of a man yourself, Cornelius," she smiled at him.

He grinned. He knew that. He was a man, strong, eager, and not evil. But he had never dared to fly. He had never learned how.

"Are you happy here, I mean, with himself, with Father?"

"Oh yes, in a way, happy enough. But he's a strange type. Not my kind of man at all. A bit soft, you know, and of course there's no future there, Cornelius."

"Future?" he stuttered. "How do you mean?"

"Well," she said, getting up again to fetch the cups, the jug, the cutlery. "If a girl is going to get married there's no use in hanging around a priest all day every day now is there? No real hope of return if you let a priest have the free range of your body. Free range . . ."

He smiled again at her lovely back, how her buttocks swelled out beautifully from below the belt about her waist, how her black hair flowed down over her back. As she stood before the Rayburn, waiting, her two hands came behind her and moved slowly on her buttocks, circling, caressing the cotton of her dress, stirring him the more towards frenzy. There was silence. Only the soft hissing of the kettle, the gentle come-hithering of her hands against her dress. She turned her head to watch him, her eyes on his eyes and he could not move, she kept her hands on her buttocks, caressing them. She smiled still.

"Would you ever take a fancy to someone like me, now, Cornelius, do you think?"

She asked it simply, with a little laugh to cover any embarrassment either of them might feel. His two fists felt hot and awkward, he rubbed them together, trying to ease the heat, trying to soothe the itch that was in them.

"Jesus, Mary Alice, sure the likes of you would never bother with someone like me!" He blurted it out, meaning it. She did not change her position.

"Well that's where you might be very wrong, Cornelius Griffin," she said firmly, her hands still kneading her own flesh through the dress, her buttocks firmly pushed towards him, welcoming him, taunting him, teasing him, driving him at once towards heat and chill. Then she stopped and her hands very, very slowly began to pull her dress up, slowly, slowly, as if distractedly, and she had turned back again towards the Rayburn, bending over it, bending well, allowing his eyes their freedom, allowing her own body its power, and the dress rose, slowly, over the hocks of her knees, over the frightening filling flesh of her thighs, up, up, up until he could see, pained and tensed and panicking, the luscious fullness of her buttocks, the soft white linen of the small pants she wore underneath. Holding her dress that way with her right hand, she moved her left and pulled that white pants tight, tighter still, making almost a white thong of them between her buttocks. She stopped that way, offering herself, promising, threatening and he could not stop himself, he shouted something incoherent to the kitchen walls, he leaped towards her and his hands clutched her buttocks, fondling them, and his face was buried in the soft, white linen of her underwear while she moved her flesh against him, pressing back against his face, driving him and herself into a frenzy of need and longing.

It was an ordinary morning. Mrs Golden was in the small meadow behind the house, hanging sheets out on her line. The line was tied to a tree on her right-hand side, and to a high nail on a shed to her left. In the centre was a long pole young Jack Golden had worked, years ago, to perfect; it was carved to a Y at the top, the bottom was pared to catch a hold in the soft earth of the meadow. Ted's meadow. Edward Golden's meadow, his space, his memory. How the years go by, leaving a weight on the life of those who go on living, under the clouds of their own, small islands.

The pole lay on the ground. The line sagged, dead and dulled, moored, the centre scarcely a foot above the ground. Mrs Golden hung two white sheets, one on either side of the centre, and two white pillow-cases. Then she put the Y of the pole under the line and hoisted it high into the air of that ordinary morning. She planted the pared end in the earth. The meadow had become a green ocean, the gentle breeze making waves, and a sailing boat floated on it, great sails and little pennants slapping and cheering in the ocean breeze. They were a great, white butterfly, wings spread to the clasp of grace.

"Where I am now, on this side," Mrs Golden told herself aloud, "is the present. The other side is the past."

She told herself that very often these days. In an effort to find some lift again out of the heaviness of the past. She watched the sheets for a while flipping and flopping in the breeze. Soon they would dry and the clapping of their hands would grow still, to a staid purity on the air. Mrs Golden was a sheet, bleached by her sufferings, hung out on the island to dry. She turned slowly towards the house.

She had grown old, too quickly, on her own. Her once tall body was stooped, her clothes were dark, her hair had grown grey and wispy. Too many burdens on her shoulders. Too many losses to support.

She could hear the mid-day bus, its engine heaving as it approached the long hill towards Golden's Cross. She paused at the back door to watch the bus go past. She heard it shuffle, change gears, slow down. It drew in by the gate to her yard, its green bulk panting. There was a long moment between times, Mrs Golden hovering between one world and the next, the bus paused, small puffs of its breath floating out on the air, the noon waiting. Someone was getting off the bus at her back gate. She had her right hand on the old loose knob of the door. When he turned from the bus and came towards her gate, Mrs Golden passed away from between her two worlds and fainted, crumbling down slowly on the concrete patch before the door.

Hurriedly, Jack Golden opened the gate, dropped his old suitcase, and ran, as well as his hurts allowed him, to gather up his mother. He lifted her. She was slight, but heavy. He pushed the door open ahead of him and carried and dragged her into the cool silence of the kitchen. He sat her down on the fireside chair and knelt before her, chafing her hands. Her eyes opened.

"Jack!" she whispered.

Then she shut her eyes and reached her hands towards him. Her fingers touched his face, his hair, his shoulders.

She opened her eyes again. She drew his face to hers and kissed him wildly on the face, on the forehand, the cheeks, the lips.

"They told me you were dead, Jack, they told me you were dead!"

He stayed there a long time, kneeling before her lap, while she touched his hair, his clothes, while she looked at him, looked into his eyes, ran her soul up and down his life, tears pouring down her face, tears on his cheeks, the world moving on again, slowly, gathering back its customary speed.

She cooked for him, hushing him, settling him back into the air about her. She grew younger, taller, straighter, she felt she could fly, she was a swan, like her sheets she was white and clean and pure, she could leave the earth and float in the breeze on an ocean of air. She fussed about him. He smiled up at her, watching her with wonder, watching the walls, the furniture, the familiar pictures on the wall, the small, red glow of the oil-lamp before the Sacred Pictures. She sat with him, then, watching how he ate, watching how he buttered his bread, laughing with delight as he drank his tea with the spoon still in the cup, though she had fought with him over it in the years on the other side of those hoisted white sheets on her line. She fed him, with anything that Mary Alice had brought of pleasure to the house, an orange, a chocolate bar, biscuits. She told him of her dream, of how he had come impossibly in and sat down to a meal at her table, how she had turned to the grate and the turf and how, when she looked back, he had just as impossibly disappeared. She would not look for one moment now, she laughed, towards the grate. In case he flew away again, like an angel, vanishing. Outside it was already afternoon, the dust of time settling where his miraculous footsteps had crossed the yard, tiny, invisible whirlpools of dust covering where she had fallen, his suitcase, forgotten, lying like an untruth where he had dropped it. Then they sat together, in the quiet of the old house, and he told her.

"I remember falling, falling, falling, the intensity of the heat all about my body, in my nostrils. The flames burned every wisp of hair I had, mother, even within my nostrils. But the fury of the fall, the way I cast my clothes off, the way I fell the last I don't know how many feet into the sea, even the parachute on fire, all of that and the waters of the sea saved me, and I remember nothing more, nothing. I know I must have floated in the sea, almost naked and badly burned, for some time. I was always a good swimmer, and something within me must have remembered that, and must have kept me afloat."

"It was God, Jack, it was God. The grace of God. I prayed for you, son, so often, so often . . ."

He reached forward again and took her hands, knowing the frail strength of them, feeling the life that trembled through her bones and flesh, trembled now with renewed vigour and determination.

"I fell like a meteor, they told me, some of the pilots who had seen my fall, trailing clouds of glory into the sea! I was picked up by a rescue launch oh I don't know how long after. They said I looked like a slab of concrete, charred and stiff, I was that cold, that burnt. But they could see I was alive. I was in hospital, in Kent, and they put me back together again. It seems I didn't come back to consciousness for a while. They didn't think I would make it. They said it was like stitching me together again, joining me up, taking strips off me and adding strips from other parts of my body. I'm scarred all over, mother, I'm ugly, my skin is white and ridged, but I'm alive and well. My right leg was very badly hurt and they've fixed that, too, but I'll always limp a little, and it will hurt me at times, I know that. But they brought me back to life. It was like starting to live all over again. Learning how. Learning again who I was. Learning my name. Discovering my past. Trying to see if there was a future.

"Because I could remember nothing, mother. Nothing. I had no identification. It was as if I had dropped out of the sky for the first time. No memory of anything, not of the accident, of the war, of you, or Gráinne, of the island, of home, nothing. That's why they didn't contact you, nobody contacted you, I was nobody, they couldn't know and I couldn't tell them. I had nothing left, nothing. Except my life.

"They were truly good to me. But it took a long time. As soon as I could move again they let me wander about the hospital grounds, around the wards, hoping someone might spot me, might know me. It was strange, I lived in a kind of bubble, knowing the names for things, knowing all that, but not knowing the names for my own life. I remember being in these strange, rough pyjamas, a light blue dressing-gown about me, even comfortable, brown slippers on my feet. None of it mine. None of it having anything to do with me. Around those fine hospital grounds, and all the world about me wholly unreal and insubstantial. I was feeling still as if I were drunk, drunk without being intoxicated. It was like living in a dream, understanding things, words, places, people, but not really being there, because I didn't remember anything, I was nobody. They had to tell me about the war, about all the casualties, and I could see them all around me, the awful wounds, I heard them at night coughing and calling and whimpering, sometimes the screams of those who were suffering most. I think I often screamed with them, I remember long periods of pain, like being on fire all over again, all over my body, but still it was as if it wasn't me, it was as if I was watching myself burn, watching from beyond a great barrier, there and not there.

"And then, one day when I was just wandering around, like a ghost, lost, unnamed, someone called a name: 'Jack!' Just that. Just the name, once, sharp and loud, 'Jack!' Like a sudden and vital crack in a pane of glass, and I was through, amazed, reborn, new. I knew it was me they were calling and I saw this man, stretched in a chair, his legs bandaged hugely, grinning up at me. 'It's Jack Golden,' he said to me and I knew at once then who he was, it was like the name was a key and the big doors creaked open. It was a man called Keane, Pearse Keane, he was Irish and we had been together at Cranwell. He was the first soldier I made friends with, the first man I flew with. I sat beside him, dumbstruck for a while, but gradually, as he prodded and pushed me, things came back, very, very slowly, like a tide coming in over flats, imperceptibly, yet every moment a little further in. In about a week's time, with Pearse's help, I had it all back, almost all. The world is still new and fresh to me, and things are still surfacing in my memory."

They sat together a long time, quietly, in the warmth of their own lives, their own company. Mrs Golden knew a happiness that was like a warm sunshine glow through her whole body. Had he been younger she would have taken him in her arms and held him tightly against her body to know the certainty of his weight and the solidity of his flesh against hers. But now it was enough to reach out and touch him every so often, his arm, his cheek, his hair.

And then he turned to her, as if he had been holding the moment at bay for long enough, he turned to her and his face was alert with expectation once again.

"And Gráinne?" he asked her. "How is Gráinne?"

"She's gone away," she answered him, reluctantly. He waited.

"Where? Gone away where?"

She looked at him. He was tensing towards her, his whole weakened body like a wild animal's, filled with expectation, with longing.

"She went to Rockford, to the nuns."

He was lost.

"The nuns? Rockford? Tell me, mother, where is she? What is she doing?"

"After you left, Jack, and after we got the telegram telling us you had been killed, Gráinne went away suddenly, in the middle of the night I believe, Cornelius took her in the car, she went to Rockford and joined the Sisters. The Little Sisters of Perpetual Adoration. She became a nun. She's a nun, Jack, she's in the convent. An enclosed order. She's a nun."

Jack stared at her while the words reached him, touching his skin from the outside at first, then slowly worked their way through his pores into his veins, touching his heart suddenly. He leaped to his feet.

"What! She can't do that! It's Gráinne, my Gráinne, Gráinne Flannery, she can't lock herself away from me like that. I need her, mother, I'm in love with her. I need her. I can't let her become a nun. I can't let her."

As he went towards the back door of the house, Mrs Golden saw him limp, how pathetic he looked, thin, dishevelled, lost again, lost to her and to himself at that moment. He turned back suddenly, from the door, restraining himself. Growing more clear. More certain.

"Where is she, mother, where exactly is she?"

She told him. And he turned from her, quickly, without another word, and was gone.

Cornelius drove him, without questioning him, glad to welcome him home, offering him friendship, care, forgiveness. He was a hero, home from the wars, wounded, but alive, and home. Jack urged him on, pushing the old car to groan and strain in its efforts to cross the counties.

They spoke little on the way, Jack's body too frayed and tense, his mind too hot and anxious. There would be time . . .

When they reached Rockford it was already dark. Cornelius drove slowly, turning in from the main road, up the hill beyond the railway station, up through the trees until they came out along a narrow street, one great, high wall along their left. Cornelius pulled the car in under the trees, pointed to the main door of the convent, and waited. Jack, impatient still, got out of the car and limped hurriedly across the road. There was an idle rustling of rooks and daws among the high foliage of the trees. He rang the bell at the convent door, pulling on a heavy, iron handle. He could hear his call echo somewhere far off in the hollows of the building. He waited. There was silence. From somewhere high in the trees came a restless movement of unsettled birds. He rang again, pulling the iron more urgently, needing a response. Above him a jackdaw complained and flew out suddenly into the darkening sky. He heard a distant shuffling sound behind the door, and then it opened. An old woman servant stood, peering out at him from around the door.

"I want to speak to Gráinne Flannery," he said loudly. "She's now called Sister Mary, I believe. It's urgent. You can tell her it's Jack Golden come to see her. Jack Golden has come back home. Must speak with Sister Mary. Please, please, please! Please hurry."

The old woman continued to stare out at him, holding the edge of the door in both her hands. Behind her he could see the faintest of lights glowing. Her mouth was open. She was ugly.

"Can I speak to her? Please!" he insisted.

"You can't speak with the sisters!" she said, as if the whole world should have been aware of the fact.

"But I must speak with her. It's terribly, terribly important. You just tell her it's Jack Golden. That's all. Jack Golden. She'll want to see me, I promise you."

The old woman grinned foolishly at him.

"You'll have to speak to Reverend Mother so," she offered, opening the door only a little wider. He pushed past her, impatiently. She closed the door behind him.

"Wait here," she said, pointing to a dark-wood seat beside another door off this high, dark hallway. She shuffled through a second door, closing it carefully behind her. He stood, impatiently, in a trap of silence. Only a small lamp burned in an alcove to his right. He could hear the sound of his own, urgent breathing. In the bowels of the building, as if it were a great way off, he heard a door close. Then silence again. He waited, shifting impatiently from one foot to the other, his head moving restlessly, seeking point. At last, he could hear movement behind the door to his left. He waited for it to open. He heard iron bars being shifted and then a small aperture opened in the centre of the door and he could see bars, like the bars of a prison cell, and beyond it only darkness. He peered into that darkness but could see nothing.

When a voice spoke to him from that emptiness he was startled and jerked back from the door so suddenly that a flame of hurt went up through his injured leg.

"What can we do for you, sir?" The voice was quiet, old, mellow. He felt a great patience in it, a kindness, a gentleness that touched him to some patience himself.

"My name is Jack Golden," he began, talking to the dark bars in the door. "I am a very good friend of Gráinne Flannery, em, Sister Mary, I believe she is now. I'm just home from being injured in the War and I must speak with Gráinne. Please. Can you ask her?"

There was silence for a while, so that Jack began to wonder if there was anybody still there, behind the grille. Then the disembodied voice came again.

"Sister Mary has joined our order, sir, of her own free will. She has taken her first vows. Vows of poverty, chastity and obedience. Vows of perpetual adoration and of silence. She has removed herself from the world. She cannot see anybody. She will not see anybody. Except close family in exceptional circumstances. Ours is an enclosed order. We do not speak with – "

Jack huffed impatiently.

"But I haven't seen her for years, and I know she'll want to see me. You see, she must think I was killed in the war. You must let me see her, you must. Please."

"I'm very sorry, but the rules of our order strictly forbid it. Sister Mary is now a contemplative sister and must not be intruded upon. If you wish to write to her you are free, of course, to do so. We shall read and discuss your letter should you write. And I beg you, sir, to maintain silence as many of the Sisters will have retired for the night."

Jack was stunned as the grille before him closed again, gently. He heard the shifting of iron bars behind the door. He was left standing in the high hallway, he felt impotent before her gentle insistence, his hands bunched into fists, his breathing loud and harsh. He could not believe he had been abandoned. He knocked gently on the door where the grille was. There was no answer. Then he knocked more loudly. He could sense the noise of his clamour like a terrible rattle about the house and he backed away quickly, opening the main door to the world outside. He backed out into the night, hearing at once the faint noise of the town below the convent. There was a soft breeze blowing through the trees.

He gazed up at the walls of the convent. Not a window was lit. To the left and right of him a high wall stretched, a wall he could never hope to climb. He stood back and searched for any movement in the windows of the building beyond the wall. He could see only the higher windows. He crossed to the other side of the street and walked slowly along, watching over at the building. There was no light, no movement, nothing. He felt as if he were a prisoner, then, a prisoner locked into the world, locked out and away from what he prized most in life. And a great fear and loneliness hit him, a great longing for the gentle and reassuring presence of Gráinne Flannery, his love, his only love.

He called her name, then, aloud, into the evening.

"Gráinne!"

The sound echoed off the high walls of the building. Birds stirred again in the high branches of the trees. Jack walked further along on the opposite side of the street, watching for a light, for a response. Behind him, Cornelius got out of the car and stood, leaning against it, watching him. Jack did not care. His need was frightful. He called again, more loudly.

"Gráinne!"

Her name, called with need, with desperate need.

For a moment he was sure that he saw someone move behind one of the windows and he stopped, staring at the window. He could not be sure. All was darkness. He called again, then, as loudly as he possibly could, calling into the darkness of his despair, calling into the great desert of his loneliness.

"Gráinne!"

He would be insistent. He knew he had been offered another chance to live. He would not easily let it go.

He crossed the street again and stood in under the high wall, below where he had thought he had seen movement.

"Gráinne!"

A long, lingering call.

"It's me! It's Jack! Jack Golden!"

There was a sudden rush of rooks from the high trees below the convent grounds and then Jack heard a scream from the high walls of the building, a faint, terrible scream that chilled him to his very heart.

She lay, like a block of ice that had melted and lay spread out on the earth, still, hopeless. Scarcely reflecting any light from the great, wild world. For days she lay and did not know anything. Stopped. Halted. Her life poured out.

And then the fever came, a heat like that of a desert sun, a dry, drying heat and her pool of water steamed and began to dry up. They feared for her, then, greatly. The nurses that came and ministered to her, passing like turtle doves through a faint dusk, feared greatly for her. Passing. Watching over her. Offering some touches of moisture, some coolness.

Jack Golden sat by her hospital bed, hours on end, watching her and scarcely speaking. And sometimes they came and shooshed him away, gently, while they tried to minister to her. Sensitive to his hurt as they were to hers. Jack sat, intent upon her, sometimes whispering endearments to her, sometimes pleading with her. And she was not there, she seemed to be shrivelling before their eyes. Burning up. And Jack saw that sad, small skull, bare almost and sorry from the terrible loss of the great loveliness of her hair.

Until the heat turned what had been left of the water into some stirring of life. She became a worm, then, wet and long and flesh-coloured, restless, ugly, despised. She was a larva, a caterpillar, beginning to feed on what was around her, repellent in her scents, her sweats, her drivelling, but they knew that now at last she was growing into something. Emerging out of somewhere. Jack watched her, and he saw the change in her and he was heartened. He began to talk to her, then. He began to mention names and places and things, the boat, the cat, Cornelius, even the butterflies and moths he knew she had kept on the cabbage-green wall of her attic room. To reach her. Wherever she was. To reach her and give her back her name, Gráinne Flannery, and to give her back her life. Sometimes she opened her eyes and watched past him, watched towards the high corners of the hospital room where the sun cast strange shadows and shifting colours. Often she twisted and turned under the sparse sheets they had over her, as if they were a burden to her, as if she would cast them off like casting off a skin, or a life.

"We used to give names to our planes," Jack was saying. "Most of the men called their planes after girls. Judith. Helen. Mavis. Joan. I called mine after birds, sometimes after your butterflies, your moths. Do you remember your butterflies? Names like *Swallow*, *Red Admiral*, such names. And the last one I called after you. *Gráinne* I called it and she was the best, the most powerful and I felt supreme in her, up above the clouds, supreme and safe and happy."

Her eyes were empty. She was gone still, squirming in some cocoon of unawareness, hiding. She was a pupa, resting from the awful predations of the world. Days more. A week. Waiting. Resting. Breathing deeply. And Jack would come and sit beside her, not daring to touch her, watching that body very slowly grow from its pale colour of near-death, to a hesitant oyster white, then towards a cream, and the slow, slow dawning of pink on her flesh was a joy to him. She was resting, resting after her long, long wars. It is a question, Jack knew, a question of being delivered from the self.

And then, one day, when Jack came into the ward he knew something had changed, some great new transformation had occurred. She was a moth, her cocoon discarded, she had bloomed at last and suddenly, back into life. Emerging from her silence and her rest almost overnight. Blood flowing again, flowing into the veins of her wondrous wings. She was wet, still, wet and shivering after the long struggle. Soon, her wings would begin to flutter. They would gain strength. She would fly. She would be beautiful again, eyes like jewels, wings strong and enamelled into loveliness.

Jack's loneliness had faded while he was able to sit by her, talking to her, calling her back. He was often alone with her, watching her come back out of the grave into new life. Today he hesitated at the door to her ward; the nurses moved with a little more ease, he could see Gráinne propped up in her bed, her head fallen sideways onto her shoulder, but they had dressed her in a pink cotton cardigan and the flowers he had left by her bedside looked fresh and filled with sunshine. He sat at her bedside and was quiet. She lay still, her breathing strong and regular, her features quietened. All morning he watched and waited. He left at noon to allow the nurses their space and freedom.

She was coming back from a great way off, a large, beautiful moth, her wings grey and powerful, decorated with wondrous, purple patterning. She knew she was resting, pausing on some dark foliage, waiting for flight. What she could remember most was darkness, a chill cocoon of darkness where she had swollen and grown towards this shape. She shuddered as she remembered it, how she had been constricted, locked away in darkness, a grub, a worm, a death.

She opened her eyes. The room was painted a primrose yellow. The sun shone in aslant from the world outside, filling the ward with a delicious, fruitful silence. She lay for a while, at peace. In the distance somewhere steel instruments scraped against a steel tray. There were flowers beside her, in a glass bowl on the small table beside her bed. She was not foolish enough to have forgotten totally what had gone before. It seemed to her now like a nightmare, a nightmare of her own making. She sighed deeply. It seemed to have burst apart only yesterday. But she knew it had been longer, her body knew it, and her mind. She had escaped. She heard footsteps pass on a corridor outside. Dust-motes stirred in the rays of sunshine. The curtains on the window were almost transparent, daffodil-yellow, with great orange blossoms. She smiled at them. They were beautiful. The day was beautiful. The world was beautiful.

When Jack arrived punctually after lunch, he pushed the door open and was surprised to see her sitting out at the side of the bed. She looked well, a little lost in the vast spaces of the hospital, but she looked well. She looked up at him. He smiled at her.

"Jack!"

The word came from her like a cry of surprise. He noticed how her face went pale, very, very pale, and her hands bunched into small fists on the covering of the bed.

"Hello, Gráinne!" he offered, quietly. "I'm so happy to see you looking so well."

She looked away from him. She was trembling. Then, to his surprise, slowly and very deliberately, she reached across the bed and touched the bell-push at the head of the steel bars of the bed. Jack moved softly into the room. He had fresh flowers in his hand, wrapped in cellophane, a bunch of rich, exotic lilies. He stood, looking down at her, lost again for words. She did not look up. She was waiting.

The door opened suddenly and there was a nurse bustling towards her. Firm, certain. A white breeze.

"Nurse," she said, in a very firm voice. "I want to make it quite clear that this gentleman is not to be allowed to visit me here. I do not want him in the room."

"What!" Jack said. The nurse turned to look at him. Gráinne was looking away, out through the window towards the sunshine.

"This gentleman has been to see you every day, Miss Flannery," the nurse offered. "He has been very good, watching over you, he has been very kind to you . . ."

"Please nurse, please. It is he who was the cause of my suffering," Gráinne said in a low, tense voice, filled with anger. "Of all my suffering, all my life. It is he who has ruined my life and he must not be allowed into this room again. I do not want to see him."

The nurse turned towards Jack, sadness and a little embarrassment on her face. She shrugged her shoulders and reached one arm to touch him.

He was lost. Utterly lost. He knew a sudden stab of pain in his damaged limbs and he gasped. He could see that Gráinne was wholly determined, her body set against him, her face turned from him, her mind and spirit locked away from him. Time, he thought, he must only allow her some time, for her strength to return, for her mind to come to terms with all that had happened. For her wings to grow strong.

Awkwardly he handed the flowers to the nurse and began to back away towards the door.

"Gráinne," he began, "I'm sorry . . . I didn't know . . ."

She did not move. Her arms were folded over her breast. She looked frail, very frail, but he knew how strong she was, how determined. He touched the knob of the door. The nurse was already fussing with the flowers, unwrapping them, fumbling with the cellophane.

"Please take the flowers away, nurse," Gráinne said, speaking quietly but firmly.

Jack opened the door and went out, dazed, into the corridor.

It was high summer of the following year when Father Wall performed the marriage ceremony for Mary Alice MacNamara and Cornelius Griffin. The priest gloried in the occasion. He admired the fine build and confidence of the young man. He already knew the beauty of the woman. He was happy for them, and he was happy for himself. There are so many things a man cannot fight against and win, not by himself, not when the flesh is so weak. What a man needs, he knew, is to be freed from the demands of the self and it is only grace, the material and urgency that comes from outside the self, that can effect the cure. Father Wall had decided he would not take another housekeeper. He would fend for himself in the silence and solitude of his home. He would continue to fight his exile, his exile in the flesh and when he was freed from the flesh he would soar high into God's kingdom.

Father Wall stood before the couple and smiled down upon them. Behind him the altar was a carnival of flowers. The priest's vestments were white with fine patterns of gold thread embroidered in sacred shapes.

"Before thou inquire," he said to the gathered people, "blame no man: and when thou hast inquired, reprove justly. Before thou hear, answer not a word: and interrupt not others in the midst of their discourse. Strive not, my dear friends, as the wonderful book says, strive not in a

266

matter which doth not concern thee, and sit not in judgment with sinners. Meddle not with a multitude of matters: and if thou be rich, thou shalt not be free from sin: for if thou pursue after thou shalt not overtake: and if thou run before thou shalt not escape."

Exactly one month later Father Wall performed another marriage ceremony, for Gráinne Flannery and a young doctor from the countryside about Rockford, Doctor Angus Walshe. Gráinne had come home from hospital, subdued, pale, smaller-looking than before. For weeks they did not see her, she kept to the store, to her room, in her attic. It was no great surprise to Father Wall when the young doctor arrived on his doorstep with Gráinne, both of them ready to discuss whatever arrangements would be necessary. They wanted to be married. Soon. He was a fine looking man, intelligent, handsome, dull. He would make a good husband. A good father. They would live in a small town in the midlands, where Doctor Walshe was getting a practice. Where the wild messages from the Atlantic Ocean could never reach. Where there was no salt on the wind and no bickering sea birds screamed. Where the only storms would be inland storms, where there would come no tempests, no exotic wild birds blows off course by Atlantic winds. They would be happy. Settled. Their feet planted firmly on solid ground.

Once again Father Wall exulted in his office. Already the summer exuberance had begun to lag, the first faint tinges of autumn had touched the leaves and the fruits. He turned once more to face an eager congregation.

"The peaceable had a vineyard," he quoted, "in that which hath people: he let out the same to keepers, every man bringeth for the fruit thereof a thousand pieces of silver. My vineyard is before me. A thousand are for thee, the peaceable, and two hundred for them that keep the fruit thereof."

Standing in a dim alcove at the back of the Church was Jack Golden, his hands held loosely before him, his body stooped, his eyes on the shifting lights from the high, stylised window.

"Look," he said deep down within himself, as one of the angels before the throne shone and seemed to move under a shifting, rich emerald light, "look, I'm a bird, I'm a bird. Watch me fly away south where the potatoes grow big as boulders on every bush and tree and flower . . ."

She disappeared then, out of his life, took flight and left him. Left the island, the county, her family; left her attic room, her kitchen garden, left the store. Definitively. Not like the swallows or the swifts, not like the white-fronted geese nor the brent, for she would not return with the seasons. She had gone, as if the sea had swallowed her, as if the horizon had melted her into its heart, as if the sky had sucked her away into its blue absence.

Jack could not cry. There was nothing he could offer the world now in exchange for peace. He sat so long, so still that once a small red squirrel came and sat on a branch above him, its tail stiff and unsubstantial as a thought, its eyes wide and wondering. And he stared back and was not interested. He was not moved. He did not care. Day after day he sat, idle, so that his mother began to wish he had not come back to her from the grave.

And the life she had regained began to slip away from her again. Slip out of her grasp as if her hands were wet with soap. Jack knew it. He knew it and he cursed himself, his lack of strength, his lack of grace. He felt heavy in himself, as if all his bones had grown thick and leaden, and his flesh had become sodden, like wet paper.

In the meantime he moved where she whom he loved so much and so poorly had moved, spending long hours in the dark cockpit of Flannery's pub, sitting on one of the hard forms along the wall, accepting the black stout from the hand of Cornelius Griffin.

"Jack," the big man would say, kindly, "how's Mrs Golden today?"

"Fine, Cornelius, she's just fine."

There would be a pause, caution opening slowly like a flower.

"Must be some meadows need cutting up at your place, Jack?"

"Must be, Cornelius, must be."

Another pause. Caution still supreme.

"Need a hand with them some day? I could come and . . ."

"Thanks, Cornelius, and no thanks. I can still take a meadow down, in spite of my broken wing. Thanks all the same."

"Don't mention it, Jack. Thought I'd offer. It's a grand place, Mrs Golden's place. A grand place."

And Jack turned from the bar and carried his stout back to the wall. The meadows swelled and swayed in the winds and grew silver under the summer sun and then yellowed, and drooped and fell down upon themselves, choking, gasping, drowning out the chances of next year's growth. Rushes flourished and the quickens in the hedges grew hard and brave and moved slowly out to invade the fields. Like bandits. Grown arrogant and self-assured. Even the hares grew big and bold, advancing into the kitchen garden as if the fruits and vegetables there had been planted only for their sake. Mrs Golden had grown too feeble to care, she had grown too sad to protest.

When Mrs Golden fell ill, Jack sat by her bed for a long, long time. She had taken to the bed in the tiny back room at the end of the twisting hallway, because she had found it impossible to climb the stairs to her own room. The room filled up again with her own ghosts, with the ghosts that haunted her poor son, and with the ghosts that had ridden on Sir's shoulders for the last, sodden years of his life. Sometimes Jack saw them, they lifted the latch on the window and stirred the curtains and climbed in, their silent laughter preceding them, the cold damp wind of their presence filling the room quickly. These were the dead, the skeletal people, flesh falling from them in long strips, they were the war dead, their eyes bulging out of their heads, their skulls blackened, their teeth and jaws breaking out of their chins and cheeks. Alive still, in his soul. Grinning at him. Accusing him. Accusing him. Pointing their sharp fingers at him, and whispering.

She saw them, too, the same ghosts, and she welcomed them, her own thin arms reaching to them, pleading with them that she might join them, might be swept away like a wisp of wind among their fine storm, and then she prayed that she might be left a while longer because every day she stayed on earth Jack stayed by her and did not spend his hours in the black hold of the pub. There was silence in the room, only her harsh breathing, and Jack's, sometimes even harsher.

Often he would lean in over her where she lay, sweating and cold, shivering and deathly still, and his lips would brush softly against her forehead and his hand would move light as a petal through the tiny wisps of her grey hair and she would try to smile her love to him but she knew that all he could see would be a crooked turn of her face, a small, pathetic leer. And she would try to move her hand, her hand that weighed as heavily as the house about her, and touch his own to tell him, to plead with him, to touch, touch, touch.

271

Jack spread the white cloth out on the little table beside the bed, he brought the two death-candles, already burned half-way down, tear-tracks hanging on to their sides, and he brought the little jug of death-water. Mrs Golden groaned and suffered. The final order of flesh falling apart. She closed her eyes and sweated, soundlessly.

After Father Wall had prayed over her, had sprinkled her with the oils that ease the passage through the rough, sandpaper duct into death, had touched her with the healing fingers of the dead Christ, she seemed to grow calm for a moment, like a baby bathed and powdered and oiled, at peace before the gentle moments of sleep. Jack sat on, watching the tiny lift of his mother's body under the bedclothes, grateful for the seeming ease of her breathing. He watched for a long time. Then he dozed.

He woke suddenly when she spoke to him. She was rising in the bed, hoisting herself up slowly to a sitting position, looking at him and smiling. She was white, as if every drop of blood had poured away into the earth. Her eyes were bright, blue and gleaming like a summer sky after rain. Her hands were twigs fumbling at the sheet. He jumped up to fix the pillow behind her head. And then her hand touched his and the chill of her flesh hurt him deeply.

"Do you know what I'd love, Ted?" she said in a firm voice.

"It's Jack, mother, Jack."

"I'd love just a small sip of boiled water that has been let cool a little. Can you get that for me, Ted? Please. With just a pinch of sugar melted in it?"

He looked at her. She was gazing up at him and smiling as if she had no care at all in the world.

"How are you feeling now?" he asked her.

"I'm feeling fine, Ted, fine, thank you. I'm like a bird, now, a small bird, maybe a wren, maybe a goldcrest, and I feel that only a tiny, tiny thread is holding me down. I feel great. Ready to fly. What I want you to do is to fix the sheet firmly about me. I'm on the other side of the sheet, Ted, fix it for me, please. Now, Ted, just get that little drop of water, there's a good man."

Jack settled her against the pillow. She folded her hands together and rested them against the sheets. Laid on top of the white sheet that he smoothed out and tucked in about the bed. Bird-claws, he thought, and that look in her eyes! She is seeing something else already, some other world, she is floating above the earth, looking down on it and it has shrunk to the measure of her distance from it.

When he came back, a small glass of tepid water in his hands, glad to think that maybe she might also eat something now, she was still sitting as he had left her, propped up against the pillows, her head resting and tilted a little to the side but he could see at once that she was dead. There was a silence in the room, a silence about her person that was tangible. All the ghosts had gone, leaving only a small shivering in the lace curtains before the window. Jack stood a long while, absorbed in that silence, envying her, almost, her quiet. She was so frail now, as if only a small percentage of her had been left at the end, the rest having flown long before, he thought a breath of wind could lift her.

They laid the coffin in the kitchen. When everything was prepared Jack hoisted his mother in his arms and carried her, out the narrow door of the little room, down the hallway, into the kitchen. She was a bundle of skin and feathers, he thought, his body not even slightly bent under her weight. The mourners in the kitchen were wholly silent as he laid her down in the coffin, straightening the shroud about her with infinite gentleness. He remembered the words of Patsy Mulqueen in this same kitchen a lifetime ago: "The dead are heavy, and it serves to quicken their sinking into the soft womb of the earth." But he knew differently, he knew that the weight of suffering her son had laid on her had been lifted by her death and that now she was free to soar into God's open, breathlessly high, turquoise purity.

Jack Golden allowed three days for his mother's presence to be quit of the house. He opened all the windows, the Atlantic winds hummed and hammered their way through, leaving the house purified and empty. He sat alone, listening, through the early hours of the night until his eyes closed almost by themselves and he dragged himself wearily to bed. He was waiting for some word, some word whispered so deeply within the darkness and the silence that he would recognize it at once and know what to do. But there was no word, no whisper of grace, and he sank more and more heavily into his own, willed gravity of purpose.

On the fourth day he pulled out his father's, Ted's, old trunk and he rummaged around inside it. Touching the past, that old, dead, heavy-weight past. His fingers touched the old, old pistol. He paused. Looking at it. In the afternoon he brought it with him to the lake below Flannery's Stores. He took the pistol and flung it, high, into the air. For a moment the sunlight gleamed off its metal as it flew, a small bird, out over the water. He laughed sadly as he remembered the kittens. The pistol fell with a dull splash into the water and the ripples quickly disappeared.

He locked the house and locked the gate behind him. He stood at the crossroads and waited. He sat alone on the bus, watching and not seeing the dead winter fields about him. The day was cold. There was a searing wind that was the advance guard of winter, the rain, driven by whips, was an admonitory rain, threatening piercing cold. The bus windows fogged before his eyes. He did not care. He did not wipe them clean.

At noon the bus reached the small square of the little midland town. The day had stilled to a steady cold and the rain had faded. He walked, alone, limping, up the street, past the station, out under old, high trees, along by a high demesne wall. He stood awhile, under the trees bared of any nests, bared of leaves, and huddled himself inside himself, listening, wondering. The walls dripped their moisture. He grew heavier and heavier within himself. So that at last he had to shake himself, force himself into movement lest he become a tree, a stone wall, a living death.

He enquired at the post office and then took a small, partly tarred, partly sand-gritted road, out from the town, moving at first between high elms that stood naked and still, as if they were watching him. Then the road began to climb and the trees gave way to bushes. He topped a hill and there below him was a lake, gleaming dully, like lead, under the early winter sky. He stopped a moment. It could be a lovely place, he knew that, a hideaway, a backwater. The surface of the water was calm, unruffled, easy. He walked on again, more slowly, the road descending always now, down towards the fields that bordered the lake.

By the time he reached the house it was already dusk, the days short, the nights long. There was a gateway. He opened the gate, careless of its grating and complaining whine. The earthen pathway wound away slowly among

oak trees, a wire fence keeping the fields from the trackway.
There were car-tracks already gouging their will into the
earth. For a while, as he walked, the lake was invisible.
Then he turned a corner and at once both house and lake
appeared, the water now only a pool of deeper darkness
beyond the darkness of the gardens. The house was a two-
storeyed, country house, lights shining from a window
downstairs. A heavy, squat, ancient house, built in the time
of the invader, for the comfort of the invader. He expected
to hear the barking of dogs, it was a house like that, a house
that ought to be bathed in gentle moonlight, a house that
ought to be brightly lit with the sounds and glitterings of
celebration, but everything was still, still with the tension
of a settling frost.

For the first time Jack stopped. He pictured himself
knocking at the door. He pictured Gráinne opening it. She
would scream at him and slam the door shut in his face. Or
she would go pale and still as death, ask him politely what
he was looking for, send him away with her coldness in his
pocket. Neither of these could he face. Neither.

And if Angus Walshe opened the door what would he
say to him?

" – I'm here to see your wife, to try and convince her to
come away with me, to tell her that I love her – " ?

A deeper sadness settled on his soul as he came up
against the great blank wall of his future. He must do
nothing to drive her even further from him. If ever he were
to have a chance, even to say to her, for he had never really
said it, never, never said it, *Gráinne, I love you, I have always,
always loved you* . . . then he must be sure that she would at
least listen, and know that perhaps it was, after all, true.

He was shivering now with the cold, his black greatcoat

drawn tightly about him, its collar turned up under his chin, his hands thrust deeply into the pockets. He moved, slowly and cautiously, around the side of the house. There was a yard, some outhouses, a stable. Already the cobbles of the yard were slippery with frost. Soon it would be deeply dark, there would be stars, sharp and deadly as thorns, still and demanding and threatening. He could make out the shape of a high hedge behind the house, he knew the lake must be beyond, close, he imagined he could hear its lapping, soft and careful, not like the male and majestic certainties of the sea.

As he came round the back of the house he was surprised to see a much brighter light. It came from a conservatory, a soft, yellow light that lit up the white framework, the scant furniture within, the plants idling away the winter. He moved ever more cautiously towards it. And stopped.

Gráinne was sitting in a wicker chair, wrapped in the soft light of the conservatory. She was still, gazing away towards the lake, though Jack knew she could not possibly see anything out beyond the glass. He crept, very carefully, to the edge of the conservatory. There was a bush of escallonia growing at one corner and he crouched behind it, watching. She was alone. Should he appear now, out of her reverie, he would come as a ghost comes, carrying the foul stench of the past with him, a past he knew he had mishandled, allowing her to slip through his hands into the darkness of another man's life.

She wore a long, grey dress, she wore a thick, woollen cardigan, she sat, her hands resting idly on her lap. She did not move, barely blinking her eyes. Jack watched her, freely, scarcely daring to breathe. Once she looked up, suddenly, as if she had heard something, an owl's scream from the distance, a night bird flying and crying low over the lake, the deep, heart-wrenching scream that grew and grew within Jack's breast in the darkness outside. Perhaps she had heard the awful drumming of his heart, the iron crying from his soul. She gazed almost to where he was, his hiding heart, his body heavy as a boulder, his dreams fallen like a pool about his feet. For a moment they almost looked into one another's eyes, he fancied he could see himself in those soft green eyes, he knew she was in his eyes, would be there forever. Then, slowly, she rose from her chair and turned towards the house. She moved heavily, too, very heavily. Jack could see, then, that she was pregnant, her hands resting on the mound of her belly. She opened the door to the house from the conservatory. Then the light went out and Jack remained alone in the darkness of his despair. Her life had moved too far away from him, too far away while his own had remained static, even dead. He could not reach her now. She was gone from him, gone as surely as his own mother had gone into the realm of the dead.

He stood up straight in the darkness. He turned from the conservatory and moved away around the angle of the house. He rounded the front of the house and began to move slowly back down the laneway towards the gate. He did not look back, not once. He followed the laneway by its ruts and clay and reached the gate. He heard and registered somewhere within him the deathly groan of its iron, its insistent clang as he drew it shut. He turned away from the gate and crossed the rough, damp earth that led towards the lake. There were a few gnarled trees and he stood among them, watching the water, listening to its patient breathing in the darkness beyond him. A few stars were visible, and in the distance the lights of a house. If he could walk away over the water now, away endlessly over the water, walk into non-existence, he would be at peace.

He walked to the water's edge. It lapped lightly against the shore. He stepped into the water. The coldness took him instantly. There was a boat tied up close to him, a small rowing boat. He untied it and shoved it out on the water. There were no oars. He climbed into the boat and lay on the hard boards. There was water about his body but he did not care. It began to drift, with whatever little wind there was, out onto the darkness. He closed his eyes, remembering his flight away up above the clouds, those days when he had shut the engine off and exulted in the glory of the purity he found there. Now the coldness was the same, pure and demanding and all-embracing. Let that purity take him now, let it draw him slowly into its cold heart, forever.

The boards on the base of the boat were hard, there were boards for seating, he was uncomfortable and shifted often. He did not raise his head. The boat drifted out slowly over the lake, the quiet fingering of the water against the keel was gentle and quizzical. Sometimes he opened his eyes and watched up against the night sky. He was so deeply sad he had grown numb. Indifferent. The stars were beautiful in their remote glittering, and once he thought he glimpsed a star shoot across the range of sky he could see. When the cold had almost burned his body into total numbness he felt almost at peace, he felt that this despair that he was drifting on would take him to its heart where he could disappear, gently, and be forgotten.

The boat drifted, out and out across the lake. Once it bumped softly against the grassy bank of a small island. Jack scarcely felt the bump. He was passing away into a silver blankness that welcomed him. Even the shivering of his body had ceased. He kept his eyes closed. He did not feel now that he could open them again.

By midnight clouds had begun to cover the sky and a small wind was gathering on the tops of the hills, preparing its descent. The lake surface rippled more angrily, the boat stopped and began to swirl, slowly, slowly. As the clouds moved over the face of the night sky the frost was overcome and a slight rain fell, like a whisper across the face of the lake. Then the winds came, gently, too, and the boat was shifted again, shifted back towards the shore it had set out from. Through the night it wandered, touching shore and grating on the rocks, floating off again, back into the darkness. Sometime before dawn it touched again, touched against the soft wet bank of the same shore, and was held among the reeds and rushes of that side.

Before morning itself had settled in, two men were down at the edge of the lake, checking on their cattle. They saw the boat, out of place among the reeds on their land. One of them waded out. He pulled the boat in and together they heaved its bulk up onto the shore where it would hold. Almost without speaking they lifted out the dead weight of the man inside and began to carry him, stumbling often, cursing the soft shoreline, the roughness of the boulders, struggling through the long line of barbed wire that marked the doctor's land. They carried him up the back field and into the cobbled yard of the doctor's house. Soon they had carried him into the modest shelter of the conservatory and laid him out on the table there. Then they stood back, caps in their hands squeezed and turned quizzically, as they watched the water drip slowly, in tiny drops, onto the elegantly tiled floor.

Gráinne felt very tired almost all the time now. There was a life growing within her, demanding the total attention of her body and her soul. She woke early, too, these days, as if the person growing within were calling to her. She lay, half aware, half asleep, while another grey day crept slowly up the curtains. Angus, solid, taciturn Angus, had been called early from the bed and for this she felt grateful, luxuriating in his absence, her life stretched taut and silent across the bed.

If it were a girl she would call her Gráinne, of that she was certain. But somehow, somewhere deep in the secret garden of her dreams, she believed it would be a boy. Then she would call him John, John Edward. She would exult in him as she had once exulted in her God, in the kisses of his mouth. She would have the joy of calling him Jackie while he struggled through his childhood; when he grew out of that name she would call him Jack, and then, when his own manhood began to weigh heavily on him, she knew the world would know him as John, John Edward Walshe. A solid name. Heavyweight. Stolid. Feet on the ground.

She was tossed out of her reverie by Angus bursting suddenly through the door of the bedroom.

"Gráinne, love, I need your help," he said. He did not often ask her help, preferring to stay at a distance from her, to conserve her, to keep her as you would keep a precious, valuable token, under glass. "There's a man brought in off the lake, he's suffering from hypothermia. A sad state. Will you please boil up the kettle and bring me in some boiled water. And I need some blankets, spare blankets. We'll get them back. To the conservatory. He's there for the moment. I've called the hospital. But they'll be some time, as usual, before they get the ambulance out for him. I need your help, dear. Please."

Oh she resented it. He was such a large man, so slow, so definite, so much – earthed. So reliable. She smiled at him, a morning smile, slow, too, and sincerely meant. He was the roof and gable wall for her, the path to the door, the mooring for the boat, the small spittle on the lake-top waves that used to be a roaring, seething sea-wave crash. She put a dressing-gown on, gathered some blankets from one of the spare rooms and moved to the kitchen. The conservatory door was closed but through the glass she could see a shape on the table, wrapped in her conservatory rug, Angus fussing about him. A strange bundle, fished from the waters of the lake, a fisherman no doubt, foolish in the weather. She boiled the kettle, her mind, for some reason, floating on warm winds of exotic landscapes where great butterflies were fluttering, where the air was still with warmth and growth, and where the deep undergrowth about her feet was rich in fruit. She found she was smiling. She shook herself. She made tea. She knocked gently on the glass door of the conservatory. Angus opened it, quickly.

"Thanks," he said, taking the tray from her. Taking the blankets.

"How is he?" she asked.

She was stretching her head around to get a glimpse of

the figure but all she could see was a dark mass, a heavy shape, a darkness.

"He'll be fine, I think, if I can gather him safely back to warmth and if we can get him to the hospital quickly."

"Who is he?" she asked him.

"Must be a fisherman, or a tourist, or just a hobo . . . Nobody, nobody, nobody."

Five

The early years of a man's life may be years of grace, slow with possibilities, years when the spirit urges time on so that great acts of flight may be accomplished soon, soon, soon, the spirit rising gradually to a great thunderclap of achieved dreams. The later years of a man's life may be free-fall, the body beginning its descent as if the early years had simply been a flash of lightning, pure and bright, or jagged and harsh. Then the spirit tries desperately to slow things down, to hold on to time as if it were a large albatross, eager to fly, to escape. Counting the days, the hours, the years. Shifting suddenly from one spring to the next, from the opening of the first snowdrop suddenly to the putrefaction of the final rose, from one emptiness to another.

"Once upon a time," Jack began. He paused, moistening his lips with his tongue. He sat back on his chair and heaved a sigh of some satisfaction. He felt light, now, in spite of the great burden of sorrow he had carried for such a long distance. The hand he held in his was still, still and warm. The body, too, was still, the face peaceful, as if all the nourishment given by light and love and hope, by grace, had taken over from the stronger, more violent and gravitational forces, to leave an aura of completion, even perfection, on the old woman's face.

"Once upon a time," he tried again, the words little

more than a whisper, yet strong in the ticking silence of the room. He found the words strange, ringing childhood bells, yet he knew that what he wanted to say could only be said by using such words, such myths. He leaned forward once more and took her hand in both of his. Then he began to speak, more rapidly, scarcely hesitating, as if he had long and often rehearsed the words.

"There was a young man by the name of Midir, a fine, handsome leader of the Tuatha Dé Danaan, the people of the Good God, the God of love and light and loving-kindness. The people who had suffered long under tyranny. Lived on an island, Gráinne, like you and me, like everyone. And one day this young man Midir went to the blessed ground where the river Boyne flows around the great resting-place of Aengus, the God of love himself. There he watched two groups of boys playing a game of hurling on the plain and there rose a great argument in the game. Midir went out onto the field to make peace amongst them but it is not easy to make peace among human beings when they are intent on making war and Midir had a spear of holly flung at him which took him in the eye and blinded him.

"Saddened at the terrible blemish he had suffered, Midir complained to the great Lord Aengus and was promised whatever reward he would ask. When he was healed again, the glorious Midir came and asked for his reward: a golden chariot, clothing fit for his rank as chieftain, and the most lovely woman in the land as his wife.

"Now Midir was whole again but the effects of the blemish were to remain with him forever, the way a lovely bird of splendid plumage may still be held to the ground by the finest, even almost invisible, thread. The way a boat, with a gash in its skin, heads out from shore" – Jack watched her carefully, he held her hand, waiting – "and must fill with water at last, must grow too heavy, and must sink. The great Lord asked him: who, then, is the most beautiful woman in the land? Midir answered him at once: She is Etáin, he said, Etáin, the daughter of the lord Ailill, she is the fairest, the greatest, the most beautiful woman in the whole land. The one without whom my life is a piece of clay, dead and useless. She is – Gráinne Flannery."

Jack paused. There had been no reaction from Gráinne. He heard footsteps pass very slowly along the corridor outside. They passed softly into silence. The night was dark along the grounds beyond their little cell and he felt his own sad weight slowly descend on him once more. He needed some sign, some word, some tiny warmth to touch him. He went on more quickly.

"Midir had to perform very difficult deeds for the lord Ailill before he would consent to give his daughter into Midir's keeping. But at last Etáin was brought back and given into the hands of Midir. When they saw each other for the first time they fell deeply in love at once, Midir and Etáin, they had eyes only for one another and there were no secrets kept between them. They were one in love, the way a river flows into the sea and becomes sea, the way one flame will merge into another and become a single hot and burning light."

He paused again, he had to. He was slightly breathless. He pressed her fingers and stood up, slowly. He sighed heavily again and moved slowly about the room, stretching his body.

"They loved each other, there were no secrets between them. They loved each other. And they spoke their love.

They were not afraid to say it, to say the words, liberating words . . ."

He stood, then, watching out the window at his own reflection, and at the darkness beyond. He knew that soon, very soon, that darkness would have entered this room finally and for ever. He knew a sense of urgency. If he could but once more kiss her, kiss her gently and without guilt, on the lips . . . He put his hands behind his back and closed his eyes. Looking at the darkness within him.

"But there was jealousy. That terrible tiger, jealousy. Midir already had a wife, Fuamnach, a big woman, black-haired, pretty, a woman who worked hard about his house, minding for him, caring for him, giving him her body and her soul. She had a right to be jealous, but that's not the point of the story. Not the point at all. For jealousy, too, is a foolishness. She cursed Etáin, cursed her with such force that the beautiful Etáin became a small pool of muddied water on the floor of her room. Fuamnach laughed with delight at her powers and abandoned Etáin to her fate. The room was hot, very hot; soon a tiny worm came to birth within the pool, the worm grew and blossomed into a wondrous fly, the fly stirred itself and rose into the air, leaving everywhere it flew a haunting music of loss and a healing fragrance of love."

The old man came back to the bedside and sat down again, once more taking in his own the old woman's hands.

"A haunting music of loss and a healing fragrance of love. A beautiful fly. Or a moth, exotic, many-coloured, a butterfly, alive and beautiful but not free. Gráinne, Gráinne, Gráinne!

"Midir, when he saw and heard this wondrous creature, knew at once what had happened. While the fly stayed near him its fragrance and its music brought him peace so that still Fuamnach's jealousy grew. She brought a wild wind to rage through the house and through the land and the fly was blown out through the open window of the house and away through the skies of Ireland. The rough, cold and angry skies. For years. Fighting the winds, the rains, the darknesses.

"The great god of love, Aengus, kept the fly safe for some time in a bower made of crystal but Fuamnach found her even there, even in the small, safe cell of the god of love. Fuamnach brought the storms with her and once more the lovely fly was tossed and whirled about the great and wearying skies of the world. Aengus was so angry that at once he had Fuamnach's head cut off. Etáin flew, lost and alone and weary. And Midir's heart was broken and he fled the lands where he had once known happiness. He fled, far away, far far away from the one spot where his heart would have known peace. There is no such thing as peace, Gráinne, there is no such thing as peace. It is an illusion we go running after all our lives while it waits within us to be discovered. The little moment of peace we do find is so fleeting it proves only that we try to make time a substitute for eternity. And it does not work, it does not quiet the ailing heart, the heart that had not known peace, Gráinne, especially when that heart knows that love was once so close, so firmly within its grasp."

He stopped again. He was speaking to her now as if he was certain she could hear and understand. He was almost expecting her to reply. His eyes were still dry though a choking sound, like the prelude to tears, came from his throat. He watched her. She seemed, he thought, a little paler than before, as if the blood had begun to slow in its final journeying round her body. He began again, speaking rapidly.

"Etáin flew and flew until she was exhausted and could travel no further. She rested on the high beams of a great hall where a feast was taking place, and because she was so weary she fell, down out of the angry heavens straight into a chalice studded with gold, filled with wine that Etar, the chieftain's wife, was just raising to her lips. The woman swallowed the wine and with it she swallowed the wondrous fly. And nine months later she gave birth to a beautiful baby girl and they called the girl . . . yes, they called her Etáin. They called her Etáin."

For a second Jack was certain her eyelids moved. He was certain of it. He could sense a slight tremor through her body. He went on, heartened, more eager, speaking more urgently than before.

"In the great fort of that country they cared for the young Etáin and gave her all the riches of their kingdom so that she grew beautiful and wealthy and was married to the High King himself, Eochai Airem, high king of Ireland, and she went to live with him at Tara.

"Where was Midir all this time? He was in the land of the dead, living in the deep dark underworld of the half-living. Like a man who had floated out on a lake one ice-cold night and who longed to die, but who did not die, Gráinne, instead he heard the voice of his loved one ringing across the darkness that he had just evaded. Or that had evaded him.

"One day, when Etáin was out on the ramparts of her fort watching the games that took place along the plain, a fine young man came towards her. He was handsome, powerful, dressed with all the glory that only great wealth and high position can offer; it was Midir, reborn, too, after all his tribulations, reborn to a new life, a stronger love. He spoke to Etáin, calling her to come to live with him in a country full of music and of fragrant flowers, a place where there is no more death, nor weeping, nor pain, where every tear has been wiped away, where there is no jealousy, where time has been forgotten and where the trees are forever full of fruits and the rivers flow with wine. She refused him, of course, for he was asking of her the absolute, the ultimate, beyond which . . . But he persisted, saying, If your husband gives you to me, will you come? To this she agreed, in all innocence and trust. And the young man went away, filled once more with hope."

Jack was tired now. Gráinne lay still and he felt that her breathing had grown just a little harsher, her flesh just a little more white. More weary. The old man felt tears, at last, hovering somewhere behind his eyes.

"Midir challenged the king to a game of chess. They played for the highest stakes they could imagine, lands, and horses, and great houses, and the king won that first game, laughing as he gathered up the pieces and ordered Midir to pay his forfeit. Midir did so and the king's lands were extended and the riches of his court grew exceedingly. Midir challenged the king once more and again the stakes were laid, arms, and chariots and great acres of forests and lakes, companies of servants and sacks of gold, and again the king won, without difficulty, and Midir paid over what he owed. When they met for the third and final time, Midir demanded that the winner be allowed to name the prize; the king, being strong and confident, agreed. Midir won the game. Then he recalled the terms of their wager and asked, as his reward, just one kiss from the lips of

Etáin. The King, terrified now of what he had promised, hesitated long. Come back after a month, he said to Midir, and you can have your prize.

"Midir went away, confident in the power of his desire, confident, too, in the integrity of the High King. But at the end of that time the King had all his warriors gathered round him in his great fort and he was determined to keep Midir out, at any cost. However, my dear and lovely Gráinne, where there is a great, deep love, there is no wall, no country, no fortress that can keep lovers from one another. He will come to her, he will come, offering her the kisses of his mouth."

By now, small tears had gathered at the corners of the old man's eyes and they were sounding in the recesses of his voice. He had leaned forward again close to the face of the woman.

"In the great hall of the fort, Gráinne, she was there, beautiful still, more beautiful than ever, surrounded by hundreds of the greatest warriors the king could command. She was sitting still, unmoving, while all that could be heard was the clanking of armour, the chinking of weaponry, the subdued, anxious voices of the soldiers. As if war could succeed in changing the world, in bringing about the wishes of the powerful. For, suddenly, in spite of all their care and caution, Midir, tall and proud and handsome, stood in the midst of them all and took Etáin by the hand. He raised her to her feet and put his arm about her waist. The warriors dared not move, for Midir and Etáin, after all those years and all those difficulties, were too close now ever to be severed again. Even by death. Above all by death.

"As he bent low to claim his kiss, slowly, slowly, he began to rise into the air above them, still holding tightly to his one great love. They rose together, there was a distant, lovely music, the hall was filled with a wonderful fragrance, and the warriors saw two perfect, beautiful white swans rise from their midst and fly gracefully together away through the skylight and rise high into the sky beyond. Together they circled the fort, flying slowly, elegantly, while only the beating of their wings could be heard by the warriors below, and then they flew together, wing-tip to wing-tip, passing at last through that turquoise curtain and away into the blue embrace of a loving God."

He stopped. She was breathing with difficulty. But her face had not changed. And then her hand, her right hand, moved with infinite slowness and touched his own and he gazed down at it with unbearable happiness; her hand opened, slowly, with great effort, and he grasped it and he knew the pressure of her fingers as she grasped his with all the strength that was left in her life. For a long, long moment they were together, their hands offering everything that they had between them. He kissed her then, gently, on the mouth, his mouth to hers and the answering pressure on his fingers gave him utter joy. He remained leaning over her, his lips to hers, and she left him then, without a sigh or a moan of pain. She was at peace. Even the tiny movement of her breathing had ceased. He imagined, however, there was the remotest shadow of a smile playing about her mouth. He felt that all her features had relaxed so that she looked as she had looked so many years before. He still felt the pressure of her hand on his. He felt the touch of her lips against his. He waited a long, long time. He wept a little, then he loosened her fingers from his, folded her hands gently together and reached and pressed the bell behind her bed.